Cetacea

Theresa Foley

6-16-2003
To my DEAR FAITH.
SWIM FREE LiKE THE
DOLPHINS.
Love
Mom

Cetacea

a novel

Theresa Foley

2001
SeaStory Press
Key West, Florida

Published by Seastory Press

305 Whitehead St., Suite 1

Key West, Florida 33040

www.seastorypress.com

LIBRARY OF CONGRESS CATALOGING-IN-PUBLICATION DATA

Foley, Theresa

    Cetacea / Theresa Foley

    ISBN 0-9673704-2-6

Library of Congress Control Number: 00-93689

Cover Art: "Cosmic Swimmers" by Atmara Rebecca Cloe, 2000,

        New World Creations; www.nwcreations.com

Book design, cover design by Sheri Lohr

For the dolphins

PROLOGUE

The silver bottle-nosed dolphin had been swimming north all morning. Now he cut through the crystal blue water and turned until his sonar detected a pod of dolphins some distance away. The silver one raced ahead.

A charioteer of the sea, he was built for speed and motion. He reached the pod and took a jagged path around the smaller dolphins, as if to evade their sonar. He was much larger than the others.

He circled twice and hung back. With his sonar, he saw them in three dimensions. He could see their muscles, the shadows of their curved bodies.

He turned the image of the pod around in the sonar center of his brain until he spotted a mature female. She was sleek and healthy, nearly as muscular as he was. He calculated her position and the distance, then swam forward. He brushed up against her a few times, making his intentions known.

She welcomed him and they swam together, warm Gulf water sliding over their sleek bodies, enacting a ritual that dated back 65 million years.

Separating from her, the silver male swam alone again. From the point of his nose to his wide graceful flukes, he was twice the length of a large man. He steered with two tapered flippers, boned appendages that had five fingers almost like a human's. His dorsal fin, made of soft tissue, was darker gray and swept away from his body with hydrodynamic grace.

The big gray dolphin circled the pod again, this time selecting a smaller female. He repeated the brief courtship, then joining her to swim as one.

Not naturally monogamous, the old gray felt a deep contentment in taking his pleasure, obeying his instincts, as his ancestors had over the ages. Locked with the small female, their bodies danced together until he broke off and moved away.

With a flip of his powerful flukes, he put a few hundred yards of sparkling sea between himself and the pod. The other males watched him closely, their clicking and high pitched song more frantic now.

After a few minutes, the males organized into a line of defense, swimming into protective position around their wards. Perhaps he was a messenger. Perhaps there was a reason for his aggression. They would have welcomed a wanderer wanting acceptance in the pod, a friendly traveler making acquaintances. But the big silver cetacean was a loner.

The pod cut quickly through the turquoise sea, leaving the strange dolphin behind, heading to the cove where they rested after feeding each day. A small, uninhabited island, ringed by a white beach, created protection for the circular shallows of sand and grass on the sea floor where the dolphins lived.

Once they reached the protected, half-moon-shaped bay, the males dropped their guard and spread out again. The younger animals frolicked, breaking the surface of the ocean in joyful abandon, leaping high in the air in the graceful, arcing dance that endears the species so well to humankind.

Near the place where the cove opened to the sea, a two-year-old swam slowly alone. She was small, with velvet skin the color of mercury. She played, her body barrel-rolling through the warm water near the surface. She would break the surface, breathe, dive down to spin, and then repeat the ritual. She danced through the sea with joy.

She had risen to the surface to breathe through the blowhole behind her head when the gray approached hard and fast from the side. He pushed against her, then down, forcing her to the sandy bottom. He felt her move, twisting, but she couldn't get away. He sensed her panic.

He wanted to take her to the south, to the big island. The place of magic awaited his return. He tried to convey to her the image of the temple, the secrets of the old way.

She lifted her tail fin up. She and the big gray joined in a motion as natural as the sun rising and setting each day. In an instant, she no longer fought, simply fell into his rhythm, and together they moved to the south, the water around them as infinite as the power in their bodies. He felt his own pain ease for a moment, then she broke away and swam back toward her family.

As she swam away, her sonar flickered over him. The sensation of tiny waves bouncing against him was almost imperceptible. She was imaging the thick white scars on the sides of his head and further down by his flippers. Then he drew up an image from his past.

In the memory, thick black nylon straps held an instrument of terror in the place marked by the jagged scars on his head. He sent her an image of the humans. His trainers had taught him how to protect. How to survive. And how to kill. The female fled and he was alone again.

He sent out sonar. The waves returned. The humans were in the water. Not too far away. He turned and headed toward them. It was time to begin.

Chapter 1

Mattie Gold turned her boat, the Paradise Diver, toward the ancient coral reef that lay due south from Stock Island. Western Sambo, the patch of reef she headed for, was five miles out in the direction of Cuba.

Havana was 85 miles further, a short distance, but one Key West mariners rarely if ever traveled due to the political situation that had divided the place for 40 years.

As the boat passed through the channel into the deeper water, a few hundred yards to port, four gray dorsal fins emerged on the surface. Mattie tracked the movement in the water, waited, and was rewarded with the sight of four dolphins leaping gracefully out of the sea.

"Dolphins to port," she shouted over her shoulder, pointing toward them. "Everybody hang on tight, we're going to pick up speed. Fifteen minutes to the reef."

Behind her, the dive boat customers clung to the benches as she hit the tops of the small waves. Each diver had a couple hundred dollars worth of gear stuffed into a bag beneath his or her seat.

Earlier that morning at the dive shop dock, her divemaster, Todd, had written eight names on the white slate that served as the passenger manifest: a young couple from Michigan; another from Tampa; two beefy men from California who worked for a commuter airline that serviced the little island; and two Navy reservists doing a few weeks duty at Boca Chica up the road.

Eight divers, half a boatload, which should make for an easy trip to the reef and back. Mattie liked driving a boat for a living, especially on a sunny day like this one. The sun beat down so bright that the sandy ocean floor could be glimpsed through 30 feet of shimmering blue sea.

The waters in the Florida Keys had been legendary since Hemingway's time, when it was said to be as clear as gin. Perhaps it was when Papa was around, but not anymore. Most days the water was loaded with sediment and particulate matter, making it more like one of those glass snowball paperweights than a glass of gin.

But on a good day, when the sea was flat, Key West still ranked among the best diving spots the continental United States had to offer. It provided a living for Mattie and perhaps another hundred or so professional divers who lived in the town.

She gripped the wheel and then reached to turn the volume up as a Bob Seger tune came on the waterproof stereo system. The customers were predominantly young, testosterone-pumped males and they liked rock music on the way out to the reef. Mattie did her best to keep them happy; it usually improved the tips.

She had turned east toward Western Sambo when she felt a hard tug on the long braid of brown hair that fell halfway down her back.

The guy from Michigan was right behind her. He was in his midtwenties, clean cut and more than a little out of shape. His tight black Lycra bodysuit squeezed his body like too much sausage stuffed into too little casing. Mattie would bet her paycheck that he hadn't had his certification card for more than a few dives.

"Hey pretty lady captain," he said, giving her braid another yank. His eyes were hidden behind a pair of cheap mirrored sunglasses that made him look like a human fly. "Out on the water every day. I'd give anything to have your job."

Mattie pulled her hair over her shoulder, out of range of his hand. "Yeah, we've got a term for that. Vacation-itis, we call it. Where're you from?"

"Michigan."

"I've got an uncle from Michigan." An uncle she hadn't seen since she was maybe ten. "Detroit. Bet you don't do too much diving in those cold waters back home. Some good wrecks up there in Lake Michigan though."

"Next year," he said, giving her a big smile and jutting out his chest. "I just got my c-card. I love diving. Talk about freedom. There's nothing like being underwater."

He was right about that, Mattie thought. But along with the freedom came responsibility, and years of disciplined preparation and even then, occasionally, the fun was spoiled by a terrible accident. Not that a novice like this guy would pay much attention to something so statistically rare.

"I'll bet you're thinking about moving down here," she said. She smiled as she thought about how long a guy like this would last outside of his cushy office job.

New divers usually didn't think about the danger that went hand in hand with strapping a tank of air onto a person's back and heading deep beneath the ocean's surface.

Mattie'd seen one body pulled from the water when a dive went bad. Any dead diver would be bad enough but it had been her boyfriend who'd been lifted out of the water that day.

Just like Detroit here, Mickey Patcher had loved his freedom and diving had been the one place he'd found it.

Mattie'd had a hard time accepting Mickey's death, but almost everyone she knew who worked in the dive business had lost somebody, and she hadn't let it keep her away from the sea. She didn't go into therapy or start drinking, she just took a few days off, shed a few private tears, and then went back to work.

"Well, you're going to get what you came for today, Detroit."

"Do you guys need some help? Looks pretty easy compared to what I do at the bank."

"So you work in a bank? Big finance, huh?" This guy had no concept of what driving a boat for a living was like.

She thought about the rainy season, the days when no boats went out, and how she and the rest of the people who worked out here didn't get paid, sometimes for weeks on end, living on peanut butter and jelly sandwiches and coconuts. And then there were the sunny days when the wind picked up and the seas were four to six. They couldn't pay you enough to go out on a day like that, but she went out anyway. No choice.

"How's about I just sign on to be your slave for a while? What do you think? I'll do anything you say, just name it." The grin again, behind those bug eye glasses. Her customer, whose girlfriend was sunbathing 15 feet away, was flirting with her.

"Just what I need, a slave. You ever been on a boat this size in a six foot chop?" she asked.

He shook his head.

"Better than weight-watchers for taking off the calories," she said. "And guess who gets to wash all the puke off the deck when all the customers are blowing breakfast?"

He shrugged.

She pushed her purple baseball cap back a bit.

"Oh hell, you're right. Look at that sky! I can't complain." Give the guy a break. The dolphins were jumping again a hundred yards to starboard and she pointed at them. "On a day like today, sunshine, dead calm. Life doesn't get any better. There's nothing I'd rather do than go diving. I don't blame you."

"Beats driving to the office in the snow. Plus you get to live in Key West." Detroit yipped like a coyote. He stared out at the water. "Is that where we're headed?"

He pointed about a mile out. Another boat was circling out there, just hanging around the same one spot.

"No, that's beyond the reef." She raised a pair of binoculars for a better look. She could see a big boat and a small inflatable raft. A man aboard the bigger boat was preparing a mammoth pile of net to be put in the water. Mattie's hands clenched into tight fists.

Todd had climbed up onto the bow, where he was fooling around with the anchor, straightening its chain and line in preparation for their arrival at the reef. The divemaster was young and strong, with short, cropped hair and a big, strapping body made for physical labor.

Mattie got his attention and pointed to the other boat. "Hey, cover boy, we're going for a little drive."

A frown crossed his smooth, tanned face. Mattie saw his lips form the words, "Aw, shit," but the roar of the engine drowned out the sound.

Todd stowed the anchor and carefully edged his way along the safety rail of the boat until he could jump down into the cockpit next to her. "That is none of our business." He lowered his voice. "We don't have time, Mattie."

She kept her heading and speed, deciding to ignore his attempt to turn her decision into a debate. As they got closer, she could make out two boats tied together out there, not one.

Todd was still frowning. "My dad will kill me if we cause any trouble."

His father, Bob Patcher, was Mattie's boss and the owner of the boat.

"If your dad says anything, just tell him you were following my orders," she said.

Todd shot her an annoyed look.

"For Christ's sake, Todd," she said, her voice rising angrily, "somebody is taking animals out of the water. I just want to see who it is."

"Can't we just do our jobs and stop worrying about things we can't control? Why do you always have to be sticking your nose into somebody else's business?" Todd's handsome features were pinched up in a frown.

"Lighten up, Todd. I don't like the looks of that."

He scowled. "All you're supposed to do is drive this thing. Every day you want to appoint yourself as representative of Greenpeace on the reef."

Todd had turned increasingly hostile towards her after his brother Mickey died. She'd been running the boat, it wasn't her fault, but who else could he blame?

But the last few weeks, Todd's anger had grown more blatant. All because she'd decided to get married. To a customer yet.

Did Todd really believe she'd spend the rest of her life mourning Mickey, who hadn't treated her all that well when he was alive anyway? Mattie had to remind herself that Todd was 21, with a man's body and a boy's emotions.

Todd turned around and moved to the back of the boat, all professional polish now. He began to brief the customers to explain the unscheduled side trip. "Okay divers. We're going for a little ride. Won't take long. We just need to check something out, then we're going straight to the reef."

Mattie pushed the throttle forward and Paradise Diver churned through the water toward the poachers' vessel. In a few minutes, she was within hollering distance of the two boats. One was a good sized fishing boat, 30 feet in length, and the other was a small, wooden dinghy with a tiny outboard motor.

A scrawny old man with a wild mane of gray hair was behind the wheel of the larger boat. His companion was a burly looking man with dark skin and a big mustache who sat inside the dinghy. They each had a set of lines attached to a sizable net stretched between the two boats. They glared at her.

Mattie waved and idled her engine. "What're you boys doing out here?"

The old man shook his arm brusquely at her, signaling her to move away from his boat.

"Those big nets are illegal here. You ought to know that," she yelled.

"Young lady," the old man shouted back, a heavy accent making him difficult to understand. "We have government permission for a limited catch. Leave us be."

The accent wasn't Spanish like many of the watermen in the area, but from Eastern Europe, perhaps Russian or Slavic, Mattie judged.

"Government permission? Since when do you need government permission to go fishing? Most people just get a license. It's a no take zone, pal." Mattie bent down to unzip her backpack on the floor. She dug into the large compartment until she found her camera.

"Get out of here," the old man shouted back.

Instead of leaving, Mattie raised her camera and began shooting. The big boat was dirty with soot, too dirty to make out anything more than a few letters of the name on the stern. The port of call was totally obscured.

The man in the dinghy bent down and pulled a shotgun from under the seat. Then the old man grinned and waved. Todd scrambled back to her side.

"He's got a gun. Let's go." Todd's jaw was set hard. He planted his feet firmly on the deck, arms crossed against his broad chest. Mattie hoped the two trappers would think Todd's anger was directed at them, rather than her.

"I wonder what they're after," she muttered. It could be turtles, rays, sharks, even dolphin, although they would be awfully hard to catch in this water.

"Let's get out of here, Mattie. We've got customers on board." Todd's fists were clenched and he looked ready to wrestle the steering wheel away from her.

"Okay, okay, just let me get a couple of pictures." She took a few more shots, set her camera down, put the Paradise Diver into gear and turned back to the reef.

The divers hadn't moved an inch from their places on the bench. They were looking nervous, except for the guy from Detroit, who edged his way to the front as the boat bumped along until he reached Mattie. He tapped her on the shoulder. "What were they doing?"

"If I had to guess, I'd say they were trying to net dolphins for some-body – a marine park, maybe the Navy. Or turtles, or rays, or even a shark for one of the aquariums," she said. "You ever wonder how they got there last time you were at a theme park, now you know."

He stared at her.

"Don't worry about it," she said. "Those boys won't bother with us. They're too busy making a fast buck."

As she neared the cut in the reef where boats could safely pass through, another boat came at them from the direction of shore. The boat was dark and low and veered off to port well before it came near the Paradise Diver. Three dark figures rode low in the small craft and gave a curt wave as they sped past.

Todd returned from babysitting the other passengers. "Special forces," Todd said for the benefit of Detroit, who was still hovering behind Mattie. Todd waved at the fast little inflatable boat. "I'm jeal-ous."

Mattie shook her head. "Those guys are nothing but trouble."

Detroit shaded his eyes and followed the inflatable's progress. "Where're they going?"

"The Wilkes-Barre," Mattie said.

"What's that?"

"A World War II battleship, 660 feet long. It's a few miles past the reef and 250 feet down. Technical diving only, cowboy," Mattie said. "Don't worry. We'll teach you that when you move down here. You've got ten grand for the classes, don't you?"

He shrugged.

"First, you get to practice up on Western Sambo," Todd said. They had arrived at the reef.

"Suit up," she shouted to the customers in back.

Mattie slowed the engine while Todd scrambled up the deck to the bow and dropped anchor. The crowd of divers in back were frozen in their seats, still eyeing Mattie suspiciously, as if they were a bunch of garden club members who had been commandeered by a sadistic taxi driver and were about to be dropped off in the middle of an urban ghetto.

"Hey, divers, what's the matter?" she asked cheerily. "You're all going diving, remember? Don't worry, be happy."

Mattie knew from the glum faces that she probably shouldn't have confronted the two creeps with the net. But if these folks were divers, they ought to be able to deal with the unexpected, even two hoodlum poachers with a shotgun. After all, it wasn't like she'd gotten into a real confrontation, all they'd done was yell a lot. Besides somebody out here needed to even up the odds for the poor sea creatures.

When the anchor was set, she shut the engine down and went to the stern. She wouldn't apologize but she was willing to explain.

"Everybody knows Key West is famous for pirates, has been for centuries. Sometimes they're out plundering the wrecks, and sometimes they're out just plain plundering. Anything anybody will pay for is fair game. Undersized lobsters, baby stingrays, they'll kill or catch anything. We had a big tame Jewfish out on Joe's Tug, big as a Volkswagen bus. Somebody shot him with a spear gun one day. That fish was like your pet dog, used to come up to divers for a handout, and some asshole just went right up and speared him at close range. Now, I don't know what those guys were up to, but I guarantee it wasn't anything nice," she said. "Usually we just take you out to the reef, put you in the water, take you back to the dock, but you just got a bonus adventure with the pirates of the Caribbean. On the house. No extra charge."

The customers just sat on the benches staring at her until Todd jumped up and started handing out pieces of equipment. "All right, time to get in the water. I'll go with you. Listen up. Here's the best way to get in and out of this boat. It may be different from the last dive boat you were on, so pay attention."

He continued giving them the standard instructions and soon the clients were smiling and gearing up.

Mattie moved to the stern and busied herself rigging lines and floats as Todd kept talking. He forgot, as usual, to tell the divers to keep off the coral, so at the end, Mattie came back to add, "Everybody listen up. Stay off the coral. Don't stand on it; don't touch it. If you touch it, it dies. It will cut you, it will burn you, it will grow if it gets under your skin."

"What is this, boot camp? You've set more rules than the NFL," said Detroit. He was loaded with gear and his face had started to bead up with sweat.

Mattie gave him a slightly forced smile. "All we're trying to do is make your dive more enjoyable. And yes, diving does have rules. I thought they told you that when you got your C-card."

"Key West is supposed to be uninhibited. I thought you guys liked to live on the edge. You are so uptight. 'Don't touch anything; don't take anything,'" he imitated her in a whine. "The reef's been there a million years, and it'll be here another million." He looked straight at Mattie. "What are you, some kind of EarthFirster?"

"If I was, I'd be blowing up this boat, not driving it," she said. He'd now crossed the line from being merely annoying to officially become a customer from hell. On days like today, the take no prisoners greens got her sympathy. But she wasn't going to debate the environment with a pale doughboy banker from Detroit who theoretically, at least, might be good for a five dollar tip at the end of an eight hour day, if he wasn't too drunk, or too tired, or too cheap.

"Hope you like wreck diving, bucko."

"I do," he grinned.

"Good, because if things don't change soon, there's not going to be a reef for long," she said. She touched his skin, leaving a white circle in a field of blazing red. "Go get in the water before you overheat."

Detroit lumbered awkwardly over to where the other divers were putting on masks, weight belts, little plastic knives and other accessories.

Mattie leaned over the side of the boat to look into the water. The smooth bottom 25 feet below them was so clear she could see ripples in the sand.

Beneath the boat, a shadow darkened the sand. An instant later, a large creature streaked past. She drew her breath in sharply, surprised by its size: ten feet or longer. Nurse and sand sharks were common to this area, but they usually never exceeded four or five feet in length. She waited for the creature to swim by again, but it had vanished. Todd came to her side and looked over.

"I just saw something big down there," she said in a hushed tone. "Maybe a shark."

"Do you want to move to another dive site?"

"No, we're running behind already. Nothing around here's going to bother them," she said. "If they see a shark, they'll just have something to brag about over their margaritas tonight."

She looked again for the big creature. About twenty feet from the boat, she could make out the edge of the reef. Hundreds of small tropical fish darted around the dark mass of coral. The little fish seemed unperturbed.

"Whatever it was, it's gone," she said. "Let's get this bunch into the water."

At the rear of the boat, Todd helped each diver take the plunge. He checked each person to make sure the air was turned on before he or she jumped overboard.

"Be back on board in 40 minutes," Mattie told each one, jotting down the time on a little white slate as each diver entered the water.

Detroit was last, naturally. He waddled to dive platform, looking like he'd been through a fire sale at a dive shop, overloaded with every piece of fancy gear imaginable, with a speargun tucked under his arm.

"Here comes the great white hunter," Mattie said, reaching for the gun. "May I have that?"

He hugged the speargun to his side. "I just bought this gun in Miami. Four hundred bucks, marked down from eight."

"Well, you can't take it with you," she said. "Too many other divers around. It's not permitted."

"Hey, I paid $125 to come out here today. You should have told me at the dock," he said.

"I didn't know you had a spear until a minute ago otherwise I would have," she said. "Either the spear stays on the boat or you do. Take your choice."

His face got red. "No way. Forget it," he said. "I want to bring home some dinner. I came all the way from Michigan to learn how to spearfish. They told me on the phone the speargun would be fine."

Mattie considered asking Todd to intercede, but why should she need a man to deal with this clown just because he had more testosterone than common sense? She was the captain, ten years older than either of these guys, and Detroit was just going to have to submit to her authority, like it or not. The trick was to get him to like it.

Todd pulled Mattie aside. "Maybe you should just let him take the gun. I don't think this guy could hit his own foot if the spear was sitting on his big toe."

Mattie shook her head. "He's been acting like a jerk since he got on the boat."

"He's booked to dive with us five days running, Mattie. We'll lose the business," Todd said. "It's your call."

She didn't want him going to Bob Patcher, demanding his money back, causing a big scene over the gun. She walked back to where Detroit was waiting, removed the spear from his gun and handed the empty weapon back to him. "How about doing a little training with an unloaded gun first?"

"That's better," he said triumphantly.

"Now get in the water, Detroit. Everybody else is waiting. Who's your buddy?"

"Arnold. You probably call him California." He nodded at a head in the water and checked his watch. "Forty minute bottom time?"

Then he leaned close to Todd and whispered loudly, "Bottom time. Love that. Sounds like chasing pussy to me."

He winked at his girlfriend, a non-diver who waved from her sun tanning perch on the front of the boat, then plunged into the ocean behind the other six divers.

They sank beneath the water, the lead weights around their waists pulling them down as they let the air out of their diving vests.

Detroit's head was the last to disappear. Mattie checked the manifest. His real name was Jim Reynolds.

"Keep an eye on him," Mattie said. "I smell trouble."

Todd pulled his mask over his eyes, popped his regulator into his mouth and dove into the sea, going straight down to join the divers on the bottom.

Mattie just hoped Mr. Jim Reynolds wouldn't do something dumb. She'd been a captain long enough to spot a diver who'd need a rescue before he even got wet. Reynolds had all the classic signs of a disaster in the making.

Chapter 2

Jim Reynolds sank to the ocean floor and rested his flippers in the sand. He landed in a field of broken purple sea fans, large brain corals, abandoned lobster traps and old chunks of metal. He spent a few minutes adjusting his diving equipment until he was no longer popping up and down like a broken elevator.

This was the life. Euphoria surged through him. Slow it down, slow it down, he thought.

He breathed slowly and calmly through the black rubber mouthpiece. The dive rig's hoses snaked around him like a mechanical octopus.

Reynolds listened to the gurgling bubbles. Through his black-trimmed mask, he saw the other divers float across a scene of underwater splendor. The water was cloudy but he could still make out fingers of undulating soft coral and dozens of tropical fish cruising past, bright as a neon dream.

A midnight damselfish with her blue dapples, flashy as the drag queen he'd seen on Duval Street the night before, darted past. He could hear the crunching of parrotfish pecking hungrily at the coral beneath him.

Reynolds wanted to inspect the coral more closely. He'd expected more of everything: more fish, more colors, more variety. Pieces of coral were broken off everywhere. The water was hazy. The reef seemed to wear a coat of gray paint. He thought he saw a white ring on one piece of coral the size of a basketball.

"Don't touch the coral," the busybody captain had said.

He went over and laid a finger against it gently. What she didn't know wouldn't hurt her. The reef looked diseased. He'd read of the mysterious ringed diseases, and if he ought to mark the spot so that someone could come back and treat the coral later. He didn't know who that might be but surely they had somebody out here to take care of problems like cancerous coral. Small tropical fish seemed to be observing him, as if they were trying to decide a safe distance.

Out of the corner of his eye, he saw a larger shape dart past. The big fish was as long as a torpedo but fatter. He did a 360-degree circle to get a better look, but it was gone. Then he heard the tinny clang of the divemaster banging his knife against an air tank to get the group's attention.

Reynolds kicked his fins furiously, trying to catch up to the others. He looked for his dive buddy Arnold, an overweight salesman from San Francisco, with whom he'd been paired on the boat.

Chunky Arnold was wedged into expensive gear decorated with splashes of fluorescent pink. In his Day-Glo outfit, Arnold was easy to spot, but Reynolds hated the idea of staying next to the fat man for the whole dive. In scuba class, they'd been taught to always dive with a buddy, but now that he was certified, he felt he could relax the rules. Seemed more a matter of personal choice than a punishable offense.

Something shiny in the sand distracted him. He turned his body upside down to investigate, but it was only an empty beer can. Then another silver flash disappeared beyond the edge of his mask before he could identify exactly what it was.

The other divers had drifted away, and Reynolds kicked harder hoping to regain sight of pink-trimmed Arnold. The big sea creature had put a dent in his bravado. Once he got with his buddy again, he would position the big guy on his flank as a barrier against any unpredictable behavior on the part of the wildlife.

Reynolds shifted the heavy speargun that was tucked under his elbow. He put the gun up to his mask and aimed at a bunch of tiny butterfly fish, just for practice.

In the distance, he saw Arnold's pink fins. He decided to try to catch up with his buddy and pumped his legs harder, sucking in air in fast hungry gulps.

He'd begun to close the gap when something hit him from the side. The gray blur propelled him 15 feet until a large coralhead got in the way.

Reynolds felt his Lycra bodysuit shred and his skin scrape the reef. Now he saw why she wanted them to avoid the coral. From afar it looked round and smooth, but up close, its ridges were sharp as razor blades.

His regulator popped out of his mouth, and he sank to the sand. He had asked for extra weight at the dive shop. Behind the counter, the kid with the long ponytail who handed out equipment had growled, "You sure?"

"I float like a cork," Reynolds had stated firmly, refusing to let the youth's disapproval dissuade him from the extra lead. Now the heaviness of the belt felt like an iron fist pulling him down.

Stay calm, Reynolds told himself. He flailed his arms until he found his air supply, then clenched the regulator between his teeth. Reynolds spit salt water through the mouthpiece, sucked in a mouthful of air and tried to regain his composure. The air tasted cool and dry, and as he exhaled he heard the reassuring sound of bubbles exit his body like a watery lullaby.

He seemed to be okay now. Something big had hit him, attacked him, but now it was gone. Who would believe it? What if the others thought he had imagined the attack?

His girlfriend would have one more reason to roll her eyes at him, as she'd done since they'd gotten off the plane, like he was some hopeless misfit who was inexplicably following her around the island instead of the guy who'd paid for her trip. He'd deal with that when they got back home.

He looked at the tears in his bodysuit and noticed brownish fluid seeping out. Blood was brown at this depth, he recalled, and he remembered something else from his scuba classes: if sharks were sighted, he was supposed to get out of the water. But he wasn't sure the creature that hit him was a shark.

Reynolds looked around for the others, but they'd vanished. Maybe he should just get out of the water. He recalled the procedure for aborting his dive and surfacing alone. Exhale, kick to the surface and make an ah sound. Or was that only for emergencies?

He was trying to remember if the regulator was supposed to be in his mouth or out during an emergency ascent when the gray streak returned, shooting like lightning across his field of vision. He wheeled to track his hunter, cursing the clumsy mask and bulky gear.

As Reynolds spun in the water, he had a moment of true clarity: Diving wasn't all it was cracked up to be and there was no way he wanted to work for that bossy girl captain. He liked his job in the bank just fine. As he contemplated his $1,500 investment in equipment and calculated how much he might get back home for a slightly used set of diving gear, a large gray snout jammed against his rib cage.

The speargun flew out of his hands and settled in the sand.

Reynolds looked at his attacker. The creature's head was pointy, not sharp toothed, and the big fish hadn't bitten, only rammed him. This was no shark. Reynolds struggled to move away. If only he had a camera instead of the gun.

The gray-skinned creature hovered nearby, a majestic 12-foot stretch of intelligence and strength. A dolphin. Amazing. He remembered the old TV show Flipper and how he'd fantasized about swimming with dolphins since he was a boy.

Then Reynolds saw the jagged scars on the sides of the dolphin's head. Looked like this old guy had been through a war.

The big gray's last hit was aimed directly at Reynolds' head. It was a strategic blow, as well placed as if the creature knew where a human body was most vulnerable. The dolphin rammed Reynolds against the coral headfirst, the blow knocking him out. His regulator slipped out of his mouth and water flooded into his lungs. Brilliant tiny reef fish darted around his body as the air in his lungs bubbled slowly out.

Chapter 3

The crowd in The Frog was thirsty, as bar crowds tend to be in the dozens of drinking establishments that run the two mile length of Key West's famous Duval Street. The strip is like Disneyworld for drinkers. They yelled for rum cocktails and frosty mugs of beer faster than Gene could pour them, leaving him no time to wonder, as he sometimes did, how he had ended up on the wrong side of the bar on Friday afternoon.

"What do you call those pink and orange ones with rum? Planter's? Right, give us a couple of those, but not too much ice."

The girl placing the order was pretty. She and her friend wore matching beach coverups with dozens of frogs intertwined in lewd acts on the front. The Frog shirt was not meant to advertise the bar but was an item tourists actually paid to wear from one the two dozen T-shirt shops lining Duval Street. Gene's two customers had gotten themselves decked out this afternoon, with their eyes traced, racoonlike, in thick black eyeliner and their lips painted bright red inside dark brown lines that had been drawn on like a cartoonist might do when creating a character. Gene liked his women natural, not that it made any difference to these two.

He didn't even bother to check her ID, even though he had a feeling he ought to. It would slow him down too much.

The combination of the heat—it was the fifth day in a row the temperature had broken 90—and the onset of a summer weekend, gave an edginess to the unruly, sunburned mix of locals and tourists.

It wasn't necessarily a bad thing that they were drinking faster than Gene could pour. He might earn an extra twenty or so in tips as a result. He mixed up the drinks and went back to the girl.

"Two Planters. That'll be twelve dollars, please."

Gene placed the plastic cups on the bar and waited for the money. After much digging through a small straw bag the young woman fished out some crumpled dollar bills.

"Twelve? Man, this place is expensive." She clung to her money and turned to her friend. "It's happy hour at Sloppy's. Do you want to go there instead?"

"They're on me, ladies." Jerry D'Argent pushed some cash across the bar at Gene.

Jerry was a thin man with skin the color of red brick. He wore a black eyepatch, leftover from Fantasy Fest the year before, that he'd decided to leave on permanently when a tattooed, big hipped Catwoman told him he looked sexy. That was what he needed to hear after four weeks on a boat diving for treasure. This week he was once again in port, where his only duty was to occupy the same stool, third from the door, at The Frog for as many hours per day as paycheck and bladder would permit.

In a gesture of acceptance of Jerry's offer to pay, the two women pulled up bar stools. One whose hair ran from dark at the roots to pale yellow at the ends smiled at the treasure diver. The other one kept her eyes on her friend and did the talking.

"Thanks, darlin'. Friendly place, Key West."

Then the women fell into deep conversation with each other, ignoring Jerry and the little pile of money he had laid out on the bar.

The Frog was a drinking man's saloon. No attempt had been made to pretty the place up with little candles on the tables or hanging plants or funny pieces of antique junk nailed to the walls like in some other bars on Duval Street. The floors were bare; the sturdy, old bar had been polished till it shone; ceiling fans churned constantly overhead in place of air conditioning. No frills. A good place to work if a man's greatest ambition was to pay the rent.

With the weekend stretching ahead, dozens of customers perched on their barstools waiting for life to happen. Tonight the possibilities were endless, ranging from a sweaty weekend fling to spending a night in jail.

The combination of tinsel, palm trees, fast money and dreams drew planeloads of tourists fattened by regular paychecks and mutual funds to the town. On the heels of the imported money came dropouts like Gene in broken-down cars, all their worldly assets stuffed into a few cardboard boxes loaded into the backseat.

As much as Key West was a refuge of last resort, it also was a place of infinite chance, which made working in a place like The Frog more than tolerable. He might earn $150 in tips in a single shift behind the bar; he might end up at a party on a million-dollar yacht owned by somebody who just happened to stop in for a drink; he might meet a gorgeous woman who was independent and low-maintenance, the elusive woman of his dreams, just when he'd given up hope forever. Or it could just be another day of pouring drinks and answering stupid questions.

He had just served another round of gin and tonics to Jerry and Melvin McDonald when Gus Williams walked in. Fish scales and blood stained Gus's arms and shirtfront. Tourists scooted their barstools out of his way for the ripe smelling fisherman.

"How's the water?" Gene asked as he drew a cold glass of draft beer. The big man just nodded.

Gene never had to ask what his regulars drank. He just set them up on sight, and for that, his customers thought they had the best bartender in town.

He had no experience mixing drinks when he'd come into The Frog six months earlier looking for work, but The Frog's owner, Rick Warholt, had taken one look at Gene's six foot height and 190 pound build and said, "Can you start tonight?" End of interview. The bar owner figured that even if Gene were a lousy bartender, he'd be able to take care of any trouble by jumping over the bar, saving the cost of hiring a bouncer.

Gene set the beer down, and instead of a thank you, Gus muttered, "Dead man on the reef today. Coast Guard brought the body in an hour ago."

Gus hadn't said it very loud but still his words rang out over the conversation around the bar like a shot out of a gun.

Jerry and Melvin stopped trying to impress two female tourists.

A few stools down, another of the regulars, Diamanda Full Moon, looked up from the astrology chart she'd been studying.

"Not a diving accident, I hope," she said. "I knew it. I knew it when I got up this morning that it something bad was going to happen."

"Hell, no. Didn't have anything to do with diving," Gus said. "Turtle trapper, the guy was. Had a live one in a tank in back. Maybe 600 pounds. My guess is he was trying to bring in another one and the poor SOB got dragged in."

Gus tipped the glass back, drank the beer in one large swallow, then pushed the empty at Gene. Gene filled the glass again and put it in front of Gus, who sat there, staring hard at the counter, drinking the second beer more slowly.

"Well, it's been a long spell. Guess we're due for something to happen," said D'Argent. He squinted at Gene with his uncovered eye. "The guy probably just had a coronary and fell in."

"Didn't look like a coronary to me," Gus replied. "Something got him. The body was torn up pretty bad. We were real close when they pulled him out of the water."

"Shark?" asked D'Argent.

"Maybe. Maybe not," Gus replied. "But there was too much left of him. Shark would have eaten more."

Gene moved around the bar, checking to see who needed a refill.

Diamanda Full Moon's glass was empty. She shook her head when he came to her. She was an attractive woman with red hair that fell halfway down her back and green eyes that reminded Gene of the color of new palm fronds.

She wore a long purple dress printed with tiny stars and moons. It hung from spaghetti straps on smooth, freckled shoulders, draping her body in folds of purple. A large clear quartz crystal dangled from a silver chain around her neck. Her bags, containing tarot cards, crystals and the other tools of a sidewalk psychic, were stashed below the bar. As a rule, the women who drank in The Frog were young and wild but not Diamanda. She was older, he'd guess around 45, and had a presence that the younger ones lacked, like an old tree in a forest of saplings. She leaned toward Gus, whose story had apparently had her in its grip.

"What happened to the turtle? I hope the Coast Guard put him back in the water," she said.

Gus just shrugged and said, "Impounded."

"For what?" Diamanda cried out. "You'd think the turtle was the criminal the way they treat him."

"The hell with the turtle. What about the dead guy? He's just trying to earn a living," Jerry D'Argent said.

She shook her head angrily, sending the long red hair flying. "Did you get the name of the boat, Gus?"

"Legal Tender. Out of Charleston," he answered.

"I need to talk to Mattie. Maybe she'll know something. Did you see the Paradise Diver out there?"

Gus shook his head.

"Mattie Gold?" asked Jerry. His uncovered eye narrowed and he raised an eyebrow. "What's she up to?"

"Working. That's all that girl does these days," Diamanda said. "I hope she's okay."

"Mattie Gold's tough as nails," Jerry said. "Nothing is going to hurt that woman. If you really have extra sensory pretension, you ought to know that."

"It's perception, Jer," she said. "But you don't need vision to know that a man who is taking live turtles out of the sea is up to no good."

"Give the poor bastard a break," Jerry growled. "He's dead, the turtle's alive, and hell, he might have just been transporting it. Maybe he was moving it to safer waters. You don't know that he was up to no good. Innocent until proven guilty; man's got constitutional rights."

Diamanda sighed. "If it's a contest between the laws of nature and the constitution, Mother Nature wins, Jerry. But I'm worried. Mercury moved into the ninth house last night. The planetary alignment does not favor the animals."

"What, are you telling fortunes for fish now? Have you met Ms. Diamanda Full Moon," Jerry said to the blonde on the stool next to him. "One of Key West's top ten psychics. She does horoscopes for turtles." He turned his attention back to Diamanda. "What in the hell are you talking about, woman? Planets are aligned just fine, just the way God meant them to be."

"The moon is full in three days, and it's Scorpionic. Plus there's been a storm raging on Saturn for months now. We could be in for a hell of a week."

"What, in the name of Neptune, is a Scorpionic moon? And how in the hell do you know that it's storming on Saturn?" Jerry demanded.

"The sting of the Scorpion, any child knows, is poisonous," she said. "The storm can be seen with telescopes. Haven't you noticed that funny feeling lately? Even you, Jerry, should be able to feel it."

"Yes, it's called being thirsty," Jerry said. "Gene, give me another damned drink. I'd feel fine if I could just get another drink."

Gene made the drink and tried to ignore the banter as Jerry continued his diatribe against anything that wasn't grounded in his definition of science. Maybe Jerry hadn't noticed the tension in the air but Gene had. It reminded him of the way he used to feel before going out on an operation. It was like walking in the dark on a canyon rim knowing you were still on solid ground but that things could change in a split second.

But he seemed to be the only one feeling tensed up at the moment. The barroom crowd kept drinking and sweating and spinning around on their barstools not bothered in the least by Diamanda's cosmic forebodings. As it should be on a little island at the end of the road that the Chamber of Commerce had labeled Paradise. The air stirred from the ceiling fans spinning overhead and the band got ready to go back on stage for another set of Reggae.

Jerry and Melvin renewed their efforts with the two women.

"Maybe you'd like to be in the photo shoot for my new 'zine," Melvin said to the blonde.

"Next time, babe. We're going home in the morning," she replied, keeping those fiery red lips on the straw in her Planter's Punch as she spoke. She drained the glass with a loud slurp.

"Hell you can't go home yet. Things are just starting to get interesting. Get us another round, Gene," Jerry called out, pointing at her empty glass.

Gene made the drinks, refilled Jerry's glass and took Jerry's money.

Jerry elbowed his prey. "Come back next year, he'll know you, remember just what you had last time you were in here." The diver tapped his forehead. "Never makes a mistake. Got a memory like a computer. Best bartender in these parts, even though that's a waste of his real talents. He used to be a Navy SEAL."

"A SEAL, huh? You really a SEAL?"

Gene shrugged. "Jerry's got a big mouth."

The blonde considered what to believe for a minute, and then pulled a small white card out of her pocket and threw it on the bar in Gene's direction. "Honey, this is for you."

Gene picked up the card and read the tiny print. It was good for a free palm reading from Hecate, one of the psychics who worked sunsets down at the Mallory Pier. He pushed it back at her.

"What am I going to do with this?"

"It's worth twenty bucks," she said. She pushed the card at him again. "I can't use it. I'm going home tomorrow."

"Great. My landlord will love it when I tell him the future instead of giving him the rent."

He started to turn away. Tourists! It was a wonder he wasn't living in a cardboard appliance box under some coconut palm the way some of them hung on to their money. Forget about that dream of saving up to buy a little place up the Keys someday.

The blonde just shrugged and picked up her purse from beneath her barstool.

"You ladies want to come to a party?" Melvin asked. "At my place?"

With a few drinks in him, Melvin would toss out the party invites like a closet society lady on Easter Sunday to any woman who gave him five minutes of her attention. Once in a while one of them would take him up on it. The ladies were moving toward the door, but they turned around to consider the invitation.

"A party? Are you going?" The blonde nodded at Gene, while her friend tugged her toward the exit.

Melvin answered without waiting for Gene to respond. "Sure he is."

"Did you really used to be a SEAL?" she asked.

"It's irrelevent," Gene said. "I'm a bartender now."

"I've always wondered about SEALs," she said. "I've heard some stories." She giggled and turned to Melvin. "Give me your address, just in case."

He scribbled it on a bar napkin and handed it to her. She shoved the napkin into a pocket, winked at Gene and left.

"Damn, Gene, I think she liked you. Maybe I should put a gray streak in my hair, some platinum highlights or something. Women love that shit." Melvin was referring to the long streak of gray that ran through Gene's dark hair from his forehead to the end of his ponytail on his back.

"Guess I better go," Melvin said, standing. "Got a connection to make."

"I'll have one more." Jerry drained his glass and pushed it forward. "Make it a double this time, Gene, seeing as how it's the last one of the day."

Gene filled the tumbler with ice and gin. He squirted tonic on top, then tossed in a tired-looking wedge of lime. When he delivered the drink, Jerry leaned forward and grabbed Gene's arm. "I'm going to let you in on something, buddy. I think we found Atlantis."

"Atlantis? Melvin, what have you been smoking?"

"Yeah, unbelievable, isn't it?" Melvin grinned proudly and sucked down half the gin and tonic in one gulp.

"I thought you were out there looking for pieces of the Atocha. You don't really believe there's a lost city out there?"

"Come on. You used to be in the Navy. You must know how much weird-ass junk is on the ocean floor. Strange things—buildings, vessels, old roads, big chunks of metal. How they got there, who the hell knows? Maybe from ancient civilizations or UFOs."

"The Navy would call that paranormal, Jerry, and if I were still active duty, I'd find an explanation for it that made sense. Atlantis is just a story."

"The hell it is. The government just doesn't want you to know. Atlantis could be right under our nose. It's the kind of discovery that makes all the BS worthwhile. My point is," he paused, "my point is a man's got to have a purpose in life. A mission. You know about destiny, about purpose. You used to be a SEAL."

"Jerry, would you stop talking about SEALs? Nobody cares about ancient history," Gene said. "Purpose is fine, but rule number one is no complications."

"Keep it simple stupid, Kiss, I know that one," Jerry said. "Taught you that in underwater demo school, right? I got to ask you, Gene. Do you miss it?"

"No, Jer, this is better. Hell, I got a job, plenty of friends, free entertainment," said Gene, waving his arm at the crowd in the barroom.

"Liar," Jerry said. "Man who worked out on the water long as you did has got the sea in his blood. You can't just give it up and finish your days on land. It's not natural."

"You're going to tell me about natural? Have another gin and tonic," Gene replied. The band launched into a Bob Marley tune, bumping up the sound by several decibels, and drowning out the rest of Jerry's lecture about how Gene ought to live out the rest of his days. Gene pointed at his ear like he was deaf and moved away.

Before the song was over, The Frog's owner, Rick Warholt, appeared out of his office in back. He was a longhaired, pot-bellied, southern redneck with a thousand dollars worth of gold chains around his neck. He came behind the bar, opened the cash register and removed all the folding money save for a stack of ones.

"Music's not loud enough," Warholt said gruffly as he passed Gene. He stuck a thumb in the air, signaling that he wanted the volume higher. "The louder the band, the more they drink. When they go on break," he gestured at the stage, "tell them to crank it up."

Gene nodded and wondered how long his hearing would hold out if he kept working here. Already the wooden floor vibrated beneath his Tevas, but he would dutifully tell the band to notch it up. Warholt should have gone back into his office by now but he just stood there, glaring inexpicably at Gene.

"Had a call for you." Warholt leaned against the back of the bar and looked at Gene with eyebrows raised as if Gene had now been caught in a major transgression. Warholt had a rule that employees couldn't take calls at work. "Told him you were too busy to talk. He said it was important. Guy named Johnnie."

"Thanks," Gene said and kept pouring drinks.

"I'm not a damned answering service," Warholt said as he walked away finally.

Johnnie had to be Johnnie Reb, who ran a dolphin sanctuary twenty miles up the Keys. Gene hadn't seen nor heard from him in months, not since Gene turned down an offer of a part-time job on the grounds that he couldn't live on a $5.50 an hour wage. Maybe he'd take a ride up in the morning. At least the prospect of an early morning ride on the Harley would give him a good reason not to sit in the bars till all hours of the night, spending whatever he'd made that day in tips.

The band took a break then and when the music stopped most of the people in the bar finished their drinks and wandered out the door. Five minutes later Diamanda was the only one of the regulars left. Gene knew she liked an occasional Cuba Libre, and he mixed up one without asking and presented it to her.

"On the house," he said.

"You're a good man, Gene Rockland."

"Don't tell anybody."

"Big weekend ahead?" When she reached out to take the drink, Gene noticed the nails, a coppery red color that matched her hair.

"Nothing special. Maybe ride my bike up the keys. Mainly, I got to work. First of the month's almost here."

She raised her glass. "Even in paradise, the landlord cometh. Maybe it's a good thing. If we didn't have bills, nobody around here would do much of anything."

"Cause less damage that way, that's for sure. I'm a big supporter of doing nothing." He started to sort the change in his tip jar and came to the small white card for the free reading.

"You going to use that?" she asked.

"Maybe."

"Well, if you want a reading, let me do it. No charge. Tomorrow if you like." Diamanda waited for an answer.

"Thanks. I'll think about it." He almost wished she was flirting with him, but that wasn't what was happening here. Diamanda was a friend, maybe even the only real female friend Gene had.

"Don't be afraid, Gene," she said.

He laughed. "Afraid of getting my fortune told?"

"No, of what's coming," she said, standing. "I'll see you tomorrow."

Chapter 4

A few hours later, Gene finished his shift and left The Frog. He walked out, his backpack slung over a shoulder, and turned up Caroline Street toward Simonton Street Beach.

He had another hour of daylight, enough time to pay his respects to the sea before he started his Duval crawl. The soft green-blue shade of the water always shifted him past the small aggravations of a day behind the bar. The island didn't have real beaches with surf and soft beige sand like the rest of Florida, but instead was surrounded by sharp little coral rock beaches. Gene had never been one for lying on a towel in the sand anyway and didn't mind. He preferred being in the water or out on a boat with the sea stretching horizon to horizon and no people in sight. Now that he earned his living on land, he was drawn to the water's edge each day as irresistibly as church drew a Holy Roller on Sundays.

When he got to the beach, the sun was still high above the horizon. He took a seat on the deserted concrete pier. Across the small patch of sand, two dirty, barefoot men sat on the porch of the bathhouse. Every few minutes, they raised small brown paper bags to their mouths to drink.

They were enjoying themselves immensely, and their conversation alternated between friendly laughter and loud cursing. Once in a while, one would take a threatening swing at the other, but the fight was more of a pastime than a serious brawl.

Key West was home to many homeless men and women, if back streets and beaches could be called home. Paradise was a palm tree and free stretch of sand to one guy, and a million-dollar mansion with gingerbread trim and a heated pool in back to another. The live and let live attitude was the beauty of the place for Gene. The cops pretty much left the beach bums and beggars alone as long as they didn't make trouble.

Whenever he saw the bums he would wonder, who had more freedom? The indigents? Or the sunburned tourists on their way to a pricey dinner and white linened hotel bed? At least the beach dwellers didn't get a credit card bill a month later for their evening in paradise.

When Gene got off work, the first thing he wanted was a drink, but the sight of The Frog's off-premises regulars, homeless Tequila Mary and two other panhandlers, out in front of The Frog made him decide to wait a while before he started spending the day's tip money on cocktails.

He stared out at the sailboats. The water's surface broke into mosaic of shimmering blue and silver. The breeze off the water cooled his skin.

Gene shut his eyes. He felt restless. The air vibrated over the little beach like the atmosphere before a tropical storm. He thought about Diamanda and her crazy talk of the scorpionic moon and the news of the death on the reef.

Maybe it would rain and the weekend would turn out to be quiet, uneventful. Maybe he'd make $600 in tips and not have to worry about money for a few days. But somehow he couldn't quite convince himself of it.

After a few minutes, he got up, brushing pebbles and dirt off the back of his khaki shorts. It was still too early to go home, so he headed back towards The Frog, looking for something to do that didn't involve drinking. That was a real challenge.

As he neared Mallory Pier, he joined a parade of people walking purposefully to the west where the sun was about to start its nightly performance. On Front Street, the crowd crossed Duval and hurried past the Pier House, the favored stop for big spenders where a room with a balcony facing the sunset could be had for about five hundred a night. Music blasted from the Hog's Breath, just a stone's throw down Duval but he didn't veer off. Instead, he stayed with the crowd moving towards the big dock where the cruise ships tied up. Everyone was headed for the same spot, a massive spit of concrete called Mallory Pier.

He caught a glimpse of the water in a space between the tall hotel buildings and saw the sun hanging low in the sky like a red beach ball. It was almost sunset.

He reached into his pocket to check his cash supply. The twenty-dollar bill that he'd earned in tips would buy him dinner and a beer.

His fingers touched a piece of cardboard next to the twenty and he had to take the card out and examine it before he remembered the free palm reading at Mallory Pier.

He stuck the card back in his pocket and continued to the pier. Hundreds of tourists were clumped around the performers and artists who were scattered up and down the pier. The card dug sharply at his fingertips as if it were trying to tell him something.

Gene knew the palm reader, Hecate, would be here somewhere.

Tim, the straightjacket man, was halfway through his escape act. The wiry little performer was wrapped in thick silver chains and padlocks. He had erected spotlights on tripods, which would illuminate his act after the sun went down. A big empty bucket sat down in front to collect money for his performance. Tim had to put his bucket out before he started since chances were he'd still be bound up in chains when the sun actually dropped below the horizon and his audience dispersed back to the bars on Duval.

The Cookie Lady nearly knocked Gene over as she pedaled by on her ancient bike, its basket loaded with sugary treats. She wore a tattered flower print dress and her hair was slicked back under a scarf.

"Chocolate cookies, coconut treats, sunset celebration is the time for eats," she yelled out. "Chickens, roosters, dogs and cats, if you think you're hungry, I'm where it's at."

People began to line up to buy her cookies and brownies.

"Who's scarier, me or the Cookie Lady?" bellowed Tim as he tried to lure some of the cookie buyers over to his act.

Up and down the broad concrete pier, artists and merchants hawked their wares. A tall man with charcoal dreadlocks peddled homemade incense. Two Caribbean islanders strummed guitars, a beat up old hat laid out at their feet for donations. A smiling hippie girl in Indian print clothes and barefeet sold falafel and vegetarian eggrolls from a rolling cart.

Gene stopped to watch a young fire-eater swallow a few sticks of flame. The gasoline smell was not as strong as the watermelon fragrance that came from the hairspray on all the tourists. The visitors seemed to be made from a cookie cutter, all freshly showered and displaying sun-pinkened skin as they lined up to spend money on cheap trinkets they really didn't need. Before the night was over, hundreds of dollars would be tossed into the money pails of the entertainers, and everybody would go home happy.

Gene remembered the first time he'd been to Key West, twenty years before. Back then, sunset celebration was just a bunch of kids playing guitar and getting high. He'd been a naïve kid from New Jersey who just joined the Navy with a patriotic idea about defending freedom. His conservative upbringing had not prepared him for the loose and wild happenings down on the pier just a short stroll from his barracks at the base. After a few months training, he'd departed to start his military career.

Things had changed in the years he'd been away. Now nobody dared light up a joint, at least not right out in public. First they ducked into an alley or the public restroom. Even the free spirits had become bureaucrats. To get a good spot on the pier, the artists and performers submitted to a lottery. Sunset had become a job and the whole point of the party was to make money.

A few paces beyond the fire-eater, the palm reader Hecate had set up her stand. She had silky blond hair and pale skin. She sat in a wooden director's chair, long folds of a dark blue skirt swirling around her slim legs.

She wore no jewelry or makeup; her skin was clean scrubbed as a schoolgirl's with only the little creases around her eyes to give away her age.

Gene knew her name even though he'd never spoken to her. She often walked past the open windows of The Frog in the late afternoon on her way to sunset. His regulars, who could provide a dossier on anyone who'd been on the island more than a month, had quickly filled Gene in when they saw him take notice of her.

"The competition," Diamanda Full Moon had said, sounding a little defensive. "But, hey, there's room here for everybody, right? The universe provides."

Key West had more tarot card readers, rune throwers, astrologists and palm readers per capita than any town in the whole state. And at $20 for a 15 minute reading, it was easy to see why. "People on vacation love to have their fortunes told," Diamanda had explained.

Now he circled Hecate's spot on the pier, hesitating. She spotted him and waved him over to an empty chair.

Gene dug into his pocket and offered her the card. "Is this any good?"

"Of course," she said, gesturing at him to sit. "Where are you from?"

Couldn't she tell if she was really psychic? Besides, his appearance ought to give away that he was a local. No watermelon-smelling hair goop or freshly ironed khakis for Gene. Instead he wore his hair shoulder-length, a later-than-five-o'clock shadow, faded, wrinkled shorts and T-shirt.

"Here and there," he answered, sitting down awkwardly.

She frowned slightly as if she heard his thoughts that she was a fraud.

"You live here, don't you," she finished for him, adding, "I've seen you around. So you'd like to have a reading?"

He nodded. She reached for his hand and as she leaned near, he smelled her perfume. The scent was light like a garden in spring.

"Is Hecate your real name?"

"Of course," she replied.

Gene had phrased the question wrong. Real was whatever a person wanted real to be. He should have asked if Hecate was her birth name.

"What would you like to ask me?"

He hadn't given that question much thought. He didn't want to know the future really, other than to know that it would be easy and simple and not like the past. Perhaps he should ask about his idea of buying a little piece of property up the Keys. He wondered if that dream would ever come true.

The palm reader's grip on his hand tightened. She turned his hand towards her, pointed his fingers skyward. She placed her slim palm up against his, matching their fingers.

"I feel much turmoil right now." She closed her eyes and breathed deeply, concentrating. "I'm sensing issues with a past lover. Someone who is no longer in the picture."

He wondered if she meant his ex-wife. Alex, the second of Gene's two ex's, lived in town. They were on good terms and she'd come around once in a while to ask him to fix her car or, as she put it, "just to make sure he was okay."

He dated a few other women, if going down to Duval Street to listen to music and have a few beers with somebody from out of town counted as a date. After the second divorce, Gene decided to take a little break from romance. He needed a breather after ten years of marriage. SEALs were notoriously difficult to stay married to and even though he'd quit the team three years back, he knew that for him, being out of the Navy would not transform him overnight into a family man. Love was one of those mysterious things, so elusive that he often wondered if it were an imaginary phenomenon, while sex was easier, especially in wild and free Key West.

"Everything's great in the love department," he said.

Hecate looked straight at him, eyes flashing, "Affairs of the heart aren't important now. Put them aside. You have a higher purpose."

Gene leaned back into the chair. A higher purpose? That was a laugh.

But he didn't feel like arguing. The psychic's words and soothing voice were intoxicating even if it were all an act.

She stopped and rearranged his hand, turning the palm down. Her eyes closed; her face crumpled in concentration.

"Give me a minute." She swayed in the seat. She cleared her throat and opened her eyes, looking straight into his. Then she dropped his hands and shook her fingers hard as if she'd just pulled them out of freezing water.

"You've been involved with the sea for your whole life, but you've given it up," she said, closing her eyes.

"Yes," Gene said. He had sailed and dived as a teen well before his 20-year stint as a SEAL. But everyone who lived on the island was involved with the sea. And if she noticed him behind the bar at The Frog, she knew he'd given up working on water.

"You've been caught up in a bureaucracy, official madness that was not of your making. Some good, some evil, some confusion."

If she were guessing now, it was closer to the truth, Gene thought. The Pentagon certainly qualified as official madness.

"You will face anger," she said softly. "You have many decisions to make; your free will will be tested."

She sounded alarmed. She was a fine enough actress to win an Academy Award, he thought.

"Breathe," she ordered. "Close your eyes and let your body relax. Breathe deeply, male air-breathing mammal."

He obeyed even though she spoke to him in words one might use to address some alien species.

"Something very important is coming into your life. It's bigger than you. Pay attention. Clear your mind," she said. "I want you to visualize a wall. Do you see it?"

His eyes were still closed and he did picture a wall in front of him. Gene nodded. It was brick, solid and high.

"Someone will ask you for help. There's a message involved. You undertake this at great personal risk." Hecate said. "Look at the wall. Do you see a gate, an opening?"

In his imagination, he could, so he nodded.

"Go through the doors," she said. "When the time comes, you will know what to do."

She ordered him to breathe and called him an air-breathing mammal a few more times, then told him to open his eyes.

When he did, he saw a lot of people standing around them, very close, listening to everything she'd said. He felt invaded, as if the audience was violating him. The psychic was smiling calmly.

Hecate's entertainment value, he had to admit, was better than the sword swallower ten feet down the pier eating his flaming, gasoline-soaked stick or the two old black men playing steel drums down at the pier's end.

Palm reading, like so much else on the island, was just fantasy and play-acting. Not to be taken seriously. He had a low-paying, thoroughly undangerous job pouring drinks. His lovers were chosen because they believed in mutual freedom. He did not have a big important mission ahead. That was reality. That was what he knew to be true.

Hecate was staring at him, her eyes cutting into him sharply. The intensity made him uncomfortable. He avoided her gaze by looking beyond her at the sun about to dip into the water.

Other people had gathered around and were waiting for him to leave the chair so that they could get their fortunes told.

"Do you have any questions?" She seemed to want to continue, and he remembered that she charged by the minute.

"No." Gene rose. The crowd drew closer in until he felt like he was the center of a three-ring circus. Gene wanted to be off the pier and away from the people. She handed him a tape of the reading and her business card. Gene impulsively tipped her with his twenty-dollar bill. There'd be no six-pack tonight.

She smiled as she took his money. He was left jangling a few quarters in his pocket. Dinner money.

"Come and see me again," she said. "I'll tell you about Atlantis, other stuff. Have a wonderful adventure."

Gene took the business card from her and headed off the pier. That last part was weird, the way she seemed to know what they'd been talking about in the bar that day. Atlantis, drunken treasure divers and higher purposes. The island was full of nutcases. He tossed the card into a dumpster when he reached Duval Street.

Chapter 5

The dolphin swam away from the dive boat near the reef but he wasn't done for the day. Three miles offshore, Sgt. Storm Davis dangled 150 feet below the surface of the clear blue sea, a thin nylon descent line clutched in his black-gloved hand. He waited for his two companions, who trailed behind on the line.

Storm and his two students had entered the water a few minutes earlier to do a three-hour training dive on the Wilkes-Barre in the deeper waters out beyond the reef.

He looked up to check their progress but could see only their silhouetted shapes against the bright backdrop of the surface. Their arms and legs protruded gracefully from their torsos, which were fat as barrels due to the double air tanks each man carried on his back. Storm continued his descent until he reached the massive ship that sat on the ocean floor at the end of their descent line.

A few minutes later, Paul Roberts and Andy Heydon, students at the Special Forces Combat Swimmer School in Key West, joined Storm at the smokestack of the Wilkes-Barre.

With one gloved hand, Storm gripped the rusty rim of the stack, an enormous tube of steel that was thick with a decade of growth. Orange plants that resembled alien life and furry green algae coated the ship's exterior.

Storm loved the old ship as much as a man could love a machine. In her finest hour, the old girl had been a warrior, nicknamed the Lethal Lady. Six hundred and ten feet long, she extended far beyond Storm's range of vision. Her superstructure loomed like a miniature city skyline.

The Navy had sunk her for underwater explosive practice in 1972. She'd tilted to starboard until a hurricane had straightened her up in the water. Now she sat erect in the sand on the ocean floor, waiting for him.

The old ship was as erotic to Storm as any woman could be, except that the feelings that she aroused in him were purer and not as confusing. His adrenaline pumped; his heart quickened; he felt excited to see her stretching out as far as he could see.

The three divers exchanged okay signs, and Storm checked his computer and gauges. Their depth was 180 feet, with an elapsed bottom time of four minutes. Each 80-cubic-foot steel cylinder was loaded with enough air to sustain them for 20 minutes, leaving extra for decompression stops on the way up.

Besides the twin 80s, which were worn like backpacks, each diver had two sets of regulators, gauges, computers, a reel and line, a bright yellow lift bag, two dive lights and two knives. With gear clipped and Velcroed to them in every available spot, they looked like Christmas trees that had been hung with a few too many ornaments. A full-sized third air tank dangled at each man's side.

So far, the dive had been textbook perfect, but at this depth, the dizzying effects of nitrogen narcosis already were setting in. Storm could see the excitement in his students' eyes as they waited for him to lead the way and he hoped they would stay levelheaded.

He motioned them to follow him and headed toward the first set of gun turrets. The armaments had pounded the Japanese in World War II but would never be fired again. As he swam past the long gun muzzles, imagining the ghosts of the men who'd served on the ship, the hair on Storm's arms stood on end. He could feel the goosebumps even under the tight skin of his wetsuit.

Storm checked the time and headed down to the main deck at 190-foot depth. Here, the ship's metal surface was rusted and hard crustaceans and fuzzy growth stuck to every exposed surface. Small tropical fish darted around, their colors muted by the filtered light, their movements magically smooth as if they were choreographed in a Disney cartoon.

On the deck, the divers unclipped their spare jugs of air and stowed them in a sheltered spot for retrieval on the return trip. Then the three men kicked their long fins to propel themselves further to the aft of the ship. They passed a dozen open doors leading to the ship's vast interior.

"Under no circumstances are you to penetrate the wreck unless I tell you to. It'll be your funeral," Storm had warned Paul and Andy before the dive began.

Getting lost inside a shipwreck was a simple thing to do. A few kicks of a flipper raised enough silt to put a diver instantly into an impenetrable fog. He could then become so disoriented he'd be unable to tell which way is up or down, let alone the direction to get out.

Storm and the students reached an open doorway about a hundred feet from where they left their stage bottles. They'd been down ten minutes, and had ten left before they had to start back to the top. It was now time to turn the dive, but first he wanted to give Paul and Andy a taste of the old girl's mystery. It would only add a minute.

He pulled a small white slate from a zippered pocket and wrote, "Two minutes. Treat." He showed the message to them and motioned to follow him. They would penetrate the interior of the ship for a few moments.

Storm led them into a passageway, then turned right into a long room full of murky shadows. He signaled them to switch on their lights and the beams illuminated a latrine. The room had a half dozen urinals lining one wall and sparse military issue sinks on the other. Paul and Andy moved slowly along. The experience of floating through a tomb-like, pitch-black head was surreal, one of the weird pleasures of very deep diving that kept Storm coming back for more.

He checked his computer. They were at 200 feet, 16 minutes elapsed time. Four minutes before they had to start back for the surface. Storm headed back to the stage bottles that they'd left on the main deck.

Because he was in front, Storm was the first to see a long silver mass of muscled dolphin extending from the corner where they'd left the tanks. The creature was enormous and at first he thought it was a shark. Storm shook his head to see if his eyes—or the narcosis—were playing tricks on him. He judged the dolphin to be about 12-feet long, probably 600 lbs., the largest he'd ever encountered.

He waved his hands trying to get Paul and Andy's attention as he watched the dolphin use his pointy mouth to open a clip that had held the bottles down. Storm knew dolphins had unbelievable dexterity. He once saw a dolphin pick up a dime from the silty bottom of a lagoon. But unclipping their tanks took as much intelligence as it did skill.

Now all three divers paid close attention, watching in amazement as the big gray mammal lifted the tank and pushed it through the water to the side of the ship. The dolphin gave the tank a shove over the side and released it. The sandy bottom was another 40 feet down.

Storm kicked over to the staging area. He wanted to save the other two bottles from the dolphin. But he was too late. While they'd been inside the wreck, the dolphin had thrown all three over the side to the sand below. If this had been a real military operation, the dolphin would have ruined it.

What was that damn fish doing? Storm had trained for a lot of military contingencies but never for underwater vandalism from a fish.

He signaled to Paul and Andy to wait, then swam over to the starboard gunwale. He could barely make out the shape of the three tanks lying in the sand 40 feet below where the dolphin had dropped them. This really screwed up the dive. He considered going after the bottles, but it would use up too much gas and all their careful planning of decompression stops on the way up would have to be tossed out the window and recalculated for the added depth and time.

Abandoning the tanks was like leaving a couple of hundred dollars lying in the sand. He couldn't bring all three back to the deck alone. The tanks were too heavy for one trip and the effort to make three trips to the sand would take too long and force a dangerous amount of nitrogen into his body tissue. He might end up dead, or at least crippled for life.

He decided to leave the tanks for another day.

He kicked back over to Paul and Andy and gave them thumbs up. They moved to the line and ascended at a slow measured pace.

Halfway up, Storm checked his air. Lower than he would have liked, no doubt due to their breathing rates being stepped up by that maritime thief. But the remaining supply would get them to the decompression station, 15 feet below their boat, where regulators were hanging in the water, connected to a tank of oxygen aboard the boat, ready to switch to oxygen hoses hanging in the water from the boat.

Storm reached the decompression station first and quickly swapped his mouthpiece for one attached to hoses dangling down from the Zodiac. Paul and Andy came up behind him.

Paul made the change to the dangling hose with no problem but Andy stopped and just hung in the water, his hand on the line. When his student made no move to switch to the surface-supplied gas, Storm kicked over to him and turned Andy around. He looked into his mask. Andy's eyes were glazed and his breathing was fast and panicky.

Storm grabbed him with one hand and dug into a zippered pocket with the other, trying to get hold of an extra clip to tether Andy to the rig before he passed out. Then Andy's head slumped to the side and he began to sink. He grew heavier and Storm's grip was slipping, and next thing he knew, Andy was loose and plummeting slowly, dreamlike, toward the bottom.

Storm thought about going after him. He didn't see he had much choice because if he didn't Andy was going to die. But if he did the nitrogen load in both their tissues meant that the chance of getting the bends would be 100 percent. He weighed his choices, one dead diver or two divers crippled for life, when an image emerged from the green-gray depths. It was that damned dolphin again, and this time the creature was pushing Andy up from the bottom.

The dolphin swam straight to Storm and handed Andy over. Storm grabbed his student, clipped him to the rig and checked his breathing. Then he stuck the regulator on the end of the oxygen hose into Andy's mouth and turned his head to check his eyes again. This time, Andy was awake, looking scared but clearly alive. The dolphin watched from twenty feet off, and then swam away.

Storm made an okay sign with his hand, and Andy returned the hand signal, nodding.

The dolphin's behavior was inexplicable, Storm thought. First it ruined his dive plan, then it saved Andy's life. The creature performed as systematically as though it had been trained for it.

Where had the big gray bastard come from? Nobody around here trained military dolphins, at least not anymore, according to what Storm knew.

At one time, the Navy had a big, top secret dolphin project at Key West. But with budget cuts and protests by fish-hugging environmentalists, the "marine mammal" program, as it had been called, had been shrunk into a small secret effort and relocated to the Navy's Coronado base in Southern California. So secret that even Storm didn't know much about it officially.

As he hung on the line timing his decompression stop, waiting for the nitrogen to wash out of his tissues so he could safely return to sea level, Storm looked down into the endless blue. He wished that the dolphin would reappear. But all that was visible were a couple of vicious-looking five-foot barracuda and a school of tarpon shooting fast to the south. Next time he met that dolphin, he'd be ready. He hadn't had a real challenge since he'd arrived in Key West and if the dolphin wanted to play war games, Storm was ready.

Chapter 6

From a bench on the dock, Mattie Gold watched the medics wheel Jim Reynold's body away and load him into an ambulance. Her dog Neptune lay at her feet, letting out an occasional whimper as if the dog sensed that something terrible had happened.

Two uniformed Monroe County Sheriff's Department officers leaned against their squad car in the parking lot in front of the dive shop, interviewing Todd. A third officer, George Means, approached her.

"Mattie, I'll need to talk to you but first I want to get their statements." Means nodded toward the boat, where four divers huddled, looking frightened and forlorn. Means walked over and handed them blank forms. "Write down everything you remember," he said.

Mattie trailed Means over to the boat. "Okay if I unload things?"

He nodded.

The divers sat and scribbled out their versions of the story. Jim Reynolds' girlfriend shivered under a beach towel. She had stopped crying on the way in and was staring into space with red-rimmed eyes. Another passenger had his arm around her.

On the dock, a small crowd had gathered to stare at the boat and emergency crew. They turned when a compact car with rusty fenders skidded to a halt in the parking lot. Out of the car, a skinny man emerged and hurried over to join the group.

The young man had pale skin and wore his straight brown hair in a bowl cut that fell just below his ears. Mattie had never seen the guy before but he got her attention as he hurried toward the dock as if he had urgent business. He might have been a geeky student from the nearby community college but his sports shirt and tie were much too formal for that and he carried a small spiral notebook of the type that reporters use.

She kept working, unloading tanks, until he came over, tucking the notebook under his arm and thrusting out his hand.

"Hello. I'm Abe Starler, with the Key West Anchor." A necktie decorated with lime green whales flopped over a camera that hung around his neck. "What happened?"

Neptune stuck his furry nose into the reporter's crotch. The dog gave him a good sniff, then backed up and growled a little.

"Neptune, leave him alone," Mattie said. "I'm a little busy now. Think I better talk to them first." She nodded at Means.

"Oh yeah, I understand," the reporter said. "I just want some basic information. You know, who was the guy, how old he was. Get a couple of quotes. It'll take two minutes, just fill me in on what happened."

"I said later."

"Aw, come on. I'm on deadline. I don't even have to use your name if you don't want."

She let out an exasperated sigh. "I said, later. Don't you understand English?" Mattie turned to finish unloading the gear.

Two of her passengers were making their way over to Means. It was the couple from Tampa, a man with dark glasses and a receding hairline, and a woman, short, plump and serious.

"Excuse me, officer," the man said. He had folded his written statement into a neat little square and played with it nervously. "How often you see shark attacks around here?"

Means frowned. "We don't. Can't remember ever having one in my thirty years. Not in these waters."

The woman tugged at his elbow. "Tell him what we saw."

The man paused, hands on hips. "We don't know what we saw."

"We saw something," she said insistently.

"We didn't see anything," he said. "Jim, the guy from Detroit, got separated from the group, and we didn't see anything. The divemaster found him, and he was pretty much gone by then."

"All right." She planted her feet and nudged him aside. "If you won't tell, I will."

"Why don't you just put it in the statement, ma'am," Means said. Sweat dripped from his forehead down his face and onto his blue uniform collar.

"Al thinks he saw a shark cruise past us just before we found the body," she said, folding her arms across her chest. "But it wasn't a shark. It was a dolphin. I studied them and all the other marine life before I ever took my first diving class. I wanted to know what I was getting into. I know a dolphin when I see one. They don't look anything like sharks."

Her boyfriend glared at her, then interrupted. "It was murky. There was surge. I don't think you could see."

Means let out a sigh. "Listen, why don't you folks just put it in the report, put your phone number on there, and we'll get in touch with you if we need more."

Mattie and the reporter could hear the whole conversation from where they were, and as they spoke, Abe Starler opened his little book and pulled a pen out of his shirt pocket. He jotted some notes and took a few steps toward the couple.

"A dolphin, you say? How big?" Starler's eyes sparkled as his pen began to soil the snowy white paper with scrawled notes.

"Who are you?" Means growled, giving the journalist a cold stare.

"Oh, sorry." Starler smiled apologetically. He stuck out a hand. "Abe Starler, Key West Anchor. Heard the sirens and just followed the noise. What happened here?"

"That is what I am trying to find out," Means said. "You're interfering with an accident investigation. I suggest you wait over there till we finish, young man. Better yet, why don't you just go on back to your office and give the public information department a call later?"

Starler shuffled away, head down, to the wall of the Dive Shop. He leaned against it, busily writing in his notebook and raising the camera to shoot pictures.

"Damn press," Means said. "Always trying to make a scandal where there ain't one."

He took Mattie by the arm and led her to a corner out of earshot of Starler and the others. The dog trailed behind, his tail down.

"Mattie, you see a shark out there?" Means asked.

She shook her head. "I don't think so."

"Anything unusual?"

"There was a dolphin. She's right about that. But I don't think the dolphin had anything to do with this. He was on the surface when they were down. He was beautiful. Friendly too." Mattie smiled as she remembered the magnificent animal. "It was funny. Almost like he'd been trained."

She'd spotted the dorsal fin about twenty feet from the boat while the divers were down. Then the dolphin had raised his head out of the water and scolded her in a high-pitched voice.

He was the largest dolphin Mattie'd ever seen and he wore a dolphin smile – all long snout and a mouthful of teeth. No one would believe it, she'd thought then. The big gray creature acted like he'd come over specifically to meet her.

"Hey, big guy. Come closer. I won't hurt you," she'd called out.

The dolphin had risen out of the water on his tail, like a performer at the zoo. Mattie swore he'd looked her straight in the eye, as piercing a stare as any man had ever given her. A chill had traveled down her spine. There was something sexual about the feeling.

She called to him again, and the dolphin plunged beneath the surface, a graceful arc of vanishing silver. But Means didn't need to hear all that and Mattie decided not to go into details.

Instead, she said, "We see them all the time on the way out to the reef, but they don't normally get near the divers. He came up and made a bunch of noise, like he was trying to get my attention. There was nothing threatening about it."

Mattie pushed the brim of her cap back a bit. "I guess I should have reacted sooner, when I noticed his bubbles. I saw bubbles in two places. I knew the divers weren't all together."

The breeze stirred the trees and the flags flying over the shop snapped in the wind.

"Mattie, accidents happen," Means said. "Diving is a hazardous sport, and these people know it when they come out here. Or at least they ought to."

Means pulled out a big white handkerchief and mopped the sweat from his forehead. "Come into my office tomorrow and we'll take a statement. I don't want to make this any more difficult for you or Patcher than I have to."

"Yeah, okay," Mattie said. She'd made an appointment to pick out flowers for "the event," as she called the small ceremony they'd planned but that could be changed.

"Got to impound the guy's equipment, though," Means said. "Rental?"

"He owned it. Everything's brand new," she said.

Means went over to get Jim Reynolds' gear as the two customers trailed behind.

"What about us?" the woman asked.

"So you think you saw a shark, or a dolphin, but you didn't see anything actually attack Mr. Reynolds? You just think you saw something in the vicinity." Means spoke in a distant, authoritative tone.

She nodded.

"It's a big ocean. Lots of big fish out there." He shook his head and smiled sadly. "We'll have the autopsy in a couple of days."

His voice softened as he raised his voice loud enough that the reporter and other bystanders could hear. "Hate to tell you, but sharks just don't bite people in the Keys, no matter what you've read in the

National Enquirer. The ocean's got its risks but there's nothing danger- ous, or mysterious or weird out there. We don't have Jaws, or great white man-eaters, or any other movie monster living offshore. You got that?"

He spit a big slimy wad of tobacco onto the ground. Means enjoyed playing the good old boy. In front of a tourist, Mattie knew he'd protect Patcher and any other local businessman until something forced him to do otherwise.

The reporter had edged closer again. The deputy gave Starler another menacing look and began to collect the tanks, weights, inflat- able jacket and regulator that belonged to Jim Reynolds. When he was loaded down with the dead man's gear, he headed to his squad car.

The woman chased after him, waving her statement. "Don't forget our reports."

Mattie returned to the boat, gathering up Reynolds' personal effects to give to the girlfriend, deciding that she'd offer to drive her back to her hotel. It was about all she could do.

Chapter 7

The bruised and battered body of a scuba diver was pulled from the waters off Key West yesterday. The cause of death was unknown, according to a statement from the Monroe County Sheriff's Department...

Starler read his words silently. The lead still had no snap, that undefinable quality that Angora Pearl, city editor for the Key West Anchor, was constantly harping about when she explained why she changed his stories.

The cursor flashed against the bright green computer screen. His eyes shifted between the smoke trail rising from his illicit cigarette and her door in the cramped newsroom. Angora would be out in a minute to check on how he was doing.

Starler lit a Camel and stared at his screen. He snuffed out the cigarette in the cold coffee dregs lining the bottom of a Styrofoam cup. He needed a lead. He had to get his opening down, and then the rest would flow into his brain as naturally as the afternoon tide slipped into the harbor.

She'd flip when she saw nothing but a blank screen in front of him so close to deadline. He could put another story on the screen, something he'd written the week before, or maybe a flash off the wires, to mislead her into believing it was almost complete. Or he could just let her panic over the prospect that he would blow the deadline, leaving a big hole in the middle of the next day's front page. It would be amusing to see her panic.

Why didn't Angora have more confidence in him? Starler always came through, even if it was at the last moment.

She came out of her office, stopped at his desk, grabbed the back of his chair and leaned over his shoulder to read the screen.

"Deadline's at eight last time I checked," he muttered as she squinted at the type. He didn't look up. Instead, he pulled out another cigarette and shoved it into his mouth.

"What's your lead? Let me have a look." She turned to pull up a chair, and he quickly punched the keys until the screen went blank again. He leaned back and lit the cigarette, blowing the smoke in her direction.

"Damn it, Starler," Angora said, waving the smoke away, "this is a non-smoking newsroom."

"Do you want me to keep writing? I haven't had a break in four hours. I'm doing you a favor smoking in here," he responded. He got up, pretending to prepare to go outside for his smoke.

"Stay, stay," she said. The pat on the shoulder she gave him was friendly but the look that accompanied it was pure disgust. Then she pinched his tie, which he'd flung over the terminal, daintily between two fingers. "Whales?"

She paused. "Never mind. A dead diver above the fold always sells, Star. I want to use this on the top of one. Let me see what you've got."

"Come on Angora, it's not finished. Have a little faith."

"Faith is for the religious, star. A killer dolphin out on the reef is a great story but if you've got a single detail wrong, the local merchants are going to go berserk. They'll be yanking ads left and right."

"I thought your job was to edit news," he replied, sitting back down. A few more months in this rathole and he'd move on to a bigger newspaper, one where the editors showed some appreciation for his talents. Angora was always interrogating him, asking about his sources, suggesting new angles, and worst of all, making assignments. Plus, she was obsessed with advertising. It was like they paid her commissions, which they didn't. Starler hated editors. So blinded by their own brilliance that they missed the picture most of the time.

"The sheriff's department was less than fully cooperative." Starler leaned back and put his feet up on the desk. "I asked them about the death. They had no comment. It's all in there. I'm sure they'd be happy if I just went away like a good little journalist and didn't cause any trouble."

"Well, if we're going to say it was a dolphin attack, you better have a couple of good sources on this. I mean, we're talking about Flipper here. What are little kids going to think when they read this?"

"Who cares?"

"Don't be a jerk, Starler. What have you got on the record? You've got something on the record, right?"

He took a drag on the cigarette and went on. "The dive boat captain, Ms. Gold, was downright hostile. That in itself is confirmation of something," Starler said. "Whenever a source starts acting guilty up goes the old red flag. She would have done anything to get rid of me. Captain Gold was definitely hiding something."

Angora cocked her head doubtfully. "Maybe she was upset."

"Upset? Ha. She didn't want any publicity. Angora, face it, everybody who profits by taking tourists out to the reef is going to say this story is all wrong. No matter what we put in the paper tomorrow."

"Starler, let's try to stick with facts. I know the truth is more important than than protecting somebody's business," Angora said calmly. "I just want to be sure this is right."

"Oh come on, don't be naïve," Starler responded.

He was wasting his words on her. Every time he tackled controversy, Angora gave him a hard time. The dying reef, the dumping of raw sewage at sea—lots of things in Key West that nobody wanted to see in print. She always wanted twice as much research and more facts than a hard working reporter had time for.

But this time there was a dead body. He wouldn't be bullied away from this one.

"This is the story we've been waiting for, Angora. A killer dolphin on the loose in paradise. We'd be crazy to sit on this," Starler said.

"A killer dolphin? I don't know," she said. "Seems like there's a piece or two missing. It's hard to believe a dolphin would do anything to harm a human. Maybe we ought to hang on another day—see if the Sheriff has something else to say."

"Wait? You call yourself a newspaper woman?" Starler cried indignantly. "Spend a few more days checking around? Wait till the guy is buried, maybe? Hey, how about if we just run the dead diver on page two in the police report, and let the Miami Herald get all the glory? Come on, Angora. I didn't become a journalist because I wanted to spend my life playing it safe."

She held up her hands and headed back into her office, muttering, "Look—just finish the story and send it to me. Fifteen minutes. Get busy."

He looked over his notes, trying to reassemble his smeared scribbling and those snippets of conversation that he hadn't bothered to write down, but still recalled, into full sentences that could be attributed to his unnamed sources.

Starler felt the words come together in his head. His fingers tapped on the keyboard at machine-gun speed.

"A killer dolphin took the life of a scuba diver in the waters off Key West yesterday."

Still needed a little more snap. Starler gave it another shot.

"A killer dolphin went berserk and took the life of an experienced diver in the waters off Key West yesterday in a bizarre incident, sources close to the attack told this newspaper."

He had a vague recollection of reading about Navy research with dolphins that taught the animals to do mean things in combat scenarios.

"The military has engaged in training dolphins for national security missions such as guarding installations and ships for many years under a top secret program. At one time, the training occurred in Key West," he typed into the story.

Better, he thought. Snappy enough that the wires ought to pick this one up.

Starler knew he'd gone a bit over the top, but every shred of instinct in him screamed yes on this one. He made a quick call to the Navy office in Key West to see what they had to say, but it was after hours and all he got was a tape recording.

"Navy officials were unavailable for comment," he typed in. That was easy.

Deadlines being what they were, Starler would go with what he had.

He punched the rest of the details into the file, feeling the head rush that a good story always brought on. Fifteen minutes later, he punched a key to send the story on its way.

Angora could still damage his masterpiece with editing. Why couldn't he have an editor who just spellchecked? As usual, tonight he would need a few cold beers just to take the sting out of her rewrites.

Starler grabbed his sport coat and knocked on Angora's door, calling out, "I'll be at Captain Tony's if you need me." Things had been too quiet in Key West lately. The headlines about a killer dolphin ought to shake things up. He had always vowed that he would make a name for himself before he left the backwards little island, and this renegade dolphin might just be his ticket out of here.

Chapter 8

The big gray dolphin caught the falling man and brought him up from the deep. Near the surface, the other men waited, and the dolphin turned the injured man over to the leader. Their eyes met and the gray recognized danger. Before the leader could approach, the dolphin kicked his tail hard and turned, pumping his flukes to get away, building up speed and feeling the cool water brush his skin. He had a long swim ahead.

The dolphin headed home, away from the enormous old battleship, still curious at the humans' predilection for placing their creations on the ocean floor. It was hard to judge the purpose of leaving a ship underwater, but then so much human behavior had no obvious explanation. They had trained him to kill, but he did not understand why.

The life force surged through him and he felt magic in his blood. It was the gift of the female dolphins from earlier that day.

They'd reminded him of the old days when he was young and swam with his own pod. Before the humans had taken him. He had been strong in body and spirit, making him a good choice for the crossover. His strength had been the means by which he had survived their abuse, in their labs, under the sharpness of their knives.

He had killed today and that also had tapped a memory, one far older than memories of this lifetime. Before he'd taken dolphin form, he'd lived as a warrior. He'd been a shape shifter, a traveler able to cross thresholds.

He'd always been a warrior, always willing to sacrifice for the Great Mother, the Earth. The dolphin was clear on what to do. More clear than the men with their weapons, their bells to command him in such a primitive way, their punishment if he chose to do something other than their desire.

For two hours, the gray swam as fast as he was able. The sun hit his right flank most of the way, warming his skin. He needed to reach the monolith by darkness when his human keepers would call him with their bell.

There might be trouble, if they knew he'd roamed so far from his pen. But as yet, with the fireball still high in the blue sky, the men would be unconcerned. He'd know their intentions by the tone of their voices as they chattered in the rapid, lyrical tongue of the long island.

The men believed the dolphin was under their control. The idea amused him. He had lived long in the free will zone and knew that dolphins, like humans, had choices.

The humans were learning, but not fast enough. They were running out of time, as was he.

He swam faster, ignoring the schools of small fish that might fill his stomach if he obeyed his instincts. No, he needed to get back to his pen; there was more to do. He'd be hungry later, especially if they cut back his food to punish him for disobeying.

He had done well today, although much remained before he could rest. He had their attention, now, he was certain of it. The time to send the message was near. The red-haired one would be their emissary; he had seen it in her dreams. He only had to draw her to him. She must come to his sanctuary beneath the blue waters.

Now he would return to the temple, where the men would call him. When the stars appeared overhead, he would visit with the red-haired woman again in the dreamtime. She would be ready.

Chapter 9

The sun was high in a topaz blue sky on Saturday morning by the time Gene Rockland turned his Harley north up U.S. 1. He headed out of Key West toward Johnny Reb and the muddy little lagoon on Sweet Pine Key.

At 55 mph the air caressed his bare arms and legs. Some people thought the Keys were too hot in summer but not Gene. As long as he could spend a few days a week riding, the temperature didn't bother him. Down here, a man didn't need to worry about having the right clothes even for things like riding a motorcycle. If a biker had leather, it just sat in his closet getting dried out.

He slowed the Harley enough to cruise through two stoplights on Stock Island. Once he passed the short strip of commercial businesses, Gene opened up the throttle and let loose.

He crossed one small key after another, with only a few houses and run-down buildings on each. Mostly the view was blue water and billowing white clouds. Shafts of sharp gold sunlight pierced the clouds in places so that the sky looked like a metaphysical visitation.

Twenty miles to the north, he reached Sweet Pine Key. He passed the flashing yellow light of the fire station and a development of modest cinderblock houses, the kind of cheap housing that seem to be around every bend in the road in Florida.

Then he slowed the bike and made the sudden left hand turn into the gravel parking lot of the sanctuary, dodging the oncoming traffic, which was doing 15 miles over the speed limit, as always. Folks may come down to the Keys to relax but they sure don't relax getting there.

Dolphin sanctuary. The name made him laugh when he first heard it. Sanctuary implied religion but Johnnie Reb hadn't been in a church in decades and this was only a sanctuary in the sense of temporary safety. The unwanted dolphins were supposed to be safe here, but that concept, like so many other conditions of life, was relative. Johnnie Reb made an unlikely guardian angel, and the sanctuary was nothing more than a small collection of cinder block structures.

Gene parked the bike, removed his helmet and put his sunglasses back on.

Johnnie Reb came out the door of his office, but he didn't look up. The small man moved quickly around the side of the building, heading for the dark green lagoon that was surrounded by tall pines except where it opened into a perfect palm-tree-lined bay.

Gene shook the stiffness out of his legs and hurried after him.

At the water's edge, orange plastic fencing had been set up to make a large underwater dolphin pen. Dorsal fins cut the surface of the water. From the fins, Gene counted five dolphins.

At a small hut with a thatched roof, Gene caught up to Johnnie, who was dumping fish into two large buckets. "Hey Reb," Gene said, clapping him on the back, "Looks like you got your hands full."

Johnnie finished filling his buckets and reached out a hand sticky with fish slime to greet Gene. "Look who's turned up. Only took five messages this time. Why are you so damned hard to get hold of, brother?" He handed Gene a bucket. "Here, help me out, as long as you're occupying God's green earth today."

They filled the buckets with small silvery fish, then made their way through thick weeds to the edge of the lagoon. A gentle breeze was blowing off the water, but all the wind did was move the heat around a few inches. Drops of perspiration formed on Gene's skin.

The dorsal fins circled faster and Gene noticed a snout or two popping above the surface. The idea was to get the dolphins to fish for themselves again after being in captivity for years, but these guys clearly were used to their daily handouts. "They catching anything themselves, Reb?"

"Nope. Seemed to have acquired a taste for dead fish when they were locked up."

"I can understand it," Gene said. "Easy to get used to three squares a day."

"Hell, I know guys who've gotten married for less than that," Reb said, laughing. He flipped off his sandals and stepped down into the lagoon.

Gene sat to take his boots off and then stepped into the water barefoot. His toes sank into the mud and the cool water lapped his legs up to his knees.

A large dolphin came up and raised her head. She swam over to Johnnie, scolding him with a clicking sound.

"Fancie. Darlin'." Johnnie bent down and Fancie raised her face to nuzzle his cheek. "Fancie, baby," he murmured, as if talking to a small child. The dolphin rubbed her snout on his cheek again and clicked softly.

"True love," Gene said.

The other dolphins circled in the water, keeping an eye on the humans and the buckets of food. They raised their heads when Johnnie spoke. He reached into the bucket, pulling out the fish by the handful and tossing them one at a time to the dolphins.

The dolphins did not push or crowd, but waited patient as a table full of restaurant patrons. Each creature had a distinctive appearance. Two big males surfaced side by side, and Gene drew in his breath sharply. The scars on their faces were familiar.

He knew these dolphins, but his only visible reaction was to pull a fish out of his bucket. "Your new girl friend come from Coronado?"

"No. She's a refugee from the sea park in Miami that went under last month." Johnnie pulled the biggest fish he could find out and tossed it to Fancie. His body language never changed but Gene could hear the anger in his voice at the mention of the marine park.

"She was half starved by the time I got up there. The place had laid off its dolphin trainers and nobody bothered to feed the dolphins. She's not military, but these other guys are. Thought maybe you'd recognize them."

"Yeah, I saw the article in the paper," Gene said. "It used names, but that didn't mean anything to me. Officially, all we had for them were numbers. I figured the Navy gave them names when they decided to release them."

Johnnie whistled and two of the dolphins came closer. "Say hello to Jake and Alphie."

"It's been a while. These guys probably came along after me," Gene lied. He knew that he would never forget even if the dolphins did.

Jake and Alphie were darker skinned than Fancie. As soon as they appeared, he recognized them. They'd been called 117 and 049 back then. The military trainers gave them nicknames but as far as the Navy had been concerned the dolphins were inventory, just like a ship or torpedo.

Seeing the rough scars on their skin and places where scar tissue covered chunks of missing flesh gave Gene the same feeling as spotting an old buddy across a crowded room. He tossed a fish to Jake and the two dolphins began to chatter excitedly at Gene.

"Hey big fellow, looks like you lost the fight." Gene reached his hand out to the dolphin. But Jake kept his distance.

"It's those goddamned Navy muzzles. Takes the skin right off." Johnnie's expression was angry. "Don't need the damned things anyway. A little kindness and they'll do anything you ask."

"Not anything," Gene said. He tossed another fish to Jake, who came closer now. He knew what the dolphins would and wouldn't do. "They're not going to behave violently, no matter what you try to teach them. Of course, there's always that hundredth dolphin who doesn't fit the profile."

Jake stopped chattering and stared at Gene.

"And the goddamned Navy will burn through 100 great animals just to find the one who is trainable. If people only knew what the damned feds were doing with their tax money." Johnnie murmured a string of curse words under his breath.

"Hey, don't take it out on me. I quit, remember?" Gene got tired of having to defend himself. He usually avoided the situation by keeping his mouth shut about his past. "You were in on it too, buddy."

Johnnie continued to feed Fancie. "How about it, old girl? Think I could train you to shoot somebody?"

Gene had to admit the bullet-firing device hadn't worked all that well. But it was better than the Navy's first weapon to kill enemy divers, which worked by having the dolphin stab the enemy diver with a cartridge. The cartridge then would release its gas into the enemy's body, literally blowing the person into pieces. The story went that 40 Viet Cong who were laying mines in rivers had been killed that way during the Vietnam War but the dolphins also killed a couple of U.S. personnel in the process.

Just how many enemies the dolphins were able to take out, if any, remained classified and probably always would be, since it was one of the darker moments of U.S. military history.

Johnnie and Gene never talked directly about such things. The conversation always delicately skirted the sensitive stuff. But Johnnie had the right connections. He would know the stories and all the gory details.

Gene tossed the last fish out to Alphie. "How long do you plan to keep them here?"

"Who knows? Maybe forever. Unfortunately for these guys, forever probably will not be all that long." Johnnie got out of the water and sat down on the grass. "I want to ask you something. What was the average age of the military dolphins you took care of?"

"Six, seven years," Gene said. "Pretty young overall."

"How long did you usually keep them?"

"We'd have them three or four years. The mortality rate was pretty high."

"Wild dolphins get to be 40 or 50. But these guys will be lucky to see 15 or 20. Once you pen these critters up, you might as well be signing their death sentence."

"You don't have to convince me," Gene said, leaning back in the grass. "Why don't you just let them go?"

"Hell, the government won't let me scratch my nose without a damned permit. And the last thing the feds want me to do is release these dolphins," Johnnie said. "Got to study everything to death. That's the government solution. Order a study and do nothing. Those NOAA scientists are going to spend every penny they can lay their hands on to prove that a captive dolphin can't go back to nature. Even though a civilized man can still survive in the woods. Why should dolphin be any different?"

Johnnie moved back to the edge of the lagoon and whistled for Fancie. She came right up to him and he rubbed her head affectionately. "Maybe they're right. If we didn't feed her, she'd likely starve to death."

Gene sloshed some water around in the fish pail, which was now empty, and climbed back onto the shore.

"Don't give up on them, Johnnie. You keep working with them, pretty soon they'll be ready to go home." He looked at Jake swimming on the surface, keeping his eye on the men. "You're not going to find freedom in the bottom of a plastic bucket of fish, are you, Jake?"

Johnnie got to his feet and picked up the buckets. He patted Gene on the back. "Come on. I'll buy you a beer."

"Maybe just one," Gene said. "I got to tend bar in two hours."

They walked along the water's edge. A few hundred feet down the shore, a small group of people clustered at the edge of the water where a bank of lights and reflectors, professional photography equipment, had been set up.

Johnnie took Gene's elbow and tried to steer him away from the water. "Let's go that way."

Gene shrugged off Johnnie's hand. "Why? What's wrong with going this way? What's going on over there?"

Gene tried to keep going toward the action.

"Nothing."

"It doesn't look like nothing to me," Gene said.

"We rented out the place to a magazine for a fashion shoot. Needed to raise a little money. Let's not bother them, Gene, they're working."

Johnnie tried again to commandeer Gene by the elbow, and then Gene saw the familiar blonde figure in a white bikini at the center of the action. The woman, the model, was tall and curvy. She reached behind her back, fumbling with the string tie at the back of the suit.

"Alex?"

"Oh. Yeah," Johnnie mumbled. "I didn't know you'd pick the exact moment she was up here to drop in. Great timing pal."

Then Alex spotted Gene and ran over to plant a big, wet kiss on his cheek.

"You snuck up here to see me, babe," Alex gushed, her excitement spilling out like warm champagne from an uncorked bottle.

"No sneaking, babe, pure coincidence," Gene replied.

"Oh sure, Gene, that's what you always say," she said, smiling. The harsh sunlight made her red mouth and white blonde hair look garish, not sexy the way Gene remembered.

"I'm a fishing dominatrix," she went on, holding up a cat of nine tails that was loaded with nasty looking fishhooks. She pointed at the other model, a young man with a long ponytail and fishing rod. "That's my victim."

Her male counterpart wore plaid boxer shorts, leather cuffs and a black chest harness with lots of silver studs and chains dangling from it.

"Got to go," she said, walking away, big and bouncy, every man's dream girl. Or so it seemed when Gene met Alex, his first week in Key West, right after he got out of the Navy. The augmentation should have been his first clue start but somehow Gene missed it. Yes, his ex-wife was beautiful but she'd trounced on him enough now that he had to work hard at raising even a slight twinge of lust for her.

Gene and Johnnie went up the hill and into the cinderblock building, where Johnnie opened an ancient refrigerator. He pulled out two bottles of Mexican beer and opened them.

"Guess your ex-wife's got her sights set on being a star." Johnnie handed him one of the bottles.

Suddenly Gene didn't mind that he'd have to ride the bike back to Key West with a mild buzz. A beer might be what he needed. Or two. "Alex's got her own ideas about life." He took a big swallow of the beer and changed the subject. "The sanctuary's looking good, Johnnie. How many dolphin you got now?"

"Five here and five at the pens on the other side of the road," Johnnie said. "We think the Navy's keeping another 100 in San Diego, but the numbers are classified. Hell, nearly everything about the program is classified for that matter."

Gene finished the beer and stood up to leave. "I got to get back."

"Wait a minute. I wanted to ask you to reconsider that job offer. I need some help, Gene."

"Johnnie, I can't do it."

"Part time then, a couple hours a week is all."

"No."

Johnnie took a big drink of his beer and put the bottle down a bit too hard so that foam erupted out of the top. "Dammit, Gene, don't you think you owe it to them after what you did? If it's just the money you're worried about, I'll start working tomorrow on getting a grant so's we can pay you a decent wage."

Gene shook his head. "I quit the business, Johnnie. I don't know how many more ways I can say it." He stood up, picked up his sunglasses.

"Yeah, I guess all those barflies down on Duval Street are more important than a couple of lousy dolphins. Those drunks really need you, Gene," Johnnie said.

"At least somebody needs me." Gene opened the door. The hot air hit him and he felt like he'd entered a sauna. Nothing like a summer day in the Keys to sweat all a man's sins out of every pore in his body. "Take good care of Jake, okay?"

Chapter 10

Mattie Gold woke just before dawn on Saturday and the first thing she thought of was the dead diver the day before. She lay listening to the old house creak and watching the sky out her window turn from black to battleship gray.

She'd made too many mistakes this year. An affair with the boss's son, who then decided to check out on her in the most permanent way imaginable just when things had gotten sweet. Then somehow a customer dies on her watch. They said bad things came in threes and she had a feeling of dread, wondering who or what would be next.

Her bed felt warm and safe. Maybe she should just stay here instead of going back out on the water. If only. She wondered if the trouble began with Mickey Patcher. The way he had excited her, not like most men, that should have been her first warning. The next time she began to feel totally alive when around a certain kind of man, she was going to turn and head the other direction. Things had been going great until Mickey. She knew the old warnings about not mixing business and pleasure but Mickey was smart, funny, and wild.

The two of them had taken the boat over to Cuba the previous autumn. Bob Patcher had them out gathering information on diving over there, getting ready for the day Fidel died, like half the other Key West business owners. They'd started the journey as co-workers and ended it as lovers. Havana had been like a dream — so far removed from her real world that none of the old rules applied. They'd stayed at the Plaza, a hotel that was old and European, with towering ceilings, lots of marble and wrought iron. So far from Key West, she might as well have been on the moon. They'd decided to share a room to save money, and events soon took their course.

Mattie had been prepared for the romance to fade when they got back to Florida but Mickey was not. When he told her he loved her, she felt like she'd stepped into a dream. She touched her neck and felt a small white medallion that hung from a silver chain, a gift from

Mickey. A glass dolphin he'd said reminded him of the crossing.

Three weeks later, she was still working up the courage to say she loved him back, and then he was dead. The victim of a freak, inexplicable diving accident, the kind that sometimes happens in technical diving and leaves everyone wondering how things could go so wrong when such care was taken to follow all the rules. When you pushed things to the limit, take nothing for granted. Bob Patcher had taught his sons well when he trained them to dive deep. Mickey'd been at 200 feet, a dive he'd done a hundred times before. He'd followed all the rules, but air embolisms don't always follow orders.

He'd been swimming around the surface after the dive, playing around, when he passed out and sank back to the bottom, where he drowned. Mattie'd been running the boat that day, and Mickey's father and brother had been there too. They had recovered the body themselves, diving deep to the bottom again to find him.

She tried not to think about Mickey much, but when she was alone in bed, her thoughts would wander back to that day. So she tried to stay out of bed. She'd get up at dawn to jog in the morning and stay up far too late at night watching old movies, and perhaps that's why she'd said yes to Sam Harbor's proposal. Anything was preferable to endlessly reliving the nightmare of having Mickey warm and alive at her side one day, and gone forever the next.

When sunlight brightened the walls of the room she rose and stumbled down the long wooden hallway into the kitchen. Neptune was waiting patiently outside her door, and he got up and padded along behind, click clicking his way down the hall as his toenails tapped the wooden floor.

Diamanda was up and in the kitchen already, wearing a chenille robe the color of key lime pie, her red hair in disarray around her shoulders.

"Early bird today," Mattie said.

"Strange dreams," Diamanda said by way of explanation. She fumbled with a coffee grinder. "Dolphins. And water. All that talking we did last night must have put your dolphin into my head."

They'd stayed up late the night before, going over the story of what had happened out on the boat until Mattie had talked the shock of another dead diver out of her. Or at least until she couldn't talk about it anymore.

Mattie went out front and retrieved the morning paper. She carried it inside, unfolded the front page and felt her stomach sink. In huge black letters at the top of page one, the paper said: "Flipper One, Diver

Zero in Deadly Battle on the Reef."

With the paper in hand, Mattie plodded back to the kitchen. Diamanda had the coffee machine assembled by now and the smell of hot coffee began to fill the room.

"This is all I need today. That little nerd reporter..." Mattie read the story aloud. "This isn't true… It's full of mistakes. He accuses that poor dolphin, and he has no proof."

"The most obvious explanation to him at the time, no doubt. You know, a reporter at a little newspaper like The Anchor isn't going to have time to find the real story," Diamanda said. She came around the counter and put her arm around Mattie.

Mattie leaned against her. "The whole thing gives me the creeps," she said.

Mattie felt tears well up in her eyes and she swallowed hard, trying to hold them back.

"Maybe we can find out what really happened. This wasn't your fault," Diamanda said.

"Everybody loves to tell me that." Mattie pulled away. If she let Diamanda smother her with warm, motherly hugs, she'd certainly end up falling apart. "Bob Patcher taught me something when Mickey died. He dealt with it, and moved on. His own son. But he didn't fall apart; he didn't let emotions stop him. You have to be strong. That's what it takes to get by in this business. Death just happens to be a fact of life in diving."

"Mattie, you aren't Patcher. You don't have to go around pretending to be a tough guy. Give yourself a break or you'll go crazy," Diamanda said. "You had a man die on your boat yesterday."

The two women stood listening to the hissing steam from the coffee machine.

"I've got to get to work."

"I think you should call in sick."

Mattie considered that. "No, Patcher's counting on me, and I need the money. You know- the wedding's coming up– I'll take time off then."

"You could postpone the wedding too. It wouldn't disrupt anybody's plans."

"What about Sam? It would disrupt his," Mattie said.

Diamanda sighed and headed toward the door, and then stopped. "Mattie, Mattie, don't rush into things."

Mattie knew that her roommate was not in favor of this wedding. Diamanda loved being mysterious, leaving things half said. After a year living under the same roof, Mattie had gotten used to it. Money, for example. It seemed to be abundant in Diamanda's life although the source of it was never apparent. Diamanda worked only when she felt like it and the rest of the time did exactly as she pleased. How she managed was a mystery to Mattie.

The phone rang and Diamanda answered it.

She greeted the caller, told him to hold and gave the handset to Mattie, covering the receiver. "It's lover boy."

"Sam?"

Diamanda nodded.

"Tell him I'll call him back later. I just can't talk to anybody yet."

Diamanda told Sam that Mattie was still in bed and would phone back, then hung up. She headed back to her room, humming Amazing Grace, her prelude to a meditation session, then turned back. "Hey, I'll help you with the wedding if you are set on it. Flowers, music, the whole shebang."

When Mattie was alone, she poured her coffee and carried it out into the garden. There she settled on a low canvas chair next to a small brick fountain and read the paper. When she finished, she sat still, listening to the splashing water and watching tiny lizards crawl up the straight trunks of the palm trees. Overhead, an early commuter flight roared, obliterating all other sound for half a minute as it headed to the island's airport.

She absentmindedly scratched Neptune's head and thought about the day ahead. The newspaper article would only increase the tension. Besides the deposition to be given to the sheriff, there'd be other reporters calling to inquire about the death and the other dive operators around town would be nosing around, wanting the inside scoop on what had happened.

She went back into the house, showered and dressed in blue denim shorts and a T-shirt with Paradise Diver's logo printed on the front. Then she loaded Neptune into her pickup truck and drove up U.S. 1 till she reached the shop.

The dive boat was tied to the dock just where they'd left it the day before. Out front, flags snapped sharply in the breeze. The sky was clear and the water had a slight chop. Perfect weather for diving. She parked and went into the shop.

She found Bob Patcher in his office behind a stack of paperwork. He seemed unaffected by the tragedy of the previous day. Patcher and his two sons had been made from the same mold. The same haircut, short and flat on top, the same lean build and sturdiness.

"How are you doing today?" Mattie asked, sticking her head in his doorway.

Patcher nodded.

"Surprised to see you today, Mattie. Thought you'd take a little time off."

"No, no, I'm fine," she said.

"Okay. You feel like going home early, let me know," he said, bending his head back over the paperwork as if nothing had happened the day before. Mattie guessed she'd better do the same.

Mattie went to the back of the shop where rental gear was stored. There weren't any customers in the shop yet so she decided to spend some time cleaning the place up. She began to reorganize the dive vests, regulators and hoses until they were neatly arranged on hangars and pegs against the wall.

When she finished that job, she went out the back door to the dock where Todd was filling aluminum air tanks at the compression station. His muscular frame, surrounded by dozens of high-pressure hoses that sprouted from the wall like a nest of vipers, reminded her of Mickey, and that small, familiar twinge of pain jabbed into her heart momentarily like a tiny knife.

It didn't help that Todd was wearing his brother's old clothes. Mickey's green cloth high top Converses, the ones that looked like tropical combat boots and a PADI tank shirt, bearing the logo of the dive instuctors' organization, that Mattie recognized from the trip to Cuba.

She pushed Mickey out of her mind for the second time that morning and walked over to brush the top of Todd's short-cropped hair with her palm. "What's on the books today, cover boy?"

"Didn't you look when you came in?"

He sounded annoyed. "No," she said.

"Everything's cancelled," Todd said, frowning. He swung an aluminum tank over to the pumping station. "We had six on the books to start, and four backed out. Can't run the boat for two divers so we sent them over to Rooker Dive."

"What changed their minds?" she asked.

"Take a guess."

"The weather."

"You're really funny. Have you read the paper? The Anchor's making this out to be Jaws 3."

"I saw it. The story is all wrong and anybody with half a brain will know it. I'm sure business will be back to usual soon," Mattie said.

"Everything's cancelled for the next four days, Mattie."

"You're joking." A loss of business was the last thing Patcher needed.

"Some joke," Todd said. He went back to filling his tanks. "Maybe we ought to advertise dolphin encounters. Make it a specialty trip, charge extra. Paradise Diver's trip to the home of the killer dolphin. Jaws South. We can do some brochures."

Patcher had come out and listened to the end of the exchange. "Todd, get back to work and leave off Mattie. The excitement will blow over in a day or two. A few days of downtime isn't going to hurt us. In fact, we can use it to our advantage."

Mattie studied Patcher's face. He looked as calm as a monk in meditation. He was one of those men whose emotions seemed to have been surgically removed, she thought, trying to figure out how he did it. She wondered if he'd lost any faith in her, but she didn't ask. All she said was, "Getting named in the paper today was something I could have done without."

"Comes with the territory, captain," Patcher replied. He began helping Todd move the tanks back to the storage area, then came back to Mattie. "What would you think of a little offshore assignment? I want you to take Paradise Diver over to Cuba for a day or two."

Mattie didn't answer. Going to Cuba would be the polar opposite of taking a few days off. Ninety miles across open water and god knows what when you arrive.

"I guess you're too busy, with that wedding coming up and all."

"No, no," she said. "What's in Cuba?"

"Good. Friends of Jose Marti have a truckload of medical supplies for a hospital in Matanzas, and they asked if we could ferry it over. You can put in at Varadero, just like before. Drop off the supplies, then take Todd over to visit one or two of the local dive operators." Patcher paused, then added, "that is, if you're up to it."

"Of course I'm up to it. I'm just fine," she said, but when she tried to smile to prove it, her jaw felt as tight as a steel trap.

"You better get busy then," Patcher said. "You'll need to rerig the back of the boat, stock up on fuel and food, get the dive gear ready. You know what to do. The weather's good for the next few days, so you've got a weather window for the trip."

Patcher's dream was to run twin dive operations in Florida and Cuba once relations opened up. He wanted to get his foot in the door the day democracy arrived on Cuba's shores.

"We'll need a third crew member," Patcher was saying, "A strong diver. Todd's not diving alone over there."

There it was, in between the lines, the one small sign that Patcher was worried about Todd, not enough to keep him from diving, but enough to want to hand select the crew.

"I've got an old friend, ex-Navy, who I might be able to talk into it. If I don't hear back from him, I'll give Jerry D'Argent a call."

Mattie grimaced. "Please, not D'Argent. He spends half his time flirting and the other half bragging about treasure hunting and trying to buy me drinks. I could use a little peace and quiet on the way over."

Todd had finished filling the tanks. "How about Bud?" he offered.

His father didn't respond.

"Bud's cool, Dad. He just finished dive master."

Still Patcher didn't answer.

"Come on, Dad, we'll behave. I promise we won't even think of going out on the town until the work is done."

Inside the shop, the phone was ringing. Todd went in to answer it, then came out to hand the receiver to Mattie. She said hello and heard an unfamiliar male voice on the other end of the line.

"Captain Gold, I was just wondering if I could talk you about the dolphin. You said later, and now it's later, so," the voice said.

"Who is this?"

"Abe Starler. We met yesterday."

It was that pushy reporter.

"What do you want?" she asked.

"I need some details about what happened out there."

"Your article says you've already figured everything out," she said. "Nobody says a dolphin killed that guy but you, Starler. I can't believe you'd print that without some kind of proof. You don't even have an autopsy report. How could you print that garbage? How could you accuse an innocent dolphin?"

"I stand behind my story unless you can show me otherwise."

"Do you know what your story is doing to our business? Maybe you ought to think about that first, before you run off and put something into print you can't confirm."

"Don't blame me. Shit happens, and it's a reporter's job to write it. Look, why don't we get together before the big meeting downtown?"

"What meeting?"

"The big meeting about the dolphin. I'll buy you a drink, we can have a nice, easy off -the-record chat," he said.

"The last thing in the world I want today is to have a drink with you," she said, hanging up and turning to Patcher. "That was the reporter from the Anchor. He says there's a big meeting planned. Do you know what he's talking about?"

He nodded. "Tomorrow at The Frog. The Chamber of Commerce wants to reassure everybody that it's safe out there. I'm going but I thought maybe you'd want to skip this one. Those guys from the boats can be kind of harsh."

He was trying to protect her, but Mattie didn't want to be protected.

"If you're going, I am too. I can handle those guys."

Chapter 11

The big gray waited in the dark water. The sun would be up soon; he felt it in his bones. He was inside his small pen, a willing prisoner of the men on the big island. The day before he had returned to the temple at sunset, answering their calls. Now they'd be back to repeat the ritual. He would be released from his cage into the darkness.

It had been the same for several moons. He would swim away from shore, the men overhead would wait in their boat, signaling him with their bell.

"Follow us, follow us, to the sacred place," the bell's clanging said.

He waited until they came and set him loose. He swam beneath their boat and away from the island.

When they arrived at the surface above the temple, he came up for air three times. Then the dolphin dove deep, circling the sacred spot and heading north again. The humans rang the bell again and again but he could no longer hear it because he was too far out. They would call him for hours. He thought the men were like machines, behaving as if they could not think. They would ring the bell over and over until he returned.

He picked up speed and headed back to the small northern islands where he'd taken the human's life. The dot of populated land at the end of the chain beckoned. It was there that the red-haired one lived. The energy, the excitement, good and bad, called to him, as always. Each time his trainers set him free, he felt the pull to the north, but only the last few times had it been strong enough to obey. To disappear from his trainers for a few hours meant punishment when he returned to the boat.

He'd go back no matter what. The dolphin had a pact with the creator. He would teach the men; he would fight them; he would stop the capture of the cetaceans. Sacred law had been broken.

Perhaps she'd come today. He had a strong feeling that she was close.

No feeling had been so powerful in many moons. Not since he'd been very young, new to this dolphin body, with much to learn when one day, obeying his inner voice, he swam far from his pod.

That day, when he was young and just learning the ways of the sea, he'd approached a small wooden boat. He'd wanted to see the humans up close, to look them in the eye. He wanted to confront the humans who'd felt like a distant relation to him. How easily they'd trapped him as he came closer for a good look. The net closed around his body, binding his flippers and flukes until he was as immobile as the primitive creatures who crawled along on the ocean floor.

The men had lifted him into the boat. His freedom had been taken, his heart broken. The weight of his flesh had been unbearably heavy without the water to support it. As he was removed from the water, he felt fear for the first time, fear of the unknown. He'd smelled the fear before it sank into his body, smelled it coming off the men. The men had been waiting on the water to take the dolphins from the sea; their small, shriveled hearts projected a darkness he'd never before experienced. Their energy swirled in circles around their hairy, fleshy forms, sucking in the magical dolphin frequencies and the healing vibrations of the seawater without honor or appreciation of the Great Mother. This boat full of men did not care about each other or him or any of the other creatures in the sea.

He didn't understand the men, but he knew he had to go with them. The men would not leave the waters, would not stop hunting his brothers and sisters until they had what they were after. They wanted a young healthy male dolphin. He heard them use the word, "specimen," as they looked at him. "A good specimen." Strong. Large. He was a prize; he knew it. The young must sacrifice; he knew that too. It was the way of the humans to make the young bear the pain.

Now, as he approached the island to the north, he remembered how suffering had made him strong. Today, a young human must match his sacrifice. But the human would not have the lifelong sentence of pain as the gray had. The child's death would be swift and effective.

Ahead he detected a small harbor, empty except for schools of fish. He would wait there. The island was crowded with humans who ventured into the water as the sun rose in the sky. So predictable. It wouldn't take long.

Chapter 12

Early Sunday morning, Woody Wilson parked his car in the middle of the gravel lot at the Key West Charter Boat Dock. Woody had come down to the Florida Keys on summer vacation from Atlanta with his wife and kids a few days before. He got out and hitched his white Bermuda shorts over his ample belly.

"Get out," he said before he slammed the driver's door shut. The passenger door opened and a ten-year-old boy emerged. The boy's head was shaved to near baldness, he wore enormous denim shorts and a cotton shirt sized for someone a hundred pounds heavier.

They strolled down the dock of the marina, a sizable operation housing a couple million of dollars worth of custom fiberglass floating palaces equipped with refrigerators, color TVs and air conditioning — all the comforts a man needs as long as he's willing to part with a week's pay for a few hours of living like King Neptune. For those with less regal tastes, a few smaller dinghies and flats boats were tied to the remote end of the dock.

Father and son strolled past the big boats as they made their way to the area at the far end of the marina reserved for the rich-in-spirit but short on cash.

"Ready for a little fishing lesson?" Wilson asked cheerfully. "Just like in the Old Man and the Sea. They teach you Hemingway in school yet?"

A blank stare from the boy. The father tried again.

"Okay, then, surely you saw Schwarzenegger in True Lies?"

Another blank look, then the boy spoke. "I have to go to the bathroom."

Wilson directed his son to the marina office to get the key to the men's room.

"It's going to be a long time on the water, so do what you need to."

Wilson returned to the rental car, opened the trunk and took out his fishing rods, a tackle box and a bag that his wife had filled with sunscreen, hats and other paraphernalia to protect her brood from the blazing sunshine.

"That Florida sun is a killer," his wife had said, handing him the sunblock. "Put it on once an hour. You don't want to die of skin cancer, and neither does Royce."

Wilson picked up his gear and returned to the dock, where his 18-foot rental boat waited. He went to the dockmaster's office, signed forms that would prevent him from suing the marina no matter what went wrong, left his credit card as a deposit and picked up the keys.

Wilson was loading the boat by the time his son finished his business. As he approached, Royce was frowning, a chronic expression that had twisted his mouth into a permanent scowl. For the life of him, Woody could not figure out why his boy was so surly. The kid had all the extravagances and treats a two-income family could provide.

Wilson wondered if his son appreciated how hard his father had worked to pay for this dream vacation. He added it up. Eight hundred for the hotel, a thousand for the plane tickets. Another five bills for food and fooling around. The Boston Whaler cost $200 to rent for the day but the father-son fishing excursion was to be the highlight of the trip. Wilson knew he needed some time to bond with his son, who was growing more distant and disrespectful by the day, so the money would be well spent. Once they got out on the water, he was sure the boy would cheer up.

"Welcome to our yacht, mate," Wilson said, motioning Royce aboard the short, open boat.

The boy climbed in, his weight causing the vessel to rock back and forth wildly. He teetered precariously, sat down with a thunk and then demanded, "Let's go."

"Lesson number one, son. A man doesn't stand up in a boat without having one hand firmly grounded. A three point stand is the secret to stability," Wilson said. He handed the boy a life preserver.

"I don't need this, dad," Royce said, grimacing at the bright orange jacket that was frayed and stained with grease.

"Put it on," Wilson commanded. Despite Wilson's investment in hundreds of dollars of swim lessons, his son was not a good swimmer.

Wilson climbed into the boat, secured the gear and started the little engine. It coughed a few times before settling into a steady rumble. Wilson untied the lines and cast off. He began to whistle again as they headed out into the Straits of Florida where the water was clear.

They reached the open water where ballyhoo jumped out of the water ahead of the boat. They motored around the island until they reached a cove a mile up from the marina. Wilson anchored, pleased to find solitude and clear skies, and instructed his son on how to bait the hook and cast.

After a few minutes, Royce was sweating profusely. He removed the orange life jacket. "It's hot," he said.

Woody considered ordering the boy to put it back on, but then decided to ease up a bit. After all, the day was calm and they were anchored in a protected cove. What could possibly happen?

Three hours later, the boy finished his third soda of the morning and casually tossed the empty can over the side. His father frowned as the can sank beneath the surface.

"How many times do I have to tell you not to litter?"

"Aw, Dad, it's a big ocean. It don't matter."

"Don't? Where'd you learn that?" his father asked, eyebrows arched.

The youth dangled his pole carelessly from the side of the boat. "When are we going back?"

"We just got here, so sit back and enjoy," Wilson said. He reached over to pull his son's pole out of the water. "Never gonna catch anything that way, buddy."

"I have to go to the bathroom, dad." The boy's voice was nasal and pleading. He removed his T-shirt, revealing tender, lily white skin where the shirt protected him. Royce's neck and arms, in contrast, were bright red from too much sun.

"You shouldn't have drank so much pop. You'll have to pee over the side," the father said. "And put your shirt on. Your mother will kill us both if she sees that sunburn."

"I don't want to go over the side." The boy placed his chin on his hands, elbows on knees, and began to tap his toes rapidly on the floor of the boat. "I'm hungry."

Wilson opened the cooler, got out one of the big submarine sandwiches and handed it to the kid, whose face knotted in displeasure. "I hate baloney. Don't you have anything good?"

Wilson took a deep breath and silently counted to ten. "Your mother got up before dawn to make these sandwiches. Eat it, fish and stop complaining. Next week, we'll be back in Atlanta and you'll wish you had this chance again."

"I hope I never come back here again in my life. I didn't ask to come on this stinking boat," the boy said, his jaw jutting out defiantly. "I want to go back to the marina. I want to go back to the hotel where there's air conditioning."

Wilson's chest felt like a balloon with a jagged piece of glass inside. "That's enough," he said. "Eat. And Royce, if the next word out of you isn't a yessir, thank you sir, you aren't getting on that damned Internet for a week after we get home."

The boy responded by taking a few bites of the sandwich. They fished in silence for a few minutes. "Sir," the son said quietly. "May I have another Coke, puhlease?"

Wilson dug an icy can out of the cooler, took a beer out for himself and opened both. "With pleasure," he said, handing his son the soda, feeling a little like a butler but pleased that Royce was responding.

Royce's lips turned up in a half-hearted imitation of a smile. Maybe the boy wasn't hopeless after all.

Wilson drank his beer and tried to relax as he watched Royce drain the Coke and casually toss it overboard, followed by the half-eaten sandwich.

"I told you not to throw the cans over the side."

"Dad, I really, really have to go," he whined. "Can't we go back to the marina?"

Wilson gritted his teeth and spoke slowly. "If you can throw your can over the side, you sure as hell can pee over the side too. It's that or hold it."

"Okay, okay." The boy stood, unzipped, his motions sending the small boat into a precarious rocking.

"Hold the side with one hand," his father advised.

The boy turned and glared, legs wobbling as he tried to balance on the unstable platform. He reached down to hold the edge of the little boat with one hand, the other digging into his shorts. A stream of yellow fluid shot out toward the water.

He was just finishing, shaking the drops off with a flick of his fat wrist when a black shape came streaking beneath the surface, heading straight for the boat. They both saw it just before the creature rammed the underside of the boat. They heard the thud and felt the boat lurch. Wilson dropped his pole into the boat, and the boy teetered left, then right, then back to the left again and into the water.

The boy thrashed a few times, sending water in all directions. Wilson tossed the orange life preserver towards him but it landed about five feet away. As the boy flailed his arms in a panicky attempt to swim back to the boat, he went under. Wilson pulled off his shoes, his eyes searching the water for his son. The water was clear and smooth, and Wilson could see a dark shape on the bottom. The shape moved away from the boat.

Wilson dove in. He went to where Royce had disappeared beneath the surface and put his head under, but when he opened his eyes, he couldn't see a thing. He kept diving down, feeling around, but his thrashing and clutching did no good. He splashed around for a half-hour until his eyes stung from the salt water, his muscles ached and panic was replaced by an overwhelming emptiness. The creature and the boy were gone.

Chapter 13

Jerry D'Argent, Melvin McDonald and Diamanda filed into The Frog Sunday morning just after opening, as punctual as churchgoers. Early arrival guaranteed a good barstool; by noon, the best seats would be taken.

Gene liked Sundays as a rule, finding it easy to keep pace with the slow and steady drinking on this day of rest.

The argument over the dolphin occurred as Jerry sucked the end of his first gin and tonic through the end of a tiny bar straw. Jerry liked to have his first drink inside him, warming things up, before he tackled the Sunday paper. He adjusted his eyepatch and then unfolded the newspaper, keeping the front part for himself and passing the other sections to Diamanda and Melvin.

"First they close the beaches because it ain't safe to swim in the water, and no sooner than they open them back up, and we get this. Scare tactics. Somebody's trying to keep people away from Key West, I'd say," Jerry said, after reading the latest headline, "Investigation Into Dolphin Attacks Continues." The singer in the band, Rolanda, came over to stand behind Jerry, looking over his shoulder at the headlines and drinking her third cup of coffee.

Melvin sped through the comics, then tossed them aside and leaned over to read over Jerry's other shoulder. As Jerry went to turn the page, Melvin reached out to get a grip on the paper, trying to yank it from Jerry's hand.

"This is bullshit," Melvin said, jabbing his finger at the headline. "Dolphins don't attack people. Period. They're intelligent, gentle creatures."

Rolanda shook her head, sending her dreadlocks a jitter. "Hell, sharks do it, barracudas bite people, why not dolphins? They got plenty of teeth. Why couldn't a dolphin go crazy and bite somebody?"

Diamanda put down the Runes she'd been playing with. "A better question is why would a dolphin attack a man? It's not natural. If a dolphin did it, there's something very unnatural at play," she said.

Rolanda peered into the mirror behind the bar to freshen her lipstick and rearrange her dreadlocks just in case a record scout from
Miami happened to be in the crowd that afternoon. "Still could be," she
said.

"No way. Ask Gene," Melvin said stubbornly. "He knows. Gene,
tell her how docile they are. The military tried to turn them into underwater goons, but the dolphins only wanted to play. They used to train
them right offshore here."

Gene polished the dark wood of the bartop with a white cloth, his
hand moving in steady circles. "Dolphins are smart. They like people.
Most of the time," he said in a carefully measured tone.

Nobody knew just how smart they really were. The scientists
learned a lot about dolphins in the 1950s, but not much new since. Gene
knew about the experiments, the autopsies to dissect the dolphin's
organs and brains. What scientists had done to dolphins over the years
reminded Gene of what people who claimed to have been abducted by
aliens on a space ship said had been perpetrated on them.

"In other words, what Gene is saying is that a dolphin could have
done it, if he were properly trained," Rolanda said.

Jerry got tired of sharing his paper and folded it back up. He
turned to Rolanda and said, "You know, I thought the music was supposed to start in here forty-five minutes ago. Why's it always late? Why
don't you get your butt back on that stage?"

Melvin looked at Jerry. "What got the first guy was a shark. It could
have been a 'cuda — they've been known to bite. Especially if that poor
sucker had speared a fish. The paper said he had a speargun."

Jerry squinted back at him with the eye that was not covered by his
pirate's patch. "My friend, barracuda don't eat divers any more than
dolphins do. For that matter, neither do sharks. Your problem is that
you got all your learning in books. You ought to get out on a boat a little more often. Rolanda's right."

Diamanda Full Moon gathered up the Rune stones and returned
them to their velvet bag. "When are things ever as simple as they
appear to be?" she said. "There are forces at play here that this newspaper reporter knows nothing about."

Melvin and Jerry both rolled their eyes toward the sky. "Diamanda,
don't get started on that again," Melvin said, shaking his head.

"You told us a million times about how the little green men came
down from the stars in their spaceships on a noble galactic crusade,"
Jerry said.

Diamanda just sat there with a dignified look on her face, and Gene decided to step into the discussion, something he usually avoided. He winked at her, then said to Jerry, "I thought you liked UFOs, Jerry. Weren't you just telling me yesterday about seeing a UFO out over the Marquesas last summer?"

"That was different, Gene, and you know it. You're taking my remarks out of contest. I actually saw something. She talks about it like it's some kind of religion." Jerry pounded his fist on the bar. "The fact is a man is dead on the reef, beaten up and bloody, his regulator torn out of his mouth by something. Drowned. Dead. On this we can all agree. It was no UFO, and a cosmic connection isn't going to help the poor son of a bitch."

Melvin nodded his head in solidarity with his drinking buddy. Overhead, the big ceiling fans danced, bathing the agitated drinkers in even more hot air.

"Story like this'll put half the folks in town out of work for a month," Melvin said.

"I agree, kid. Whoever wrote this is just plain irresponsible," Jerry added. He looked at his watch. "Hey, it's after twelve. Time for lunch. I'll take another gin and tonic and a bowl of that popcorn."

Diamanda looked at Jerry with the type of patient expression a teacher might reserve for a slow child. "The dolphins are here for a reason. We all need to pay a little more attention to what they're trying to tell us."

"You know, nobody's going to pay you for that in here. You ought to get on back down to the sunset, you want to sell all that voodoo, mumbo psychic shit," Jerry said, stirring the fresh drink with a little red straw. "We are realists, living in the real world."

"Don't pick on her," Rolanda said. She came over to put her arm around the psychic. "Let me tell you about dolphins. When I worked on the catamaran last summer—you know, when I was trying to make a little extra money to go back home to see my mama in Jamaica—we'd have to stop at least once a week to fish some crazy snowbird out of the water after he or she jumped in 'cause they just couldn't resist swimming with the dolphins. Hell, once they saw dolphins, these people didn't care if they were three miles offshore and couldn't swim a stroke. They'd jump right in, like the dolphins had some kind of mind control. People go crazy over dolphins. They'll do anything to get near them."

Jerry removed the straw from his drink and scratched the skin under his eyepatch with it.

"Okay, so we're going to tell dolphin stories now. Well, I've got a dolphin story too," he said. "I knew this lady who went to Australia to hang out on the beach. One day, she sees all these dolphins out in the water, their cute little fins poking up, waving at her, inviting her to come on in. She gets all excited, starts jumping up and down, and tells her friend, 'I'm going out. I have to swim with them.' So she plunges into the water and swims out to the dolphins. Turns out they weren't dolphins at all — they were tiger sharks. They ate her."

He and Melvin looked at each other and laughed loudly, clapping each other on the back.

"That's a horrible story." Rolanda shuddered. She gave Diamanda a hug as she turned to go on stage. "I'm going to play Three Little Birds, and dedicate it to your dolphin."

"So now it's your dolphin," Melvin said to the psychic.

Rolanda walked across the room and climbed the stairs to the stage, where her guitar player was waiting. Her walk was slow and dramatic as a thoroughbred's, hips rolling and head tossing as if getting there was half of the performance. She didn't seem to care that it was only half past noon, the bar was near empty and nobody was watching.

As they began to play, a somber, solidly-built man came in and took Rolanda's empty seat at the bar. He had the sturdy body of a weight lifter and closely cropped hair. The regulars did not greet him with their usual friendly banter, just stared at the stranger in his black T-shirt and khaki shorts that exposed legs as thick and strong as tree trunks.

As soon as Gene came over, the guy smiled, and Gene held his hand out to greet him.

"Haven't seen you in a while, Storm," he said. Gene set a coaster in front of the man.

Storm ordered a beer in a gruff, no-nonsense tone. When Gene brought the drink, he waved away the man's money, saying, "This one's on me. Don't see you down here much, buddy."

"Been busy," Storm replied in a tone as serious as though he carried the weight of the world on his shoulders. "TDY," he added.

Sgt. Storm Davis was Army Special Forces, assigned to the military combat swimmer school at Trumbo Annex. Gene knew what TDY, the military acronym for official travel, meant but didn't bother to ask where. Offshore meant some clandestine destination, probably a god-forsaken spit of strategically important sand, where Storm would have spent a few weeks training young thugs to kill one another more efficiently.

Gene had known Storm for the better part of a decade. They'd first met during a war game in the Indian Ocean. Even though Gene was Navy and Storm Army, all the divers bunked together aboard the ship. The two units worked as one to capture an old freighter that had been hijacked by terrorists, the mission turning out so well that it didn't even make the evening news. But it did form the kind of ties that lasted.

Storm tipped the beer back and half of it disappeared down his throat. "See the paper today?"

Gene wiped the bar in steady circles, no speck of dirt in sight. He nodded.

"Something's up, buddy. Can we talk in private?" Storm looked around for a private corner.

"Not here. I'm working," Gene muttered.

Storm finished the beer and motioned for a refill. "What time you off?"

Gene looked at his watch. "Three more hours."

"We need to talk. Got a job for you," Storm said.

Gene refilled Storm's beer and set it down gently. This time he took the money. "I can't help you, Storm. Sorry."

Storm stared into the white foam that capped his beer, his crew cut head bent over, face tilted so that Gene couldn't see his expression. He spoke in a low voice. "Gene, I'm not asking for much. Just a drink and talk. All you gotta do is listen. Come on. Trust me."

Gene had spent his whole life trusting men like Storm, all too often ending up on a trip to hell with no way back. He'd worked hard to change that lifestyle but he still had to remind himself that he didn't owe Storm or the Navy a thing. The days of getting dragged into other people's troubles were over.

"I'm glad you're not asking for much," Gene said. The hairs on his arms and back were standing on end, sending off alarm bells off in his head. "For a minute, I thought you wanted something."

"So meet me later, what do you say? How about the Compass Rose? I'll buy."

Gene had no desire to hear Storm's pitch, which most assuredly would involve a secret operation. Some enticement or threat would be used to drag Gene into it, and he'd get nothing but a headache in return. That was the problem with special ops. When you did a job right, nobody would acknowledge it. When you did something wrong, it was a different story.

"No. Not interested," Gene said. He picked up a bar towel and began the slow circular polishing once more.

Storm signalled him to come back over, and then spoke in a whisper.

"Look, buddy, I'm doing you a favor. If you don't come down and talk to me, friend-to-friend, you're going to get an official call. Then you won't have any choice."

Gene's grip on the towel tightened until dirty gray water dripped out. "What do you mean, no choice? I'm out. Retired, remember?"

Storm leaned over the bar. "Gene, we got a problem out there. Now you and I can fix it ourselves, quietly and professionally. You're one of the few guys around here qualified to help me. Or you can refuse." He paused. "The big guys will be down here quick as lightning, your service file in hand. They'll find ways to convince you that I can't even begin to imagine."

Storm had stopped whispering and was talking way too loud now. The other patrons at the bar had begun to listen in. Diamanda was sitting next to him, appearing to be focused entirely on those Runes but Gene knew that she was listening to every word.

"All right. All right," Gene said reluctantly. "I'm off at five. I'll meet you at the Rose."

Storm polished off his beer, held his thumb up and grinned at his little victory, then walked out the door.

Gene would let Storm buy him beer and listen to what he had to say but there the line would be drawn. He already knew what Storm would say—the moral imperative, right against wrong, life versus death, the argument that a man of conscience had no real choice. He didn't even know what the mission was but he knew the rallying cry. A SEAL would be sucked in every time by a speech like that, and Storm knew just what buttons to push: patriotism, expertise, that good old sense of right versus wrong.

His shift would end soon, so he started to clean up. As he waited for the night bartender, Ripper, to arrive to take over, Gene vowed that he wouldn't let some damned military operation interfere with his carefully constructed life of blissful ignorance of world affairs. He didn't watch CNN or read the paper. He didn't belong to any military clubs or even subscribe to Soldier of Fortune. He'd spent the last six months setting up a totally uneventful existence. He wasn't about to let a sob story from Storm change it.

The palm reader's strange warning Friday night crossed his mind, then Gene shook his head. He wasn't going to let a fortune teller influence his thinking either. He knew what was real. This business with the dolphins didn't involve him. Diamanda could be right about the dolphins being in trouble. That diver and the turtle trapper, well whether the dolphin had anything to do with it or not, they were already dead. When all was said and done, neither he nor Storm had the power to change a thing.

Chapter 14

After work, Gene strolled up Margaret Street through the old neighborhood of Victorian mansions on his way to the Compass Rose. The cool of the evening had not yet set in and heat rose in waves from sidewalks that had baked all day in the tropical sun. Even though he took his time, his T-shirt was sticky with sweat after only a few blocks.

Night jasmine was in bloom all over the island and by this time of evening, its sweet scent hung in air like an old lady who'd doused herself with a little too much French perfume. Everywhere he turned, the sweet air brushed against his bare skin like warm satin. But the magical atmosphere came to an abrupt end the moment he opened the Rose's door and the greasy odor of stale beer and burgers hit him.

The off-the-beaten-path Rose had the singular attraction of being half the price of the tourist traps down on Duval Street. For ten bucks, a guy could get a belly full of fish sandwich and beer that would cost three times as much a few blocks closer to main street.

But the Rose's drawbacks were many. No live band, no charming island ambiance, no frozen rum concoctions made with fresh fruit. Just an oversized TV screen and the game of the week.

Once Gene's eyes adjusted to the dark, he spotted Storm at a red gingham covered table toward the back of the room, a draft beer planted between his elbows. Except for two skinny men with greasy ponytails twisting down their backs and long hairy beards hiding their faces, the place was deserted.

Gene sat down wearily and ordered a beer from the young, gum-popping waitress.

"Okay, you got me here, Storm. Now what?" Gene asked when the waitress was gone.

"Relax. We'll get to that in a while," Storm said. "We've got plenty of time."

"Maybe you do but I've got plans," Gene said. It wasn't an outrageous lie. His cat, Tugger, would be waiting for a meal.

The waitress brought a tray with two beers in big frosted mugs. Storm took a sip and grinned. "Hey, did I tell you, we've got the new Lar Vs over at the school? You ought to come over and check them out one of these afternoons."

"Great. New toys. Is that's why you wanted to meet with me? Need an old timer to help evaluate the hot new machines?" Gene knew that wasn't what Storm wanted at all. This was diver small talk.

A Lar V was a rebreather. It looked like a chest-mounted backpack with hoses for breathing. The device recycled a diver's breath, eliminating the bubbles that usually give away a diver's presence to a gunner on the surface. Unlike regular scuba equipment, the rebreathers were silent, a big plus for either a military operation or getting close to fish. Professional photographers loved them. And a diver equipped with a rebreather could stay underwater far longer without running out of air.

"No, we've had them out a few times. But I'd like to get them into action, see how they perform in a real op. You wouldn't believe some of the stuff we're doing at 250 feet these days. Using trimix, heliox, even talking about getting a couple of hard suits down here next year."

"You're making me feel obsolete," Gene said. He looked down at his body. He was still in good shape for a guy in his 40s, but his body was softer and had padding in places that used to be tight and hard. "Once you quit, you can't go back."

"Don't underestimate yourself." Storm winked. "I'd take a cunning and wily old coyote like you over a youngster any day. That's why I wanted to talk to you."

"I was hoping you'd get to that before we drank up half your paycheck. I'm only going to disappoint you by saying no."

Gene looked up at the TV screen. A CNN reporter stood in front of a bunch of palm trees on a breezy white sand beach. Gene recognized Fort Zachary Taylor, the most picturesque beach on the island. He nudged Storm and yelled to the guy behind the bar, "On the TV, it's Key West. Turn it up a minute."

"A third mysterious death has struck in the Florida Keys. This time it is a young boy missing out on the reef, which follows separate incidents Saturday that took the lives of a fish collector and a scuba diver. Authorities have no official comment but sources tell us that something in the water is attacking people. Does Key West have a homegrown version of Jaws? No one knows for sure, but some kind of killer is at large at sea," the reporter said, and then the image switched to a war zone someplace on the other side of the planet.

Storm let out a low whistle. "Looks like our boy just upped his body count. We've got to do something about this."

"We?"

"You and me, buddy. I've got a plan. Operation Wet Night. What do you think?"

"Very sexy name." Gene picked up his glass.

Storm's gaze settled on the red gingham cloth as he kept talking. "That dolphin is military. I can't prove it yet, but I swear it's true. And this boy's smart. Dangerous too. Worse than having a renegade missile flying around these islands."

"You're worse than the drunks in the bar, Storm. What do you want to pick on a poor old dolphin for? Count me out."

"How can you say no? Hell, I haven't offered you anything yet. The dolphin's got to be brought in."

"Why are you so sure it was a dolphin?" Gene said. "What about a shark?"

As if anybody on land could understand an event that happened far from sight in the mysterious waters five miles out. The sea had her secrets and that was the way it was meant to be.

"What about a plain old heart attack? The fish collector could be some old, out-of-shape drunk whose body just gave out on him while he happened to be leaning over the side of his boat," Gene continued, wanting to throw as much cold water as possible on whatever idea Storm was hatching. "And maybe the diver had enemies and he was killed in a freaky murder by fellow human beings. Have you checked his credit record, seen if he'd taken out an insurance policy lately? People are a helluva lot meaner than dolphins, as a rule."

Storm leaned close. "Gene, I've seen the dolphin with my own eyes. He's smart." He scooted his chair closer to Gene and lowered his voice. "I was out on the Wilkes-Barre the same day the diver got it. The dolphin was there. He was going for us too. Believe me, this old boy knows what he's doing, and we haven't seen the end of him. He's been well trained. If he is one of yours, I have to hand it to you. You did a helluva job, my friend."

Storm flashed Gene one of his million-dollar smiles. He apparently thought he had Gene convinced.

Many military divers were afflicted with severe, and sometimes dangerous, overconfidence. Gene used to wonder sometimes just how smart the guys were who were picked for the truly dangerous underwater military assignments. There was a fine line. Typically, the divers were far above average when it came to understanding the technology and physics involved. The common sense quotient was another matter, and some men seemed eager to rush into a deadly situation simply for the thrill. Eventually Gene realized that men often were handpicked to do the job because of those very traits. The men who would blindly follow orders even when the odds were clearly against them often rose to the top in the military hierarchy.

Storm ordered two more beers, then returned to his sales pitch. "We've got a military weapon gone haywire on us, Rock." Gene could hear the eagerness in his voice. "The DOD's lost a lot of our expertise since the program was descoped, with the cutbacks in personnel and a lot of the old timers getting out. I could use your help."

Gene shook his head. "You know, Storm, I've worked real hard to simplify my life. I like it nice and quiet."

"Hear me out, that's all I ask." Storm gave him another ear-to-ear grin like he was selling used cars to a guy who couldn't get credit anywhere else in town. "I could handle it myself. Go back out to the Wilkes-Barre with a spear gun and wait for the dolphin to come back. But no. I've given it careful consideration, and the best solution is a sanctioned exercise to eliminate the threat."

Storm leaned forward, excited, his hands clenched into fists.

"Come on, Gene. These days, the guys don't see a lot of real action, especially in the water. Sure, we get down to Central America once in a while or get to ride shotgun on some damned peacekeeping mission." He paused to drink his beer, wiped the foam from his lip and continued.

"We're graduating kids who are warriors in name only. They haven't been tested, not like in the old days. A search for a real predator, an intelligent one, not some damned military game, would separate the men from the boys."

Storm looked over his shoulder, as if some enemy agent might have followed him into the Rose and was now listening in. He lowered his voice to a whisper. "I've asked for permission to locate the released units and eliminate them."

"Eliminate, as in kill?" Gene said. This was serious madness. He was angry now and not caring if it showed. "You're not thinking straight, pal."

"Hey, you saw the TV. The body count is going up. The last thing the Navy needs now is more bad publicity. The story gets out that the killer is one of theirs while they're still reeling from last year's scandals, there's going to be hell to pay back in Washington. Between the admirals caught with their pants down and the cadets caught cheating on exams... if there's even a chance that a military unit has gone AWOL and is endangering the public, well, you'd be surprised at what the brass will approve when it comes to keeping up image at budget time," Storm said. "The Cold War is over, Rock, unfortunately for all of us, but a fact of life. If it was up to me, I'd let the old boy go. What do I care if a dolphin takes out a couple of tourists? But it's not up to me."

"I can't believe you'd get permission."

"Let me worry about that, Skunk. I want you on my team. You're a specialist; you'll be compensated."

"I told you I was through."

"You're never through." Storm gave him a hard look. "Gene, you are the only one around here with experience with those dolphins. You have information that can't be obtained by looking up old records. You know they don't give us low level Army guys access to classified Navy data. Ninety percent of what I need is inside your head already. Hell, you were at Coronado, what, two years? Anything those dolphins have been trained to do, you would know, one way or another."

He was right about Coronado. Gene had been stationed at Coronado, the Navy base in San Diego, twice. First in the 1970s when he was a new recruit to SEAL school. Fifteen years later he went back. Gene wondered where Storm picked up that little detail.

The second tour, Gene's official job description was Navy marine mammal trainer. In simple terms that meant he taught dolphins, seals and whales to plant and detonate bombs, guard harbors and kill enemy swimmers. The program was a PR nightmare for obvious reasons. For years, the Navy refused to confirm even the existence of a marine mammal project. But pro-dolphin extremists like the Sea Shepherds and Greenpeace knew all the details and regularly blew the whistle. Finally, the Navy had admitted publicly that the dolphin-training program existed but only the most innocuous tasks such as harbor guarding were acknowledged.

Gene had never told Storm of his own involvement. The Navy's dolphin program was still top secret.

"I can't talk about this stuff. You know that," Gene said.

"You can if you're part of my operation. Besides, the activists blew the lid off it a few years ago," Storm replied. "It's an official open secret just like the spook satellites."

Storm laughed and finished off his beer.

"Just pick up the Herald and you can read about how the Navy is still trying to figure out what to do with the assets," Storm said, waving the waitress back over to their table.

Gene had seen the news stories. Hundreds of dolphins were still in the Navy program, kept in tiny pens off the southern California coast. And trappers were still hired each year to catch new dolphins to replace the program's casualties.

"It's not going to be as easy as you think, Storm. Besides, you've got plenty of talent at the school. You don't need me."

"Kids half your age, Rock. Sure, they're strong, they do anything they're asked. But man, I need you. You're the only one who can help me understand exactly what we might be up against."

"If you can't do it without me, guess you don't have a mission."

"Please?" Storm put on his best imitation of a pleading look.

"Don't you have something better to do with your time? Jeez, I know we've been at peace a few years now, but you'd think an Army ranger would have a bigger, meaner enemy to fight than a dolphin. Can't you find a terrorist or some third world dictator to practice on instead of some poor old dolphin?"

Storm sat up and slammed his open palm hard on the tabletop. "He's a damn serial killer, and he fucked up my dive on the Wilkes-Barre Friday. That fits my definition of a big problem."

"Somebody else's problem, Storm. Unless you make it yours."

"Maybe how that dolphin got out on the reef is somebody else's worry, but what's happening offshore affects me and all my divers. It's like having your neighbor's dog crapping in your front yard. You got to stop it the minute it starts or you are going to have to clean up the same mess every day. I don't have to go on the damned Internet and read the Greenpeace page to know that the Navy's dolphins have been released into the water around here."

Storm crossed his arms over his chest and pouted for a minute, then flagged down the waitress for another round and continued his attack. "Here's the offer. You help me plan the op. You are treated as a full team member, my second in command. We'll pay you the top outside expert fee, fifteen hundred bucks a day, for as long as it takes. What do you say, Rock?"

"That could be a hell of a lot of money. Why don't you drive up to the sanctuary and talk to Johnnie Reb?"

"What do I want to talk to him for? The guy's manic."

"He knows a lot."

Storm leaned forward in his chair, planting his elbows on the table, his biceps bulging till they strained the black T-shirt. "Johnnie Reb may have screwed up big time. He let those dolphins out and we know it."

"You just don't get it," Gene said.

"Get what?"

"Johnnie's dolphins didn't do it. Any dolphin that was good at killing things would never be released by the Navy. They only release the old, the sick and the hopelessly untrainable—the dolphins that would rather starve to death than to hurt a human being, and believe me, that describes most of them," Gene said. "Dolphins can be mean if they've been abused. That part is true. They will fight back. But you will never convince me that a dolphin is a serial killer."

"Then you tell me. What the hell is happening out on the reef?" Storm asked.

Gene swallowed the last gulp of his beer and signaled the waitress to bring the check.

"Man, I don't know what's happened to you," Storm said, his smile gone now. "I remember a time when you would see something that wasn't right and be the first guy jumping in to fix it. But look at you now. Working behind a bar all day, drinking down on Duval Street all night, pissing away your life."

Storm shook his head and looked at Gene with disgust. "Without your help, I'm afraid there's going to be a bloodbath."

Gene was silent.

"You have till tomorrow to change your mind," Storm said. "I've got visitors flying in from the Pentagon."

"The Pentagon? I thought you said it was a local operation."

"I called Loring. I had to."

Gene's stomach sank.

"Don't worry. It's not a problem," Storm said, "he's only going to observe. He'll be down for a couple of days, take a look around, rubber-stamp the paperwork. He won't be looking over our shoulder every second."

Loring was a four-stripe admiral who had run a mission that got four SEALs killed. The SEALs were assigned to secure Manuel Noriega's airplane on the runway so that he couldn't use it to escape when the U.S. forces went into Panama. Loring wanted maximum public relations benefit out of the operation and had insisted on a show of force that had SEALs parading down a runway in the open. The men were virtual sitting ducks for snipers but the press pool got great footage of the whole show, operatives being mowed down in action and all.

Gene had been a mid-level advisor stationed at the Pentagon in a desk job at the time. He had just washed out as a dolphin trainer out in

California, and the Panama fiasco was all it took. Two months later he was out.

Gene stood. "All you had to do was mention Loring and you would have saved yourself a lot of time and trouble. I'm sorry the military dolphins are going to take the blame, but I don't want to hear another word about this." Gene headed toward the door in a daze.

Chapter 15

Back at The Frog, Ripper was working the bar, his hair dangling in two tight skinny braids that hung to his shoulders Native American-style. The place was nearly deserted. Gene took a barstool and ordered a draft. Ripper set the beer down and Gene pushed a ten at him, but he waved the money away, shaking his head, the Geronimo braids swinging back and forth beneath a red bandana headband.

"Don't you have someplace better to go on your night off?" Ripper asked.

Gene shook his head. "One beer and I'm going straight home."

Rip's jaw worked over a wad of gum as he spoke. "Hear the news? Looks like the dolphin got another one."

"I saw something on CNN."

"Kid was dragged out of a Boston Whaler." Rip grinned. "Poor little devil didn't even have his pole in the water. Couple guys in here from a fishing charter told me the Coast Guard's still searching for the body. Too bad. Really ruined his vacation." He laughed. "Key West is such an exciting place to visit."

Gene finished his beer and Rip refilled it. He made no move to take Gene's money, which lay on the bar.

A steady stream of people filed through the back door, stopping to order drinks at the bar and then heading to a room in back.

The men who filed in appeared to have been dressed on a production line in the same T-shirts, shorts, white socks and soiled athletic shoes. Most of them had blue-ink or full color tattoos peeking out where ever bare skin showed. All were deeply tanned.

The next time the back door swung open, a husky guy with a large video camera and lights, the big kind TV professionals use, hurried through it. He wore ill-fitting pants that sagged below his belly and his hair flopped down into his unshaven face. A better looking fellow with blow-dried blond hair, holding a microphone in one hand and notebook in the other followed him. They went directly into the back room without pausing to get a drink.

"What's going on?" Gene asked, motioning toward the back.

"Dive operators and fishing guides are having a little pow-wow," Rip said. "Warholt loaned them the backroom."

"The dive boat captains and fishing guides together? What could be important enough to create such an unholy alliance? On a Sunday yet?"

"Sea monsters, dead bodies. The usual. They're afraid the publicity's going to ruin their business," Rip said. "Wonder if they heard about the kid. Tourist trade is really going to suck now."

Diamanda came in through the front door then. She walked slowly, with her head high, as if she really were a temple priestess and The Frog some sacred site. She wore a white dress that hung to the floor, gold chains circled her waist; more gold dangled around her neck. She must have come straight from working the Mallory Dock crowd. She always earned more tips when she read cards down at the pier if she dressed the part of gypsy fortune teller, and Gene guessed she'd brought in a fortune this night.

"What kid?" she asked as she took a stool at the bar, overhearing Rip's remark. Ripper mixed her a rum cocktail and repeated his story about the latest death on the reef. Gene guessed that Rip would tell the tale of the dead tourist boy a hundred times before his shift was over. If he got a dollar tip each time, it would be a good night. No sooner had he finished telling Diamanda what happened before Gene heard the bartender repeat, "Heard the news?"

Jerry D'Argent came up to the bar to order and Gene was surprised to see Alex tucked cozily under his arm. She wore a tight black dress and red lipstick.

Jerry pulled a fat roll of money from his pocket as Rip finished his headlines. "A bottle of champagne, and give my friends whatever they're drinking." He nodded at Gene and Diamanda.

Alex was doing her best to look seductive, and the act was working on Jerry. Gene wondered if he was feeling jealous but the more he looked at the two of them, the less he cared. That little achy feeling that usually crept from his mid section into his throat when he'd see her around town was mysteriously absent. Instead, Gene was relieved to see her on the arm of D'Argent. Better than prowling around Duval Street on her own. Maybe he was finally over her. He was better off alone; it had just taken him a long while to discover that.

As soon as Jerry led Alex off toward the meeting room, a bottle of cheap champagne in one hand and two plastic cups in the other, the back door swung open and more of the watermen filed in.

Behind a couple of Cuban fisherman came Bob Patcher and his crew. The three of them made their way up to the bar. Patcher was lean and tough looking, as though the years on the water had reduced him to his essence. He reminded Gene of a high mountain alpine tree that years of wind and rain had stripped down to its trunk and branches. In his wake was a woman who Gene recognized as Mattie Gold. She had a large dog in tow. Bringing up the rear was Todd Patcher, Bob's youngest son, but Gene was so busy watching Captain Gold that he barely noticed Todd.

He'd met her many months back at Goombay, one of the local street festivals where Key Westers danced and drank out of the way of Duval Street and its tourist hangouts. Now, as then, she had an inaccessible air, her eyes hidden behind dark glasses. With her hair pulled back from her face and no makeup, she looked like a grownup tomboy. A pair of black jeans cut off well above her knees showed off long, athletic legs that were butterscotch-tan from the sun.

Mattie Gold looked distinctly unhappy. To be expected, Gene thought, after bringing in the dead diver on her boat. Pretty brave of her to show up in the midst of the crowd of watermen.

Patcher edged into the bar next to Gene and nodded. "Hello, Gene. Something wrong with your answering machine? You never return my calls."

"I've been meaning to get back to you, you know how it goes."

"I could use you out on the water," Patcher paused. "Got a trip to Cuba coming up."

Cuba, now that sounded a lot more interesting than Storm's offer. At just 90 miles away, Havana was a lot closer to where they were sitting than was Miami, even though the politics made the two places seem vast distances apart. But you could be there in a few hours on a fast boat, twenty minutes on an airplane, if flights from Key West International to Havana hadn't stopped 40 years earlier. Havana, city of unfulfilled dreams, was said to be part Casablanca and part trip to hell. But getting over to the island wasn't easy.

"I didn't think Americans were allowed over there," Gene said.

"If you've got connections, you got nothing to worry about."

Gene looked at Patcher skeptically. "Taking a big chance, aren't you? Between getting crosswise with the State Department and the anti-Castro loonies in Miami, you might lose your boat over there or worse."

"Nah, we've got permission. We're running hospital supplies."

"Is that what your call was for? You want me to help you deliver hospital supplies to Havana? What do I look like—the Red Cross?"

Gene shook his head. Storm played on his sense of patriotic duty, while Patcher was mixing bleeding heart sympathy for the Cubans with some misguided notion of getting into business over there. Sometimes Gene was thankful the Navy had turned him into a cold-hearted bastard who knew how to say no.

"Besides, we've got an emergency going on right here in Key West," Gene said, nodding toward the back room. "How could you even think of leaving with all the excitement right here in your own backyard?"

"Those guys?" Patcher laughed. "They get all stirred up over nothing. This business will blow over fast."

Todd nudged his father. "Come on, Dad, let's go get a seat."

"In a minute," Patcher said. "You know my boy, Todd?"

Gene shook the tall young man's hand.

"And Captain Mattie Gold?"

Instead of holding out a hand, she removed her sunglasses and examined him, slowly. Gene wished he'd gone home and gotten cleaned up after working instead of going drinking with Storm. He felt like an old head of lettuce at the end of a hot day at the market.

"We met at Goombay, on the street. Last year," he said.

She had been with Mickey Patcher at the little street festival in the old black neighborhood of Key West called Bahama Village. It was just a week before Mickey died. They'd had been laughing and dancing to Reggae music in the middle of Petronia Street.

"Nice to see you again." She finished giving Gene the once over and turned to Patcher. "I'll go get us some seats."

She walked away, an entourage consisting of Todd and the dog, close behind. A skinny guy in a tie who'd been drinking at the bar jumped off his stool to follow. He hurried to catch up to Mattie and caught her elbow. She turned, and Gene heard her say, "Leave me alone, Starler."

She left the guy standing there mid-sentence.

Patcher was still hanging around at Gene's elbow, apparently wanting to get an answer about Cuba. Gene didn't feel like giving him one just yet.

"Hey, I was sorry to hear about the accident," Gene said.

"Once in a while something bad is going to happen. It comes with the business, Gene, and you ought to know that."

Then Patcher got tired of waiting and followed his troops into the back room, leaving Gene alone at the bar with his beer. One little dolphin had created quite a circus.

Gene could hear the meeting getting going, and now the bar was as dead as a funeral parlor, so he picked up his beer and wandered toward the back room. He could use a little free entertainment.

Inside, the windowless room was crowded and the air thick with smoke. He found a spot against the back wall, next to the skinny guy who'd chased Mattie Gold down.

"Dolphins are sweet, harmless creatures," George Flowers, head of the local chamber of commerce, was telling the captains, divers and fishing boat guides who had packed into the meeting. "Wasn't Flipper a resident of our very own Florida Keys? Now the Anchor expects us to believe that Flipper's gone bad. Last thing Key West needs is for the rest of the world to think our beautiful sea is full of blood-thirsty killing machines."

He paused to wipe his forehead with a monogrammed handkerchief. The good life that came along with his position glad-handing the restaurant and hotel owners around town had encouraged George Flowers' passion for the complimentary doughnuts, cocktails and free dinners that were one of the only perks of the job, and an enormous weight problem proved it. In keeping with his position as a businessman, he wore a dark blue sports coat and tie, but in the true spirit of a local, his feet were shod with Birkenstocks beneath the suit.

"We can exert enough pressure to stop these inflammatory stories. Sign the petition. I urge you to sign the petition. Object to these sensational stories and demand that the Anchor acknowledge the safety of the waters surrounding our fair isle," Flowers said. "We've got six million tourists a year coming to the Keys to enjoy our waters, and we want them to know that nothing out there is going to hurt them."

A few of the men gathered around ready to sign, end the meeting, and get back to the bar. They jostled each other, their elbows jabbing out like the wings of large, overfed birds.

Smitty Smith, a fat, puffy-eyed, charter fishing boat owner, parked himself like a traffic barrier between the crowd and the petition. "Mister Flowers," he said loudly, wiping his watery eyes with a dingy handkerchief, "How about answering a few questions first? I'd like to know a little more about what happened out on the reef. You say it's safe. You say it wasn't a dolphin. Okay. You owe us some kind of explanation that the public will believe. What killed those fellows?"

Flowers looked annoyed. "That is a matter for the sheriff's department to handle. Who's ready to sign?"

"Aren't you going to answer our questions?"

"No, I'm not."

"Well that's a cowardly way to run a meeting. There are lies, lies and damn lies," Smitty said.

A man wearing baggy shorts imprinted to look like a huge can of Budweiser beer jumped to his feet.

"Right on, this plan is garbage. It enrages me," he said. "The government has no right to tell us what we can do. NOAA stinks."

A tall man with shaggy brown hair that fell into his eyes and thick glasses joined him.

"I'm a live rock collector," the new speaker said, "and I want to say, this whole thing is unconstitutional. The constitution was not written with ink, it was written with blood. Who the hell do they think they are? They have no right to do this. The constitution is not toilet paper."

"What do you think we're talking about here?" Flowers asked, shaking his head.

"The marine sanctuary. We'll do whatever it takes to stop it," said the Budweiser shorts man.

"Wrong meeting," yelled a voice from the back. The crowd booed.

George Flowers' bright red face turned a more fiery shade. He pounded his fist on a nearby table and said, "This is not another public hearing on the marine sanctuary. This meeting has been convened to discuss the two deaths just offshore."

"Three," shouted out a voice from the crowd.

"Okay, three. Tomorrow the Anchor's gonna run another story about the killer fish that got the kid from Atlanta, and next thing you know the networks are going to be down here just like they were during the Cuban rafter invasion, enjoying the sunshine and conch fritters and beautiful women and scaring the hell out of the rest of the country," Flowers scowled. "And we all know how good that was for business. Room occupancy in Monroe County dropped 40 percent for two whole months. Hell, CNN's here already."

He gestured toward a TV crew whose camera panned the room. Several watermen waved and preened at the camera when they noticed the lens aimed at them.

A tattooed man in farmer style bib-overalls held up a copy of The Anchor and slapped his hand against the newspaper headline. "This is worse than the National Inquirer. I'll bet this guy, Starler, has never even been out beyond the reef. He doesn't know the difference between a grouper and a 'cuda. "

Flowers picked up a large pink conch shell that had been sitting on a nearby table and blew out a piercing sound to quiet the crowd.

"One last time, let's sign the petition," Flowers said. "The tourist trade for the rest of the summer is about to be flushed down the damn toilet. You remember the time the paper said barracudas were leaping out of the water like some kind of goddamned flying vampire fish to bite people in fishing boats on the neck? Well, here we go again."

Flowers pulled a gold pen out of his pocket and turned once more to the crowd, his face glistening with perspiration. He walked dramatically over to the petition and began to sign it.

"Hey, Flowers, what if the reporter got it right? What if it was a dolphin?" cried a voice from the back.

The skinny guy next to Gene shuffled forward, planted his two feet shakily on the ground like a man trying to withstand a gale force wind and losing the fight. "I'm Abe Starler, from the Anchor," he said, blushing as he straightened his tie and jutted out his skinny chest.

"I have one question," Starler said, his voice climbing an octave. "The attacks could have been one of those military dolphins from Sweet Pine Key, the ones that were released last month. Where's the Navy? Why don't you get them to show up here and give us an explanation of what's going on out there in the water?"

The notepad dangled by his side as he waited for a reaction.

The room was silent, and then a commotion started in the back, which ended when the crowd parted to allow a stooped man with bushy gray hair to shuffle to the center. The old gent wore a Salvation Army special olive green polyester leisure suit.

"I would like to speak," he said. He spoke with a thick Eastern European accent. "My name is Valeri Ruykov. We can eliminate this problem for you. I have spent my life studying the dolphins. And my colleague," the old man indicated a swarthy fellow who had moved forward to join him, "is Mr. Mordent. He is experienced in trapping things in the sea. You may have seen him on television. He starred in the National Geographic shark show."

"Hold on, Mr. Ruykov. Who invited you? This is a meeting for locals," Flowers said, turning to appeal to the crowd. "Mr. Mordent is a shark hunter. We are not going to hold an open season on dolphins in the peaceful waters surrounding our little paradise."

Ruykov waved his arms as if Flowers was a gnat. "Aughh," he rumbled, "We don't want to kill anything. We will simply capture the dolphin and take him far, far away. It's a big ocean."

"We can handle this ourselves," Flowers said, planting his feet wide in a fighting stance. "No bounty hunt."

"You are making a big mistake," Ruykov said "I'll give you some time to think it over. Our fees are reasonable."

Flowers looked around the room, then shook his head. "The answer is no."

Smitty stepped forward. "Not so fast, George. I can't afford to lose a week's worth of business while I wait for you to handle things. This fellow says he can handle this problem, maybe we ought to hear him out."

Patcher had been sitting, quietly watching the discussion, and now he slowly stood to speak.

"You people are overreacting," Patcher said. "I advise all of you to let this blow over, and get back to business."

D'Argent got up out of his chair and flung his arm around Patcher's shoulder. "Bob's right. There's no proof there was a dolphin at all," D'Argent said. "Maybe that diver just had some kind of convulsion down on the reef. All you've got is this newspaper article saying so."

Smitty sputtered and held up a hand, then shouted out, "Patcher, your crew should have known exactly what happened to that guy. But the crew doesn't seem to know much of anything," he said. "The men on my boats never would have handled it that way."

The way it came out, with the word men twice as loud as the rest of the statement, made it clear that Smitty was taking aim directly at Mattie Gold. As if the diver would have been fine if only a man had been running the boat that day.

Bob Patcher looked at Mattie Gold, who was still sitting quietly on a stool nearby, and then turned back to the crowd. "My crew played it by the book, Smitty," he said in a measured, even tone.

"Why are you protecting her?" Smitty continued.

"Mattie Gold's as fine a captain as any in the charter boat fleet," Patcher said. All eyes were on her as the eye of the storm now stalled directly over Mattie's head. Gene wanted to see how she would handle it.

"I can speak for myself, Bob," Mattie said finally. She stood up, calm and unemotional as if she handled verbal assaults from a roomful of angry men every day. "There was a dolphin. That part is true."

She looked around the room at the men, her brown eyes intelligent and unflinching. "It could have been trying to warn the victim, or warn me, that something was wrong. The diver was in bad shape when we brought him up, but I'm afraid this is one accident where we may never know exactly what happened. I cannot tell you that a dolphin killed anybody. You can speculate all you want. It's not going to change things."

Diamanda was right behind Mattie. With her long red hair, white dress and gold jewelry, she looked the part of an ancient oracle. The room was silent.

"These accidents are a warning, but not the first ones you're getting," Diamanda said. "The dolphin strandings, the extinction of the whales. The reef is diseased. The beaches are contaminated. There is something strange going on out there. But I am warning you – do not harm any dolphin." She looked straight at the old Russian and continued, "A bounty hunt is the last thing you should be considering."

Smitty slammed his fist on the table next to him. "You work down on Mallory Dock, not out on the water like the rest of us. Maybe you can afford to close down business for a few weeks, but the rest of us can't. That dead boy didn't get much mercy."

Diamanda touched Mattie's hand and Gene heard her say softly, "It's time to go."

As he watched Mattie and Diamanda make their exit, Gene decided he'd had enough too. He followed the women out, catching up to them in front on the sidewalk.

"Mattie," he called out.

She turned around to see what he wanted. Once she stopped and waited for him to speak, he wasn't quite sure what to say.

Then her chin jutted out, and her eyes flashed in anger, as she prepared to defend herself against another verbal attack, guessing that this man had followed her out to continue the criticism that had started inside. "What is it?"

"You're going to Cuba?" Gene heard himself stammer like a teenager.

"That's none of your business."

"I just wanted to say… be careful. It can be dangerous over there."

"Dangerous? You've been there?" she asked.

"No. Not exactly. I'm thinking about going, but haven't been there yet."

Mattie's eyes narrowed. "Then, what do you know about Cuba?" She waited for an answer.

"Look, I've worked with these dolphins," he finally said. "There are things you don't know. The government's involved. I just think you ought to be careful."

"Yeah, thanks," she said in a dismissive tone. "I really need another one of you guys telling me to be careful. You used to be a SEAL, right?"

He heard the disdain in her voice, like SEALs weren't to be trusted. He also was surprised that she knew that much about him. "A long time ago," he responded.

"Thanks for the tip, frogman. I don't need to be rescued." She turned away. "Nothing's going to happen in Cuba that I can't handle."

Chapter 16

By sunrise Monday, Paradise Diver had been on the water for an hour. Mattie was headed south to Cuba, five more hours of sea ahead of them before they made land. From her perch high up on the flying bridge, she could see for miles in all directions, and every way she looked the view was the same endless blue.

Mattie's love of the sea was in her blood. Her earliest happy memories were of the times she and her mother had spent on the water, sailing or whale spotting along the northern California coast. Her father had been a seaman too, not that he'd taught her much. He'd sailed into the sunset when she was still a toddler, leaving her mother to raise Mattie on her own. When she was younger, Mattie had been angry at him, a feeling that sometimes transferred onto other men. She felt cheated by his absence. As she grew older, she accepted the tendency of certain men to not be there when it counted to be the world's way of teaching her to be truly independent.

A boat, unlike a man, was straightforward and easy to control. On the water, she could think more clearly. She welcomed the long crossing to Cuba. The angry watermen, the death of Jim Reynolds, the nagging feeling that maybe she'd been too impulsive in accepting Sam Harbor's proposal—all of it faded when she concentrated on guiding the boat in the direction of the horizon. Today, the weather was perfect for crossing the Florida straits. A crystal blue sky was dotted with dainty white cotton puff clouds, the kind that pose no threat to boaters, just decorate the sky.

On the starboard side of the boat, she saw movement in the water, then sleek shapes just below the surface, moving fast as lightning. Mattie waited and a few seconds later was rewarded with the sight of three jumping dolphins. They made a half dozen joyful leaps through the air, graceful as dancers, before disappearing back into the sea. Excitement surged through her. She hoped the dolphins would stay with the boat for the crossing. She needed all the luck she could get today.

"Dolphins bring magic," Diamanda liked to say. Nothing was dull or boring with her roommate around.

Diamanda never let on that she'd started out as a serious marine biologist. On the contrary, her roommate would rise in the morning to announce that she'd received a message from the cetaceans during the night. "The legions and the Dakinis are fighting it out in Guatemala," she'd say. Or, "Let go of material things, girlfriend, until the moon passes through Saturn's house. " Later, Mattie would pick up the newspaper there would be a story about a revolution in Guatemala, or the economy tightening up north. It was impossible to tell how she got all that eerily accurate information.

Mattie headed south, deep in thought, her crew suspiciously quiet somewhere below. Only an hour out and already salt from the sea air had formed a rough sandy layer on Mattie's cheeks and neck. She felt her skin baking in the hot sun. She needed some cover before the sun grew more intense. Time to rouse the boys, her so-called crew.

"Yo, Todd," she yelled to the deck below.

No response so she yelled again, louder, straining to be heard above the engine's roar. Still, nothing from Todd or Bud. Mattie craned her neck and saw two pairs of hairy brown legs stretched out on the main deck below. The four feet were pretty much identical, wearing the same two pairs of black Teva sandals, propped up side-by-side on the engine hatch cover like a matched set.

She wondered if the boys were sleeping. They'd gotten an early start, arriving at the marina before dawn and spending several hours loading up the boat. As the boat pulled away from the dock on Stock Island, Todd had opened the ice chest and pulled out two beers.

He had tossed one to Bud, popping it open with a cheery, "Breakfast of champions."

She slowed the engine and leaned her head over to view the lower deck. There they were, napping like a couple of kindergarteners. Mattie could see that Todd was not going to be terribly useful, at least not on the way over. At least they'd done a good job of loading the boat.

Cardboard boxes covered with blue tarp had replaced the dive gear and the dozen paying divers that usually were jammed in the back. The spot where Mattie gave CPR to the stiff body of Jim Reynolds just two days ago was buried under donated cartons of baby formula, tampons and ballpoint pens.

Eight black air tanks sat strapped in a row to the sides of the boat, and two large white fuel drums rested near the stern. The boys would refuel the boat's tanks with the drums once they dropped off the medicine. They had to bring all their provisions along since they couldn't depend on being able to buy fuel, food, water or anything other than cigarettes, beer and some very strong coffee once they got to Cuba. Her previous visit had taught her that much.

Mattie drove the boat in relative quiet, listening to the engine and the wind until her peaceful contemplation was interrupted by a war whoop directly behind her, followed immediately by icy cold metal against her neck. Mattie smelled beer breath and spicy aftershave. The unmistakable signs of Bud.

"Beer, Cap'n?" Bud asked, brown eyes twinkling from beneath a wide brimmed straw hat. He was fit and tanned, just like Todd, but with short curly hair streaked blonde from the sun. Bud was an incurable flirt, always laughing and teasing. Mattie had noticed the times he'd come out diving with them, how the female customers always seemed to flock to Bud, asking for his help and leaning on him just a little bit more than was necessary as she bumped the boat along over the waves. She was about ten years older than him, but that didn't stop Bud.

"No thanks, Bud. Designated driver, remember?" She thought about asking him to take the wheel for a minute so she could go below for sunscreen, but decided not to. "You guys take it easy on the beer, okay?"

"Don't worry, captain. We can handle it," Bud said. "All we got to do today is cruise across the straits, right? No real work till tomorrow."

Mattie sighed. "Just take it easy. I may need you guys."

"Relax, captain. We're ready. Couple a brews never got in my way," Bud said.

Mattie frowned.

"Come on, Mattie, who says we can't do the job and still have a good time? I promise I'll be in tiptop shape for the dive tomorrow." Bud threw his arm around her shoulder and squeezed. "Chill out, okay? You've had a rough time lately."

Bud removed his hat and put it on her head, tightening the brown cord up under her chin. "Here you go. Looks better on you than on me anyway," he said.

He went below, leaving her alone again.

Mattie picked her binoculars up to scan the horizon. Another boat, about the same size as theirs, was behind them, moving slowly in their direction. She could make out two men inside.

She slowed down until the gap narrowed, then looked through the glasses again. It was the funny little old Russian, Ruykov, and his shark-hunting accomplice from the watermen's meeting the night before. What were those two were doing so far out? Shark hunting, perhaps? She hoped they weren't out hunting the gray dolphin.

She sped up, trying to put some distance between them and when she turned around 15 minutes later to check for the Russian and his accomplice, they were nowhere in sight.

The only life visible behind her was Bud, hanging on in back as he emptied his bladder into the sea. She heard Todd's voice, loud and happy, making fun of his friend. Mattie kept an eye on Bud. The last thing she needed was a man overboard. She didn't want any more mistakes on her watch.

Chapter 17

Gene locked his bike in the alley behind The Frog and went in whistling a cheerful tune, his spirits lifted by the sunny Monday morning. He was clean and freshly shaved, and he'd pulled his hair back into a neat little stub of a ponytail. He was ten minutes early for a change, and being early felt good.

Each tendon and muscle in his body was alive. As he came through the bar's open door, the odor of last night's stale beer hit his nostrils, but for once the smell didn't bother him.

Rip was behind the bar, pigtails swinging as he set up ashtrays, bottles and coasters. All Gene's normal duties were done. The liquor bottles were out of their locked cage and lined up neatly in front of the mirror behind the bar. Normally there'd be a sticky, stinking mess from the night before.

That should have been the first clue that something was wrong. Gene checked his Rolex to see if he were late. Rip shouldn't be here for five, six more hours.

Warholt couldn't have scheduled two bartenders on a Monday afternoon. It was always slow then, and the last thing Gene wanted to do today was share tips. Rent was due soon and he needed every dollar. Rip dumped a bucket of ice into the stainless steel ice well, and the pieces clattered as noisily as hail falling.

"Thanks for setting up," Gene said, lifting the wooden plank and slipping behind the bar. "What are you doing here?"

"Gene, buddy. How's it going?" Rip gestured at the tiny office in back. "Warholt said he wanted to see you."

"Okay," Gene said, smoothing his hair back. He sucked in his stomach and tucked in his shirt, then breathed out, wondering why he was trying to make a good impression on Warholt. He turned back to Ripper to try again. "What are you doing here?"

Rip shrugged. "The bossman told me to be here by ten, so here I am."

Rip wouldn't look him in the eye. That should have been his second clue. Something was definitely wrong. He straightened up to his full five foot 11 inches and headed back to Warholt's office to find out what was going on.

The bar owner's cubbyhole was cluttered with invoices, dirty bar glasses and pin up calendars from liquor distributors up and down the Keys. The scent of stale cigarettes hung in the air. The furnishings were sparse and stained, and everytime he came in here, Gene thought he was entering the office of a monk who had fallen into the gutter. One cigarette butt smoldered in an ashtray while another dangled from Warholt's lips. The joke was that the only way the boss knew it was time for lunch was that his morning pack of cigarettes would be empty. Only it wasn't a joke.

The bar owner sat at his desk, his eyes fixed trancelike on a wall calendar picture of Miss July straddling a beer keg and wearing a red, white and blue boa constrictor and matching bikini.

"You wanted to see me?" Gene said.

Warholt snapped out of the coma. He motioned Gene to come in.

"Close the door," he said. Gene's boss was a real slob, forty pounds overweight, with gold chains hanging in the rolls of fat on his lumpy neck. Flesh and metal were layered like some kind of human terrine.

Gene tried but boxes of paper bar napkins and Styrofoam beer cups blocked the way. Finally, Gene gave up and just leaned against it.

"You wanted to see me?" he repeated.

"Sit down." Warholt raked paperwork off a metal folding chair to make room. Gene did as he was told, as obedient as a juvenile delinquent in the principal's office, and continued to wonder what he did wrong. Warholt wasn't the kind of guy to call you in for praise.

The fat man could bitch and moan, scream about the customers or the service all he wanted and Gene wouldn't let it get to him. Gene decided when he quit the Navy that he wouldn't ever again allow a so-called superior to control his life. Warholt was not going to ruin Gene's day. He could yell until he turned blue. He could demand that the whole bar be scrubbed top to bottom. He could rearrange the schedule so that Gene wouldn't make a dime till later in the week. It didn't matter.

Warholt opened the top drawer of his desk and pulled out an envelope and handed it over.

"Your paycheck. I'm letting you go."

Gene was stunned. He hadn't considered getting fired on his imaginary list of how far Warholt would go to ruin his day.

Warholt removed two pink squares of paper from a bulletin board next to the phone and handed them over. Gene held the pay envelope between his thumb and index finger, barely touching it, as though it were a piece of hospital waste that would infect him.

"You mean you're firing me? What for?"

"You had a couple of calls this morning. One from a woman. A customer, I believe." Warholt shook his head in disapproval. The employees were not supposed to date customers. Warholt said it caused trouble.

"Don't take it personally, pal. It also got back to me that you were in here drinking yesterday for free. I like you, Gene, but a place like The Frog has got to maintain some standards for its staff or all hell will break loose."

Could The Frog's owner get rid of him that easily? Gene wondered if Storm had anything to do with this. If Gene were suddenly unemployed, Storm's offer to join a military mission for some quick-and-easy money would be harder to turn down. But the Army could hardly have the kind of clout to get somebody fired at a little rathole bar on Duval Street. Gene told himself to stop being paranoid. He'd simply screwed up. It wasn't the first time. He'd thought his job, as unchallenging as it was, was safe, and it was not.

The stuffy air in the office suddenly felt suffocating. Heat rose from his solar plexus to his chest, into his head.

He thought of waiting for Warholt in the alley after The Frog closed. Pummeling the boss man into a bloody heap would feel good. But what would he be fighting for? A lousy job behind a bar, working terrible hours for minimum wage for a jerk who didn't particularly like him. He didn't need The Frog, and he sure as hell didn't need the fat man's blessing.

He got up, pocketed the envelope and taking the messages. Storm's name was scribbled on one. The other was from Alex. Gene crumpled the messages and threw them into the overflowing garbage can next to Warholt's desk.

He marched out of Warholt's stinking little cesspit of an office back to the bar and instantly transformed himself from employee into customer.

"Give me a shot of whiskey and a beer," he said to Ripper. He wondered if the drinks would be free today.

Rip put the shot glass down and poured the whiskey. "Bad news, huh?"

Gene shrugged as Ripper set the beer down on a coaster. Rip was silent. Gene knew he was waiting for the money. He reached into his pocket and pulled out a fistful of change. He was counting it out to pay for the drinks when he felt a gentle touch on his shoulder.

"What's my favorite bartender doing on this side of the counter?" Diamanda Full Moon bestowed her most beautiful gypsy smile on him.

Gene grunted to acknowledge her and tossed back the shot. He followed the sear of the whiskey with a large swallow of beer and waited for the heat of the alcohol to spread from his throat to his midsection.

Diamanda sat down next to Gene and ordered coffee. She wore another one of her classic going-to-an-ashram dresses, this one purple with splashes of gold. "I came in here to talk to you, but I thought you'd be working."

"I just got liberated," he laughed, "and it actually feels pretty good."

"Liberated?"

"Fired," he said. Now that the word had been spoken, he liked the way it sounded. "Fired. Warholt fired me."

"How generous of him," she said, reaching an arm around his shoulders, but not sounding all that sympathetic. "Are you okay?"

"I was thinking of moving uptown anyway. To a higher class joint. This place is a dump. Patrons are nice, though," he said, toasting her with his beer. "Hell, I needed a little vacation anyway. Bar jobs are as easy to get in this town as coconuts. They practically fall off the trees and hit you on the head."

Ripper delivered her coffee, which she doctored up with milk and sugar, and then turned her attention back to Gene.

"When one door closes, another opens. What are you going to do with the opportunity?"

"I don't know." Gene didn't feel anywhere near as bad as he thought he should. He assumed the reality of the situation would take time to set in. He couldn't afford to be out of work for long. "Take a vacation. Catch up on my reading. Lie on the beach."

The morning's paper was lying on the bar, and Diamanda caught sight of the top headline. "It's getting worse," she said reading out loud, "Another Dolphin Attack Leaves 10-Year-Old Tourist Missing In Action."

Gene shook his head. "Don't believe everything you read, Dee. No matter what the newspapers or boat operators say, it doesn't add up. I know a little bit about dolphins."

"Then you know our brother is trying to tell us something," she said. "And I intend to find out what it is."

"Brother?"

She nodded. "You know what I mean."

Gene drank his beer. "I heard you at the meeting last night. But I don't know what he'd be telling us. The scientists have been trying to talk to dolphins for years. And they've come up empty-handed."

She finished her coffee. "Let's go. Come on. We have important things to do."

She hopped off her stool, tugged at his arm until he got down off his, and then led him out the door. A couple of drinks on an empty stomach and Gene had no will power to resist a pretty woman's whims. It had been a long time since he'd had beer for breakfast, and now he remembered why, but hell, he had nothing better to do. They could have a few drinks, share a few laughs, he'd forget about how pissed off he was at Warholt and then he'd go home and nap through the hottest part of the day.

Diamanda guided him up Duval St. by the elbow. They passed the La Concha Holiday Inn. In the windows, oysters and cold beer rested on thick, white beds of shaved ice. In the upscale souvenir shop next door, a thousand different pink flamingos flew at him from the windows. Gene wondered how so many shops stayed in business when all they sold was worthless trinkets. The tourists seemed to have nothing better to do than wander up and down the street charging large bags of junk on their credit cards. Enough to keep Key West humming anyway.

It seemed pointless, and he despised the affluence, the work ethic, the normalcy. He'd take being a misfit any day. They walked east on Duval, where traffic was backed up for several blocks by a slow-moving, lane-hogging pedicab.

Across Petronia, they reached the glass storefront office of the Key West Anchor. Longhaired, shabbily-dressed protestors circled the newspaper's offices. The marchers carried placards that read: "Dolphins Have Rights Too," and, "Messengers From the Stars."

Diamanda tightened her grip on his elbow, propelling Gene straight toward the insurgents. They were sweaty, pierced and too young looking. A little too sincere for Gene's taste, and with a glint that could be suppressed insanity in their eyes.

Squatting at the perimeter, snapping pictures was Abe Starler, the reporter from the night before. A small plastic badge hung on a chain around his neck.

Diamanda left Gene leaning against a palm tree, trying to blend into the background as she went to talk to one of the marchers. She chatted the protestor up for a few minutes, ignoring Gene, until she headed back his way. He feared that she would join in, or worse, try to drag him into it, but instead she took his arm and steered him down the sidewalk.

"You don't look well," she said. "Protests make you nervous?"

"I've been the one they're protesting against too damn many times," he said.

"Things change," Diamanda replied.

After a few blocks, they turned on a narrow side street. The lane's thick trees and plants created a green tunnel to the houses, which were packed so close their walls almost touched.

Wild cats slept in the shade of tall palm trees. Little gray geckos streaked across the path, darting so fast that they seemed like optical illusions created by the heat.

The passageway through the foliage led to a tangerine house with a white door and shutters. Diamanda opened the gate and went up the steps. She unlocked the door and let him in.

Inside, the front room was dark and cooled by a ceiling-fan spinning overhead. Three large cats draped themselves across the furniture like stuffed pillows. The room smelled of burning incense.

"Sit down, my dear. I'm going to make us some tea." She pointed to the sofa.

"How about a beer instead?" he said.

She gave him a skeptical look. "That can wait."

Diamanda disappeared down the hallway to the back of the house. The sounds of water running and china clattering drifted into the living room and then she came back through the doorway carrying a tray laden with a black teapot and two mugs. She settled down next to him on the couch.

"I remember the first time I got fired," she said, as she poured the tea, its spicy aroma mixing with the incense smell. "Sixty-nine. A California marine park. I'd just gotten out of grad school. What a sweet, naïve young thing I was. I was working as an assistant dolphin handler. In the beginning, I loved the job. Taking care of the dolphins was play, not work to me. But by the end of the first six months, three of my babies had died. Each time, my heart broke. I was crying at work every day, but I couldn't bring myself to quit. When they finally fired me, it was a relief."

"They fired you for crying?"

She laughed and her green eyes sparkled. "No, for talking to the dolphins. I knew exactly what they were saying, whether they wanted to tell me about work or play. Sometimes I would get bigger messages. The other assistants didn't like that one bit, and started to complain about me. I was a little too far outside their reality, so finally the director fired me. He said I had a personality disorder. Hard to believe. I mean this was California in the 60s. You'd think anything would go."

She shook her head. "I decided the best therapy was to get out of town, so I hit the road for a long time. Finally I ended up here."

"So you got fired, too," he said. "Never thought I'd wash out as a bartender. Considered it my retirement job."

Diamanda touched his hand. "You'll be fine. As they say, the universe provides for the little sparrows, so why not you?"

"Good, then the little birds can pay my rent," he said.

On the small coffee table sat a polished clear crystal skull, about the size of an apple. Gene picked it up, feeling its smoothness.

Diamanda moved closer to him on the couch. "I want to tell you about my dream. You were there, and so were the dolphins. I could see you swimming with them. One of the dolphins kept swimming off, and then coming back. Finally you followed him. Then I ended up in the water alone with the dolphins. I could feel them against my skin and I heard them speak. It was soothing, like being rocked to sleep. The dolphin dreams have been coming since just before the attacks started. Something's definitely going on out there."

She sounded like a nut but Gene didn't care. Today, he decided, anybody who'd gotten fired over a dolphin was a hero in his book. "Diamanda — a dream is just a dream. The dolphins are intelligent, misunderstood creatures. But in the end, that's all they are."

He had just said exactly what he thought, but the words brought the same uncomfortable sensation that he'd had when he saw the protestors. In the Navy he had said things on occasion that he only half believed in for expediency. He'd been properly trained to parrot the government line, whether it was the truth or not. It always made him feel queasy like this. Why was he doing that now?

But Diamanda was having none of it.

"You don't really believe dreams are meaningless, do you? Or that dolphins are just animals with cute faces put here on Earth to entertain us at theme parks? Gene, you know so much more than that."

"I'm talking about what's happened out on the reef. An accident is an accident; a dream is only a dream."

"Sounds like you've already made up your mind and nothing's going to change it."

"You're wrong, Diamanda. I have an open mind."

"Have you? These dolphins are conduits, like antennas pointed at the stars. It's there for you too, at least if you are aware and sit still for long enough to hear."

Gene didn't mind if Diamanda was getting galactic telegrams, but he was a practical guy and he wanted her to know it.

"I don't want to argue with you," he protested. "You believe whatever you want, Dee. But I'm the kind of guy who likes proof."

Diamanda tossed her red hair back defiantly and pointed at a newspaper lying on the table near the tea. "What kind of proof? There it is in black and white. Is just seeing something in the newspaper enough to make you believe? If it is, you're just like almost everybody else. But I don't think you are like that, Gene. I know you aren't," she said. "How do you know what's true, what to believe in?"

Gene thought about the question. A long time ago, he would have come up with a scientific test, but as the years had passed, he began to lump the scientists into the same category as politicians and bureaucrats. Self-promoting, uncompassionate, or worse. Where did a man turn for truth in this day and age?

"Instinct," he finally replied. "I trust my instincts."

That was what carried him through years of hard-edged discipline. He'd lived overseas and snuck off countless times to secret destinations to do dirty work for the good old U.S. of A. He'd followed orders, even when the mission was the kind that a man didn't want to think too long or too hard about. A SEAL wouldn't be able to do as he was ordered if he didn't.

"Yes, I would imagine you have a good instinct for self preservation."

"Don't get me wrong. I've made as many mistakes, believed in as many fairy tales, as the next guy," he said. "When I enlisted, I was a dumb kid from New Jersey who thought he could change the world. Becoming a warrior seemed like a simple way to do it. I believed in what I was doing every time I went off on assignment. Until they sent me to train the dolphins. I couldn't do it. I had a lot of time to think."

In San Diego, he'd happily reported to his dream assignment working in the Navy's secret marine mammal project. During an endless summer of southern California days, he spent the daylight hours out on the ocean and the nights haunting the familiar watering holes he'd discovered years before as a recruit. He slept in the same soft bed each night, no longer having to endure the hardships of being an active team member on assignment.

In San Diego, he'd also found that the Navy had crammed his

pupils into tiny pens, isolated and unable to see or touch each other. The dolphins were alternately starved and then rewarded with dead fish as part of the training method; they had heavy equipment and muzzles strapped to their bodies. He never deliberately abused them but they were subjected to conditions that Gene thought were similar to prisoners of war. He was able to teach the dolphins certain tasks, like search and recovery operations, but when he needed to show them the more violent and aggressive missions, the dolphins often played dumb. He wasn't supposed to talk of his work, which remained classified. But he wanted Diamanda to understand.

"I worked with the dolphins for a few years. They may be the smartest animals on the planet, but they will not do tasks contrary to their nature," Gene said. "I spent two hard years learning that lesson. And then I just couldn't do it anymore. Not for all the glory or money in the world."

When he couldn't get his dolphins to perform, he caught hell from the higher ups. And then Gene, almost against his will, began to question things. He'd begun to think about war, death and the value of life. Did a single life have almost no value or was it more precious than gold? He'd been taught to kill, and was supposed to teach the dolphins the same lesson. It hadn't worked.

"I don't know what I believe in anymore, Diamanda," he answered her, slowly, truthfully. "But I don't think a dolphin is out killing people on the reef." The crystal skull felt cool in his hand. He didn't want to put it down.

She looked at the crystal in his hand. "We've got to find him. You like that?"

He nodded.

"It's yours," she said.

"You're awfully generous," he said. "What did I do to deserve this?"

"Are you willing to help us with the dolphins?"

"Us?"

"Mattie and me," she said. "We're on the dolphin's side. It's a small team."

"Everybody wants to go dolphin hunting," Gene said. "First Storm, with his crazy plan, and now you women."

"Storm,'" she said, nodding as if she'd known this all along. "He's the big guy who came into The Frog Sunday. Gene, you've got to stop him."

"I don't think so. You know who that guy is?"

Diamanda reached out for his hands. She gripped them hard and frowned. "We've got to get to that dolphin first. To protect him. We need to move fast."

"Whoa," said Gene. "I didn't say I was going to help you. I don't want any part of this business."

Diamanda got up and brought the telephone to Gene. "I want you to call your friend and find out was much as you can. Please. I promise you won't regret this."

He put the crystal skull down and stared at the phone, shaking his head. "Military operations just aren't my thing anymore. I've worked really hard to get out of that business."

"Would you do it as a favor to me, then?" she asked. "Just talk to him. The dolphin needs someone on his side."

"The dolphin needs someone on his side? What about me? We all need somebody on our side, and right now, I think I need to look out for myself, not the dolphin."

"Please," she said quietly. She reached over to touch his shoulder. Her green eyes looked directly into his, pleading with him, and he felt his resistance breaking down.

"Okay." Gene picked up the phone and punched in a number. Just a phone call, a conversation. No more. He'd limit himself to words. He liked Diamanda and Mattie Gold. An unlikely pair, one so flighty, the other so solid and down to earth. If he had to help someone, it might as well be the women.

On the tenth ring, the locator at the base answered.

"Patch me through to Sergeant Davis, please," he told the operator.

Chapter 18

The dark brown shadow of Cuba appeared against the blue horizon where the sea met the sky. Mattie checked her instruments and took a heading. The Loran had stopped working once they were out of range of Florida. Cuba didn't have the necessary stations on land to send out the signals for navigation into the country.

"Todd, bring me my Magellan," Mattie called to her crew down on the main deck. She would rely on satellite signals and some ancient charts to get the rest of the way in.

A minute later, Todd climbed the ladder to her perch on the flying bridge. One hand clung to the aluminum ladder while the other held two cans of beer. He reached the top and offered her one of the beers.

"No, thanks. You guys lay off the beer for a while," she said. "I need the GPS unit and the charts."

"Got you covered," he said, pulling a black satellite navigation unit, about the size of a deck of cards, out of the pocket of his shorts. The nav chart was folded and stuck in his back pocket. "Sure you don't want a cold one?"

Mattie shook her head, took the GPS receiver and switched it on. The small green screen glowed and then flashed the warning, "Battery Low." The device beeped three times and shut itself down.

"Todd, go get the extra batteries, please," Mattie said.

Todd stashed his beers under the seat and climbed down the ladder. A few minutes later, he returned, empty-handed.

He still held a beer can in one hand. He was frowning. "Bad news. Guess I forgot to bring them."

She'd been holding it all in and now she let it loose. "I can't believe it. Do I have to take care of every little detail myself? Todd, when are you going to start taking some responsibility for things? I've just about had it. You'd think I get something better than a couple of kids to take to Cuba if this job is so damned important."

Todd scrunched his shoulders and sank lower into the seat as if he were trying to disappear. "Sorry, Mattie."

Just before they'd left the dock, she'd double-checked the engine oil and discovered that Todd had forgotten to fill that up, too. She had controlled her temper then, but now she wondered how many other mistakes he'd made that were still in store for her. "What did you guys come over here for anyway?"

Todd stared down at the can of beer clutched between his thighs as though he were being hypnotized. He wasn't going to respond.

She took the beer out of his hand and poured it over the side into the water. "There. No more beer until the job's done."

"Aw, Mattie." He gave her a petulant look.

"A woman wouldn't get away with half the shit you guys pull."

Mattie thought about all those watermen at The Frog the night before and their implication that a boat captained by a man would have prevented the death on the reef as if somehow a person's sexual organs were involved in a rescue.

"So I forgot the batteries. What's the big deal?" Todd shrugged. "People have been sailing to Havana for centuries without GPS. A captain as good as you are shouldn't have any problems."

"Tomorrow, Todd, you need to take care of the details yourself. I'll be on the boat, not there to bail your sorry ass out if you forget something."

"Okay, Queen..."

"What did you call me?"

"You heard me."

"Did you say queen?"

"Yes. Ice queen. You honestly didn't know that's what they call you?"

Mattie's nose tickled and eyes itched like she might start to cry, but willed the tears that were welling up to go away and glared off at the horizon instead, thankful for the dark glasses.

After a few minutes of silence Todd tried to backpedal away from the revelation. "People respect you, Mattie," he said. "It's just that you're so intimidating."

"Intimidating? Me?"

"Yes, you."

"Tough." So the hardcore, macho men in the diving world thought she was made of ice? She didn't really care if they were intimidated; she wasn't about to start acting incompetent just so the men could feel superior.

Then she saw a huge dolphin leap out of the water some distance from the boat. He was enormous, and as soon as she saw him, she knew he'd come again.

"Look over there, Todd. It was the dolphin," she said.

"A dolphin or the dolphin?" Todd asked.

"The one from the reef," she said, shading her eyes and scanning the water in case he reappeared.

"The killer? You've got to be kidding."

"Who says he's a killer? We don't know that."

"Well, you know what I mean. There must be ten thousand dolphins between here and Cuba. What makes you think it's the same one?"

She didn't have an answer but she was quite certain. It was a little weird. Now she remembered what that ex-SEAL had said out in front of The Frog the night before.

"The government was involved and to be careful," he told her.

But this dolphin didn't seem dangerous to her.

"I know him now," she said. Cuba was looming larger on the horizon. "Hand me the nav chart."

Mattie had navigated her way into Varadero once before without Loran and she was confident she could do it again. As they drew closer, she began to recognize landmarks.

She used a factory smokestack to get her bearings and the hotel rooftops against the skyline to navigate toward the harbor. It was one o'clock. They'd made good time crossing. With any luck, they'd dine in Havana tonight, although that didn't guarantee much as far as getting a decent meal went. Last time she was in Havana, she was happy if she could just identify the food on the plate.

Bud climbed up the ladder to join them. "Havana manana, baby," he said. "Look at that skyline—so this is Cuba."

"Welcome to infamous Varadero," she said. "Endless white sand, world famous beaches, and dirty old men on cheap sex vacations."

"Well, we're not dirty and we're not old. The babes ought to be ready for some young blood tonight," Bud said.

"They're not going to be interested in you, Bud, unless you have a thick wad of money to flash around. The women are in survival school here. If they fall in love with a foreigner, romance generally has nothing to do with it."

"Yeah? Well, we'll see about that."

"Not here. Varadero's just the place to tie up for the night." She patted his arm consolingly. "Hey, you still get Havana."

She pointed the bow toward Varadero and slowed the engine,

watching the depth finder more closely as the water got shallow. The boat churned ahead and the hotels got closer and bigger until they no longer resembled toy buildings on a game board.

In the distance, a small boat motored toward them, starting and stopping, lurching forward as its old engine coughed in protest. Finally the boat drew near enough for her to identify it as a 1950s era pleasure craft. The old vessel had peeling paint and more than a few holes above the waterline.

"A gunboat," Mattie muttered. "It's the Cuban coast guard. Go below and get out the fenders."

Bud nodded and climbed down to the lower deck. Mattie saw two young Cubans in mismatched blue uniforms crewing the old vessel. The Cubans looked even younger than Todd and Bud, and she guessed that they were still teens. They pulled up alongside the Diver, their engine idling loudly and belching out thick black smoke. Mattie slowed Paradise Diver to a crawl.

Todd pointed to a battered machine gun mounted on a metal tripod and bolted to the bow. "What the heck do they need with that thing?"

"Welcome to the land of Oz," she said quietly, then yelled to the Cubans. "Buenos dias. Habla inglés?"

The taller of the Cubans responded in rapid-fire Spanish.

She couldn't understand a word of it, her Spanish vocabulary being limited to what was needed to get a coffee or a beer. Todd and Bud stood side by side, staring at the Cubans. They didn't speak Spanish either but as they were your average testosterone driven young men, they had to try out their own Spanglish to see if it would work where Mattie's had failed.

"Let me try," Bud yelled. He moved to the side of the boat, cupped his hands around his mouth and shouted, "Amigos. Cervesos for amigos?"

He grabbed a couple of beers out of the cooler and waved them around but the Cubans just stared back icily at the hyperactive Americans. Then he pointed to the cartons stacked in the stern of the boat.

"Medicino," Bud shouted. "Por hopital." He pointed to the boxes again. "Varadero. OK?"

Then Bud tossed the two beers through the air to the Cubans. The tall Cuban caught the beer cans in midair. The beers disappeared like magic below deck. The Cuban turned to Mattie and shouted at her in English, "Follow me, please."

Paradise Diver fell in behind the gunboat and the two boats headed into the harbor. At the mouth of the concrete-walled harbor, dozens of people from the town stood, waving at them as if they were on floats in a parade. The whole place seemed to be on a big holiday, where nobody was working, and everyone had time to come down to the port to greet the newest ship to arrive in town.

Beyond the harbor was the one and only marina in the town. The marina could accommodate dozens of large boats but most of the slips sat empty.

On the dock, a small army of Cubans milled about waiting for Paradise Diver to pull into one of the empty slips. Mattie counted a dozen men, all wearing official looking brown uniforms. Even from a distance she could see their clothes were faded and shabby.

A tall, heavy Cuban in a dark blue shirt with epaulets was the first to greet them. He waved them into a slip with a fist punctuated with a thick cigar. The other Cubans moved quickly aside when he came down the dock, deferring to him silently.

"Buenos dias," Todd said politely as he tossed the line to one of the smaller Cuban men who scrambled around the dock following the directions of the big guy in the blue shirt. All of the Cubans watched Mattie and her crew with suspicion.

For the first time in her life, Mattie had the cold sensation of being a criminal. The place brought up old memories. The Varadero marina hadn't changed at all since she and Mickey made their trip last fall. She remembered the cement steps and the buildings on higher land. The Cuban flag still flew from a pole planted in front of low cinder block buildings on shore.

Now the head Cuban stepped close to the transom where Mattie was rearranging the lines of her boat. His uniform was in better condition than the other men's and he wore a thick brown leather belt and boots, the signs of his rank.

"May I have your passports?" the man said in excellent English. He stepped over the transom onto the deck without asking her permission to come aboard.

"Certainly," Mattie said. At least he spoke English. That should simplify matters slightly. "I'm Captain Gold. Todd, go below and get our documents."

"How long do you plan to stay in Cuba?" the man asked.

"One night," she said.

"What is the nature of your visit?"

"We've brought hospital supplies for the hospital at Mantanzo. Humanitarian aid. They're expecting it. We're going into Havana for the day, coming back tomorrow to meet with the hospital people, and then heading back home. Here, here, you'll see, it's all approved." She handed him the State Department papers approving the trip from the U.S. side and their three passports.

He examined the papers for a minute. "Please wait," he said, then headed up the steps, taking their passports and the official documents with him.

"Might as well relax," she said, turning to Bud and Todd. "This could take hours."

She climbed up to the bridge, folded the chart and put it back into the waterproof pouch. Then she began to stow the rest of the gear they'd used during the crossing.

"We're the only boat in port," Todd said. "How long can it take?"

"It can take as long as they want it to," she said.

"Anybody want a beer?" Bud asked, pulling a handful of cans out of the ice chest.

Mattie shook her head. A dozen Cubans squatted on their haunches, like birds watching picnickers from a safe distance, hungry but not brave enough to come close.

"Maybe they want something to eat," Todd said. He went back to the cooler for the sandwiches.

"Sandwich?" he offered the Cubans. "Cervesos? Come on, it's good, have some, amigos."

The Cubans would have none of it. The thin, dark men had nervous eyes that jumped quickly around as if just listening would bring trouble. One of the Cubans scooted closer. He kept staring intensely at Todd, and finally he was brave enough to speak.

"Aspirin?" he finally inquired in a small voice. He flashed a nicotine-stained smile and held out an empty palm.

"No, no, no, you no want aspirin," Todd said. "You want cervesos. Cervesos, yes?"

"Aspirin," the man repeated. He turned away at the offer of the beer.

The man's sad expression drove Mattie to raid the boat's first aid kit for a couple of aspirins. She called him over and placed them in his palm. He studied the pills, then carefully placed them in his pocket, still looking rather disappointed.

"He wants the whole bottle, captain," Bud said.

She went back to the kit and took the whole bottle out, handing them over. "He needs them more than I do," Mattie said.

This time, the little man smiled enthusiastically and nodded in appreciation. "Gracias, senorita."

Then they settled in for a long, dull wait.

Six hours later the officer returned with a sturdily built woman. She was in her 40s, with short clipped hair, bright red lipstick and a plain brown dress. A large, old-fashioned stethoscope hung around her neck.

"Dr. Rivero will now examine you, with your permission," the officer said.

The doctor shook Mattie's hand.

"A woman for capitan," she smiled appreciatively. "This won't take long."

She looked into their eyes and ears, examined their arms, hands and faces, and then made notes onto a clipboard.

"You stay long in Cuba, captain?"

"No, only a few days," Mattie said. "Then back to Key West."

"It's too bad. You should stay longer, see Cuba."

"I'll be back again," Mattie said. "Some day I want to see the whole island. Spend some time here."

"You bring medicine?"

"For the hospital at Mantanzo."

"That is good." She took Mattie to the center of the boat, away from the men and spoke quietly. "They have no thread for the surgery, no gloves for the surgeons, no aspirin. The doctors are excellent, but the situation is not good. The children, they suffer."

"Yes, well, we're happy to help," Mattie said awkwardly.

The doctor shook her hand. "Good luck," she said.

She signed the bottom of a long form and handed it over to the officer.

He studied the paperwork, then asked her for forty-five U.S. dollars for Cuban visas.

"Highway robbers," Bud griped, digging into his pocket. "How much is that in pesos?" He reached into his other pocket, and much to Mattie's surprise, pulled out a fat roll of Cuban currency.

The officer shook his head, frowning. "No. Dollars. Only dollars. No pesos."

"We're in Cuba, surely you take Cuban money," Bud protested.

The officer's eyes narrowed. "Where did you get that Cuban money, gringo?"

Mattie stepped between them and held up her own U.S. money. "We have dollars. We want to pay you in dollars. Forty-five, right?"

She pulled out fifty and gave it to him.

He studied the money suspiciously, just as he had the medical forms, then stamped each passport and handed them back, without supplying either change or an explanation of where the extra five would go.

"You are free to go," he said. "You must be back within 48 hours."

He and the doctor headed up the steps.

A few minutes later, Mattie and her crew were hurrying up the crumbling concrete steps to the taxi stand in front of the marina, where a lone driver leaned against a dark blue 1950s sedan. He smoked a cigarette and gave them an indifferent stare. They were the only paying customers in sight, but then, he was the only driver and obviously knew who would hold the upper hand as they bargained for a ride.

"Havana," Mattie said, hoping the driver understood English. "How much?"

He frowned. "Havana? No. No, Havana."

He didn't want to go, but then maybe it was an act, designed to get her to pay more.

"Havana?" she asked again, pulling some cash out of her bag. She showed him three twenty-dollar bills.

He shook his head.

"Let me try," Bud said, stepping forward. He flashed the thick roll of pesos. "What about these?"

The man shook his head and glared, as if Bud had offered to punch holes in his tires rather than give him money. The driver turned to Mattie and held up eight fingers. "Eighty dollars, Havana."

She added another twenty to the three she'd already offered. He nodded, then opened the back door to the cab, and they climbed in.

Wedged in between the boys, Mattie felt warm and safe and protected even though logically she probably wasn't. She leaned against the back seat, which was covered in a cheap polyester fabric. Beneath her feet, the floorboard was hot as an iron. She looked down to see large rusted hole, and through it, the pavement.

They headed west toward Havana on the coastal highway, the car's engine complaining on every steep hill, of which there were many. Mattie figured the old sedan had lasted for forty years since the revolution and probably would live another two hours, the time it would take to get into town.

She was exhausted. It would be close to midnight by the time they got to the city. She'd been up at 3 a.m., off the dock around sunrise. The steady rhythm of the tires contacting the asphalt made her sleepy and she closed her eyes, but sleep did not come, perhaps because of the thousand and one bumps that pitted every mile of the coastal highway. Then a series of deep potholes jarred her into sitting upright, and she decided to stare out the window at the dark Cuban countryside instead of trying to sleep.

Bonfires illuminated the road and moonlight provided enough light to see the outline of trees up the tall hillside that rose on the left hand side of the car. To the right, only an occasional light flickered out on the ocean.

Every so often, they would pass a huge clump of pedestrians, all of whom seemed to be walking vigorously down the middle of the road. The driver veered each time he came to a crowd of people or a wandering cow, and the swerving was fairly regular since large quantities of livestock were wandering loose on the highway. Each time the car lurched, Mattie shifted heavily against one of the boys. They smelled of the afternoon's beer, sea spray and sweat, familiar, masculine scents that reinforced that sense of security that she'd felt after getting into the taxi.

She remembered the edginess from the first time she was in Cuba. Imminent danger lurked but it never actually surfaced. Maybe that was due to Mickey. When he had been around, she'd found herself drifting through the days and nights as if she were in a long, vivid dream.

And tonight Cuba seemed a dream again as the fields and forest gave way to high rise apartments and small tracts of houses, the suburbs of Havana. The lights stretched to the edge of the sea. Here, unlike Florida, the coastline was almost in a natural state. Back home people and boats lined the edge of the land, every inch put to use, and it was good to see any land that the developers hadn't turned into a huge parking lot. Here the shoreline was more natural, perhaps like Florida used to be, long before Mattie got there.

Before long they were in the heart of Havana and the taxi was zipping through the uncrowded city streets and stopping at the Plaza, the same hotel where Mattie stayed the first time. Familiarity. Familiarity is good, she thought. The Plaza rose several stories and had an arched white marble promenade running along two sides of the building. Inside, she remembered, was a long, ornate entryway leftover from the old days when the hotel had been a grand old dame to rival the elegant hotels of Europe.

At the entry to the lobby, a guard opened the door to admit them. He scrutinized the group quickly, then waved them in as soon as he saw they were not of Cuban nationality. Cubans were not allowed in the Plaza unless they had a good reason to be there as Mattie had learned during her first stay.

Bud and Todd lugged the gear up to a carved wooden counter, where a clerk was busy with paperwork. He finally looked up.

"Two rooms," she told the clerk, a neat man wearing a suit two sizes too small. "How much?"

"You pay in dollars?"

"Of course," she said, wondering how different the price in dollars would be from pounds or yen or even pesos, if they even took pesos here. At least Bud was not leaping forward to offer his Cuban money this time. She had instructed him in the cab to keep his pesos in his pocket until further notice. As the clerk watched, she plucked her own roll of money out of her pocket. The roll was getting thinner. Her three hundred dollars would be gone soon at this rate. Then maybe she'd be grateful for Bud's Cuban money.

"One hundred twenty each room, with breakfast," the clerk said.

"No, no. That's too much. Seventy-five. No more."

"Ninety."

"Eighty-five, breakfast included." She wanted to finish this business and get to bed.

"Very good." He fished below the counter for two keys.

He traded her the keys for a stack of American money. No credit cards from the United States were taken here. The Cubans couldn't collect on them because of the embargo.

She looked at the keys. Rooms 304 and 306.

She handed the boys the key to 304 and turned back to the clerk. "Can I have another room, please? A different floor perhaps?"

The clerk sniffed and said, "Something is wrong?"

"306. An unlucky number," Mattie said. She didn't want to tell him that, against all odds, he had put her in the same room she'd shared with Mickey, and she'd be damned if she were going to have to be reminded of that all night long. The clerk pulled another key from a rack on the wall and handed it to her.

She thanked the clerk and turned to the boys. "Have a good time, and try to get some sleep tonight. Remember you have to dive tomorrow."

"Come to the Floridita with us, just for one daiquiri," Todd said.

She waved as she stepped into the wrought iron cage of the elevator. The gate slid closed and she ascended alone. She had no energy to venture out to the world famous Floridita for a drink.

On the fourth floor, her room had two narrow beds and ceilings about 18 feet high, exactly the same as the one she'd just rejected.

Mickey was going to haunt her tonight no matter where she tried to hide. Maybe once she married Sam, the whole darn thing would be easier to forget.

Then she remembered that she was supposed to call Sam back the day before, and she'd completely forgotten in the rush to get ready for the trip to Cuba. The Plaza had no phones in the rooms. Sam would just have to wait until she got back home tomorrow night.

She lay down on the coarse white cotton spread, rubbed her fingers against its stiffness and remembered making love with Mickey the first time in that very hotel. She'd hoped the crossing of the Florida straits would bring some closure to their sad love affair, sort of a symbolic burial at sea for memories. Instead, the trip had only brought him back to life, if only in her mind. How often did people mistake beginnings for endings, she wondered. A tear caught in her eye as she fell asleep.

Chapter 19

J ust before sunset, Gene arrived at Louie's Backyard, a restaurant housed in a large pink mansion on the eastern edge of the island. Storm and a silver-haired man waited for him at a small blue tin table on the oceanside deck.

For a Monday, Louie's was busy, packed with the usual money crowd—politicians, realtors, and yachtsmen—people who wouldn't be caught dead in The Frog. Just looking around could put a dent in your credit card. Louie's was not the kind of place where guys like Storm normally went for a good time.

Storm's companion was a compact little man who looked like he jogged a few miles every day of his life. His body was trim as a teenager's but his face more like an old shoe, all leathery and weathered. Gene had never been formally introduced but he would have recognized Admiral Frank "Eagle" Loring anywhere.

"Storm. Admiral." Gene nodded and pulled back a chair. He held out a hand. "I'm Gene Rockland."

"Good to meet you, Rock, or can I call you Skunk?" the admiral said. His white shirt and shorts were as clean, crisp and wrinkle-free as a military uniform. Small sharp eyes peered out from behind silver wire framed glasses. "I'm Frank Loring. Storm's told me a lot about you. Used to be one of the Navy's best divers. SEAL team three, right? Those boys miss you, I hear."

Gene gave a noncommittal shrug. "I've heard a lot about you too, admiral."

The waitress came and Gene ordered a beer. Storm and the admiral asked for more scotch. Storm seldom indulged in hard liquor, preferring beer, but tonight was not to be an ordinary night, that already was evident.

The waitress delivered a fresh round of drinks. Loring took a large gulp of his Scotch, set the glass down and turned to Gene.

"Storm tells me you're working in a bar or some crazy goddamned thing, Skunk," Loring said. "Maybe it's none of my business, but you ought to be using your skills."

"The bar suits me just fine," Gene said, bristling at the old man's use of his nickname. Loring must have pulled his file. The streak of gray hair, already showing 20 years earlier, had earned him that handle, Skunk. Gene decided that the admiral did not need to be enlightened as to his present employment status.

"Come on now," the admiral continued. "We spent half a million bucks training you, Skunk. That's a helluva lot of a capability to go to waste. A guy leaves the team, he still has a high market value. You play your cards right, you could be a rich man."

"I like tending bar, admiral," Gene said quietly.

The waitress brought their drinks and the conversation paused for a minute. The admiral stirred his scotch, took a big swallow and gave Gene a broad smile. "I'll put it to you straight. Gene, the country needs your help. We got a couple of AWOL units out on your reef, causing all kinds of havoc," Loring said. His voice raspy, as if he had a mouthful of gravel.

"This bullshit," Loring went on, "about a killer dolphin—the Navy does not need any more trouble—the politicians are on us like a cheap suit already what with all the hoopla over sexual harassment and the academy scandal. The last thing I need is a bunch of publicity about a Navy-trained fish causing trouble in paradise. You with me?"

Gene shrugged. He knew better than to argue, even if he was no longer in the admiral's chain of command. He kept a blank expression, calmly replying, "A dolphin's not a fish, sir."

The admiral blinked and held his fire. Gene could see his mental machinery calculating his next strategic move. He twirled his glass and the slivers of ice clinked.

"A porpoise, a fish, a tactical unit. Call them whatever you like, son. We want that dolphin taken out," he said softly. His eyes were watery from the scotch.

"Storm told me," Gene said. "Frankly, the whole operation sounds a little inhumane if you ask me, sir."

"Now don't get excited, son," Loring said in a soothing tone that Gene didn't like. "We'd never hurt those animals willingly."

Loring smoothed his silvery hair down around his temples. The cocktail waitress stopped to tidy up their table and Loring smiled up at her.

"Thank you, darlin'," he said, raising his glass and giving her a wink.

Condensation had pooled on Loring's scotch glass and when he lifted the drink, water streamed onto the blue tabletop. Loring didn't notice until the drips made their way to the table's edge and over onto his crisply pressed shorts, forming a dark wet spot. He brushed at the dark spot, which made no difference except to spread the mark.

The waitress hurried away, turning before the admiral could catch the amused look on her face.

Loring snapped at Storm, "Bring me a towel."

Storm went obediently to the bar and brought back a stack of little white paper napkins. The admiral mopped at his pants with the napkins, tossed the wet clump back onto the table and turned back to Gene. "Now what were we talking about?"

Gene shook his head. "For a minute, I thought you said you wanted to kill the dolphins that have been released out of the military program. But I'm sure I wasn't hearing things right. That would be a real public relations nightmare for the Navy if it ever got out."

"No, no," the admiral said. He banged his fist on the table. "A last resort, Skunk. Killing's always a last resort."

Gene glanced at Storm to see if he wanted to voice a second opinion. But Storm just sat there passively watching Loring and Gene spar. "Why doesn't the Navy just stay out of it, admiral? With all due respect, even if a Navy dolphin did it, how's anybody going to prove it when your program is top secret?"

"You mean your program," Loring snapped back. "I'm a problem solver, Rockland, not the one to blame. I didn't create this goddamned mess. You did."

Gene jumped in his chair as if he'd been knocked over. "Hold on. I didn't have anything to do with what happened out on the reef this week."

"Well, you may not have been out there but you are in the thick of it. Least that's what our records indicate. Yes sirree, you have a central role. You were one of our top dolphin trainers. That's why Storm said we ought to at least give you a chance to help fix things."

"Help? What are you going to fix? You have no evidence that Navy dolphins, or any dolphins for that matter, killed any of those people. All you have is speculation. Now you and Storm want to mount some half-assed operation that makes about as much sense as when you sent SEALs into Panama." Gene stopped. As soon as the words were out, he knew he'd made a mistake. He clenched one fist inside the other, feeling the metal chair bite into his back and arms.

Loring's face turned bright red at the mention of Panama. His hand began to rattle the ice in his empty glass noisily. Finally Storm sat forward, hands clasped, ready to mediate.

"Gene, we thought you'd want to help," Storm said. "I checked the records. You trained the units we released last month. They're your pupils, Rock. We figure those are the ones most likely to be causing the problem."

Storm shifted uneasily, his weightlifter's body too big for the flimsy metal chair. "Now, I know what you're going to say—we don't know that Squid or Orna or the others did it, but they could have. They are your responsibility—they need you now, just like delinquent children need the attention of dutiful parents. You owe it to them to take care of this mess before things get any further out of hand. If we can catch them, maybe we can find some evidence of whether they did it or not."

"You guys are crazy. I didn't teach them to kill tourists," Gene said. "I'm not going down for this. You guys are going to have to find another scapegoat."

Storm and the admiral exchanged an unhappy glance and then turned to stare at the sea as if it might hold an answer to their dilemma. The sky had turned darker and almost matched the blue-gray of the water as darkness closed around the island.

Storm signaled the waitress for another round. When the drinks arrived, Loring polished off half his in a single swallow. The scotch seemed to revive his fighting spirit, as he turned back to Gene. "We'll take care of you if you take this assignment on—job down at Boca Chica, or back in Washington, or hell, whatever you want. Storm tells me you want a little cottage up the keys, you can have it."

"You really think I'm for sale?" Gene asked quietly.

"Be realistic, man. Everybody's got a price," Loring said. He let out a tired sigh. "And if you won't help, somebody else will. We'll go to an outside contractor or simply offer a bounty. Like you suggested, let the locals handle it."

An outside contractor meant one of the fishing guides or adventure hunters from the local crowd of crazies. Half the dolphins in the Keys would be slaughtered. Gene felt a wave of nausea. Diamanda had begged him to get as many details as possible on the military plan but he'd heard about as much as he could stand. As he thought about the best way to make his excuses and get away, George Flowers lumbered up to the table.

Storm pumped Flowers' hand and held out a chair. "Admiral, this is the local businessman I wanted you to meet. George is head of the Key West Chamber of Commerce."

Flowers lowered his bulky frame into a chair, groaning at the effort, and ordered a beer. He wiped his palms on his baggy white shorts and adjusted the gold chain that peeked through his open collar. His shirt was a tropical pink number with enormous flowers printed on it.

"Real pleased to meet you, admiral," Flowers said deferentially. "Whatever I can do to assist you on your visit, all you've got to do is ask. This community really appreciates having the Navy around."

Gene had gone this far to get some intel on the dolphin operation, and Diamanda would certainly want to know what Flowers had to do with the fiasco, so he forced himself to sit still for a few more minutes to listen and see what would be revealed next.

"Storm tells me you want to run some exercises out on the water. The chamber is at your disposal, admiral." Flowers wore a smile like the Cheshire cat. "What exactly do you need?"

"That all depends," the admiral replied, "on our friend Gene. We may need a little help; we may need a lot. Skunk, you've had some time to think it over. Should we contract this out or do you want to get on the team, give old Storm here a hand?"

Storm leaned over and spoke quietly to Gene. "Come on. Forget the past. The dolphin needs you. I need you."

Loring murmured, "Think about that big bungalow up the keys."

"Gene, I'll call your boss at The Frog, get you out of work if that's the problem," Flowers said. "Hell, do you good to get out on the water for a day. I'm going to bring Abe Starler, that kid from the Anchor, with us."

Loring downed the last of his Scotch and turned to Flowers. "He's not working there anymore, so that's not a problem. Might help you find a new job."

How did Loring know that? It had only been a few hours since Gene was fired. He felt like a trapped animal. He was fairly certain that the same atmosphere hovered over Louie's waterfront patio that had engulfed the commanding officers on the Titanic, the Lusitania and the Hindenberg.

"You guys are out of your minds," Gene said, standing up.

"Suit yourself, Skunk." Loring turned back to Flowers. "Looks like I need a boat and crew."

"I'll have one first thing in the morning."

"The boat's got to be fast, and we want one big enough to get a ways offshore if we need to, make it look like a bunch of guys out on a charter fishing trip," Loring said.

"And a crew that knows how to keep their mouths shut," Storm added.

Gene realized then that these men were quite serious about exterminating dolphins. Diamanda was right. He should do something, anything, to interfere. For the first time in his life, Gene understood why responsible people some times turned confidential matters over to newspapers, hoping that a little exposure would stop something crazy from going ahead when all internal checks and balances had failed. He'd been taught as a SEAL that loyalty to the team was the first rule. Whistleblowing was something that a SEAL would never do. But if you couldn't turn a matter over to the proper authorities to handle because the proper authorities who the very people screwing things up, what were the options? One was to stop consorting with the enemy, Gene thought.

He stood up. "Thanks for the drink, Storm. I'll be seeing you."

Before they could try to argue him out of leaving, he hurried up the wooden steps and out the front door. Behind him, the sea and horizon were black. Lightning bolts across the water split the sky far away in the direction of Cuba. The lightning flash reminded Gene that Mattie was over there. He wondered if she was safe.

Chapter 20

The dolphin's pen was small and cramped. The water thick and brown as Cuban coffee from the silt stirred up on the shallow bottom. Every time he turned, his tail touched the mud, adding dirt to the mix. When he surfaced, oil stuck to his skin and petrol fumes seared his lungs.

Just before sunrise, the humans came and opened the gates to let the big gray out. Then they moved down the dock, opening the pens of the three others.

The gray dolphin heard the raspy low voice of the small bushy-haired human, the one called Ruykov. The other men did as he said, even though the old man did not come to the pens often. The bushy headed one spoke in a rough language, and the dolphin's distrust of the old man was strong.

The old man climbed into the boat with the younger men in dark green uniforms and the boat headed out to sea, its bell beckoning the dolphins to follow. The big gray took the lead, with the other three dolphins trailing at a distance. The men would try to teach the dolphins to act as guardians and warriors. The three smaller dolphins would not be able to feed until they returned to the pens that night. The humans had seen to it by strapping a muzzle on the snout of each. But not the gray. He was well trained already and needed no muzzle to guarantee his return.

Their voices carried through the water. He measured each by loudness, tone and frequency. The dolphin was wary of the men, as he knew the frequencies were too low.

He felt rebellious. He might get away for a few hours but escape from the men was out of the question. His agreement with spirit must not be broken.

The dolphins swam together to the temple. The other three swam in a wide circle, diving deep to the tip of the crystal temple. The clanging from the humans' bell was fainter down here, the water more peaceful. The three dolphins stayed together, circling over the temple, but the big gray continued descending until the light was dim and he had to rely entirely upon his sonar to determine his surroundings.

The red-haired one already was listening, waiting for a sign. She waited at night, in the dreamtime. The deaths on the water would draw her out, and she would bring allies. These warriors would transmit in the higher frequencies, the beautiful ones that had almost been lost over the years as humans played with their electronic creations and the electromagnetic outpourings changed their bodies in response. The friends of the red-haired one would receive his message, and then he could be free.

He went deep until the pressure closed in on him like a tight velvet embrace and then he turned north and began to swim hard and fast again to the little island. He was already picking up another frequency. He felt it vibrate in his body, a strange sensation beckoning him closer.

A vision lurked at the edge of his awareness. The visions guided him in carrying out his part of the pact. As he swam north, he broke the surface periodically to take sweet air in through the blowhole on the top of his head. As the air filled his lungs, the vision moved from the edge to the center of his mind. Now he could see what must happen. Excitement surged through his body.

He had crossed the water three times now to carry out his mission. Today was the fourth time, possibly the last. He hoped that with what he did today, the humans would finally listen despite how hard that was for them.

Chapter 21

Delicate little waves stirred the blue waters of the bight. The sun glared hot and intense in all directions, even though it was barely eight o'clock in the morning. Storm Davis had just finished taking inventory of 15 boxes of gear brought over from the Combat Swimmer School when a short, khaki-clad figure came strolling down the dock.

"Good morning, sir," he said to Loring as the admiral approached. Storm executed a small but perfect salute. The formality was unnecessary since they were supposed to be posing as regular guys out for a little fishing expedition on the boat that had been chartered for them by George Flowers, but Storm didn't want to get off on the wrong foot with Loring. That would come later, he was pretty sure.

As Loring got closer, Storm could see the admiral's face was already flushed and his neatly pressed cammies were soaked with sweat. Loring returned the salute, then slapped Storm on the back.

"Didn't sleep worth a damn," the admiral said. "Flowers had me out at the tittie bars till oh-four-hundred. Got more per capita on this little island than any place I been since Bangkok. But hey, I guess that's why you call it paradise."

Storm dug a bottle of water out of one of the boxes and offered it to Loring. "Have some water, sir? Dehydration will sneak up on you in this climate."

"Don't worry about me, soldier. I spent half my life in the tropics. Hell, my longest tour was the South Pacific. I remember one time back in '72 when it didn't get below 98 degrees for 45 days running. I'll be fine." The admiral mopped the moisture from his face and neck with a khaki handkerchief. "What's the plan?"

"We're heading out to the reef, where the unit struck the first time. Make a little dolphin music, see what we stir up," Storm said.

"Great," Loring said. "It's your op, sergeant. Just consider me an observer."

Next to arrive was George Flowers, who strode up to the pier with Abe Starler in tow. Flowers wore his trademark Hawaiian print shirt and a baggy pair of shorts, a more sensible outfit for a day on the water than Loring's combat getup. Starler, on the other hand, had dressed up like he was on a job interview. He wore a pair of brown polyester pants, a button down shirt and a tie with a red, white and blue flag theme printed on it.

Loring greeted Flowers with a hearty, "Look what the cat dragged in," punctuated by another friendly thump across the back.

Flowers carried a huge ice chest on his shoulder, large enough to hold a week's supply of beer. The cooler wobbled precariously until Storm stepped up to lift it out of Flowers' hands before the cooler and its precious contents plunged into the water.

"Storm, meet Abe Starler," Flowers said, clearing his throat noisily and launching a large glob of spit into the water.

"Greetings," the reporter said, nodding. He fumbled with a heavy bag of camera equipment as he tried to extract a hand to offer. "Abe Starler, Key West Anchor."

"Hi," Storm said tersely as he pulled Loring aside. "Why are we bringing the press?"

Loring frowned. "What are you worried about?"

"Maybe we ought to wait until the mission is complete before we try to get it into the papers."

"Relax, sergeant." Loring pulled the khaki handkerchief from a back pocket and mopped at his neck. "Didn't anybody ever teach you anything about public relations?"

"This isn't about public relations, sir, it's about mission protocol."

"Don't argue with me, sergeant. Let me tell you something," Loring said. "You get the press in your pocket by being nice to them. Take them with you everywhere. Give them a taste of being on the inside. Something to brag to their girlfriends about. Next thing you know, they think the Navy's the best thing ever happened, and you got yourself a positive story."

Flowers appeared at Loring's side.

"Son, it's like this," Flowers explained, speaking slowly. "We take Starler out there. If there's no dolphin, he sees the waters are safe. Great story. He writes it up, no problem."

Loring nodded as Flowers spoke.

"If there is a dolphin, he sees that the Navy and the city, working hand in hand, have a plan to eliminate the threat to our visitors. We are ensuring the safety of the waters together. The tourists can sleep safe and sound; the public has nothing to worry about. Another good story, thanks to our friends in the Navy. There is no way we can go wrong."

Storm's jaws clenched. His teeth began to grind. The Navy? The head of the Chamber of Commerce ought to know the difference between Army and Navy personnel. Oh hell, let Loring and the Navy take all the credit for now. At least until Storm knew how this was going to turn out.

Loring pulled out a pair of sunglasses. Like the hankie, they had a brown khaki pattern that was not any standard military issue that Storm had ever seen. Must have bought them at some designer military boutique or out of the back of Soldier of Fortune magazine.

"Just wish Flowers would have brought along a female reporter," Loring was saying as he donned the shades. "Oh well. We're going to have a helluva good time today anyway."

The boat captain, who had remained discreetly out of sight till now, came down the dock with two buckets of dead fish for dolphin bait as Storm had requested. Storm's students from the school, Andy and Paul, emerged from the SportFisher's air-conditioned cabin and loaded the smelly cargo.

Fifteen minutes later, the boat cleared the Palm Ave. Bridge and was headed out of the bight into the open water. On the way out to the reef, the men divided into two groups. Storm and his students congregated in the bow where they'd have a clear view of the water ahead and other boats in the vicinity.

The admiral, Flowers and the reporter formed the observation team in the stern, settling into big sturdy chairs that were bolted down to the deck for deep-sea fishing.

The late morning sun beat down hard but the boat moved at a good clip, and the breeze kept them cool. For a half-hour, they plowed through the clear turquoise water until they were about five miles out. When they reached Western Sambo where the scuba diving death occurred, Storm told the captain to slow down so he could look around. He hoped none of the local dive boats would be around. He preferred to attract as little attention as possible as they started to troll for the dolphin.

"Things seem awfully quiet out here today," Storm said to Andy, who was scanning the water on the port side. "Why don't you go wire up the sound system?"

He told Paul to stay on the bow and watch for dorsal fins, then edged his way to the stern, where the party was in full swing. Loring was busy unwrapping a cigar the size of a cucumber. The admiral handed the stogie to Flowers, who ran the thick roll of dark tobacco under his nose and groaned with pleasure.

"Cuban," Flowers said, letting out a low whistle. "Fifty bucks a pop for these babies in Miami, if you can find them. Where'd you get this?"

"In the military, we got a policy called don't ask, don't tell, and it's good for cigars as well as other matters." Loring unwrapped a second stogie, taking a big greedy whiff before cutting off the end.

They leaned together to shield their cigars from the breeze as Loring struck a match. Starler stood to the side, like an unpopular kid in a schoolyard, watching suspiciously and then pulling out a long notebook from his polyester pants pocket and scribbling some notes.

"Sir, I want to give you a few more details on what we're about to do," Storm said to Loring.

Loring blew a cloud of brown smoke around Storm's face. Then the admiral yipped like a cowboy in a rodeo. "We're going to get ourselves some AWOL sailors today. Yessiree, I can feel it in my bones. We are in for action."

Paul and Andy came aft from the cabin like a pair of pack mules under all the equipment they would use to lure in the dolphin. Paul carried a black rubber box that looked like a stereo speaker in a raincoat. It was attached to a chain and thick cord. Andy had a large wooden box full of electronics and wiring bundled in tight black coils.

When the gear was unpacked, the back of the boat was jammed to the gills. Storm's men set up the underwater sound system around the admiral, who didn't move from the throne-like fishing chair where he sat with a beer in one hand, Cuban cigar in the other. Andy set the black speaker box, its large coil of line, and a pile of chain near Loring's feet.

"All this damned technology is making me thirsty," Loring said to Flowers, who caught the admiral's drift and went to the cooler for another round. He returned with two beers, slipping each into a bright pink foamie beer holder. Flowers handed one to Loring.

"To paradise, George," the admiral said, holding a foamie, decorated with palm trees and pink pelicans, high in the air.

Flowers sat down and popped the top on his can. "You ought to come down more often, admiral."

"I plan to. Sergeant, I'm ready for your little briefing," Loring summoned Storm.

Storm leaned in close to Loring, as did Starler who didn't want to miss a thing.

"What we're about to do, sir, is drop a speaker into the water." Storm pointed to the black rubber box. "It's sort of the reverse of a hydrophone. Instead of listening to what's going on underwater, we broadcast our own sounds. First up will be dolphin tapes made by the scientists in San Diego."

Loring nodded.

Storm continued, "The tape contains computer simulations of their language. Gives them a few commands, like return to the boat pronto. If our guys trained the units, they should come right over when we call them even if they are off without supervision. If we can get them to respond, to come to the boat, then when we put our team in the water tomorrow with dive gear on, Operation Wet Night will work like a charm. We'll get them in custody, off the reef, and the situation will be over."

"The U.S. Navy saves the day," the admiral said.

"Don't forget the Army, sir," Storm said. "I'm a ranger, remember."

"Hell, I know that. Course you'll get credit too. What's the contingency plan? What if the dolphins don't come? What if they aren't ours?"

"We thought of that. Then we change to a different tape... Jungle drums, Celtic chants, all the tricks the dolphin huggers use when they take out the tourists to meet the dolphins. Sounds crazy but it seems to work around here," Storm said. "Dolphins come over out of curiosity. At least we'll get a good look at them."

"Okay, drop that little sucker in, let's get started." The admiral leaned over toward Flowers. "George, go get me another beer. I don't want anything to disrupt me once we get started."

Flowers went to the cooler and returned with three cold ones.

"Here you go, son," Flowers said, holding out a beer to Starler.

"Sure, why not?" The reporter smiled and opened his beer.

Flowers and Loring began to move in tandem now like they were choreographed. They did everything together, taking long slugs and placing the cans in holders on the arms of each fishing chair, like these were dance steps.

Storm turned to Paul. "Let's get moving."

Paul picked up the speaker and dropped it over the side. Andy let the cord and chain play out about 25 feet, then hooked both to a steel cleat that kept the rubber-coated wiring from trailing any further behind the boat. The excess cord and chain were piled close to Loring's feet. Dangerously close.

"Nice rig," the admiral said. "You boys are doing just fine."

Flowers waved his cigar. "When's the dolphin sonata start? I can't wait to hear it. You guys sure you don't want a drink?"

"We don't drink till the job's done, sir," Storm said tersely. "Rule one."

Loring pounded his fist against the railing. "Hell, I thought we agreed that this trip was not official business, sergeant. Just taking a look around. Hell, this," he held up the beer, "isn't a real drink. It's just a beer."

"That's right," Flowers said. "We'll open my Johnnie Walker when you get the killer. Then we'll have a real drink."

Starler scribbled in his notebook, the beer tucked under his elbow.

Flowers got up and put his arm around the reporter. "Stop writing down everything and just have a good time, okay? There's nothing dangerous out here. You can quote me on that."

Storm went to the gunwales and checked the speaker chains. They were nice and tight, the equipment deploying neatly into the current. The speakers trailed behind the boat.

Starler still hadn't stopped writing. Storm came over and tapped on the notebook with his finger. "Starler, this is my operation and I've got to tell you, the whole day is off the record. We're not ready for any publicity yet. Not till it's over."

The journalist stopped writing. He aimed his pen at Storm like a gun. "Too late for that, Sarge. You've got to lay out the ground rules at the start, not halfway through."

Then the crew turned on the underwater audio and squeaking, chattering sounds could be heard. It was the Navy scientists' training tape.

Storm leaned over the gunwale to look for dolphins.

"Nothing," he muttered. "Switch the tape."

Drumming and chanting soon replaced the dolphin chatter. It wasn't long before a slick dark dorsal fin split the water a few hundred feet to starboard. Storm's pulse quickened as the fin approached.

"I'll be damned," he muttered. "It's working."

It had to be the big gray from the Wilkes-Barre.

"Look," he yelled, pointing at the fin, which had surfaced again about 100 feet away. The dolphin made his way toward them, gracefully breaking the surface every 25 feet or so, blowing a spray of water toward the blue sky.

"Sergeant, you're a genius," Loring said, as Starler made meticulous notes.

Now the dolphin was 15 feet away, close enough for Storm to see jagged white scars on the creature's skin. "That's the one," he yelled. "I recognize his markings."

Then the dolphin dove.

The admiral looked puzzled, unlike Paul and Andy, who were hooting and hollering victoriously.

"We lost her, we lost her," the admiral yelled. He leapt to the rail, and they all followed, crowding together to look for the dolphin. Loring and Starler were side by side, gripping the railing when the dolphin emerged from the water close behind the boat, its body half out of the sea, suspended by the gyrations of its powerful tail. As the dolphin levitated, heavy sheets of water sprayed over the men and they jostled each other trying to avoid the deluge.

In the pushing match, Starler's notebook slid out of his hand. He reached down for the pad, catching it mid-air before it dropped into the sea. But the maneuver had left him dangerously off balance, bent in half, one hand on the boat, the other reaching down, his polyester-covered butt pointing skyward.

The dolphin came closer.

As the dolphin dropped toward the boat, Starler was pinned neatly beneath. Storm would recall later how he wanted to laugh at the sight of the skinny arms and legs flailing like the limbs of a rag doll from the edges of the dolphin's torso, until he'd realized what was happening. It really wasn't funny, a man was in peril, but the dolphin gave them a toothy smile as if he'd been trained to do this little trick as part of the show at a marine theme park, and that dolphin grin made Storm want to laugh too.

Storm waited for the dolphin to release Starler but the creature didn't budge.

"Oh hell, he's fucking with us again," Storm said. "Andy, give me a hand."

Starler was teetering up and down dangerously. Before they could push the dolphin away, the journalist lost what was left of his balance. He slid into the water, as slow as the Titanic but just as inevitable, the weight of the huge dolphin dragging him down.

With a flip of his wrist, Starler tossed his notebook up and it landed back in the boat. Then he hit the water with a splash and sank.

"Man overboard," Loring shouted. "Man overboard. Quick, throw him something; throw him a life vest, anything."

Loring looked around for something to toss overboard. Storm saw him grab the black rubber cord of the speaker. Loring tossed the line over. Unbeknownst to him, the speaker cord was all tangled up in the fabric of his heavy green fatigues.

He reached down to untangle his leg as the line unreeled over the side. It whipped past him until all that was left was the silver chain at the end, which caught his wrist. He kicked at the mess until the chain had his ankle too and the tangle was more tightly knotted around him.

Then the black cord grew taut and the fiberglass on the boat where it was wrapped around a cleat let out a painful creak. The cleat snapped and flew into the water taking the rest of the speaker cord, which was attached firmly to Loring now, with it. As the silver chain flew into the sea, the admiral followed it.

Storm watched in disbelief as Loring disappeared behind Starler.

"Stop the boat, damn it," Storm shouted. "Man overboard."

He tore off his shoes, grabbed a mask and fins, and jumped into the water. The captain circled for twenty minutes before fishing Storm out, having found no trace of the two men or the dolphin. It had all happened so fast. Storm climbed aboard, nearly knocking over George Flowers, who was staring, granite faced at the water as he watched the day, and possibly the whole tourist season, go down the drain.

The dolphin had just upped the ante considerably. Operation Wet Night had gotten off to a bad start, but, with a missing admiral, it would be easy for Storm to convince the Pentagon bean-counters to give him the resources necessary to get that dolphin.

For Storm, this was as good as a declaration of war.

Chapter 22

The big black Harley purred beneath Gene as he followed the familiar ribbon of asphalt up the Keys. An artist's pallet of blues and greens surrounded him. Shimmering water stretched to Cuba on the right and on the left to the north where the shallows of Florida Bay met the Everglades.

Another perfect day, and Gene had decided to use it to go up and see Johnnie Reb, ask him why he hadn't shown up at the watermen's meeting. Being out on the water would have been better by far but the last place Gene wanted to be was out with Storm and the admiral.

When he reached Sweet Pine, Gene pulled into the parking lot of the dolphin sanctuary and parked the bike. He found Johnnie sitting in the dark inside the office building. The place was more of a mess than it had been a few days earlier and so was Johnnie. His hair was hanging loose and stringy past his shoulders and his face was covered with a two-day growth of beard. When Gene came through the door, Johnnie didn't even bother to get up.

"Twice in one week, Rock. Key West must be boring you," Johnnie said. He had his feet propped up on a battered gray metal desk. Junk covered every inch of the desktop except for the small space where his dirty bare heels rested.

"It was a nice day for a ride. Thought I'd stop in and see how you're doing. That's all," Gene said. Empty beer bottles spilled over the top of the trash can. Not a good sign. "How are the dolphins?"

Johnnie just shook his head. "Everybody's interested in the same damn thing. You want a beer?"

"Little early for me," Gene replied.

Johnnie went to the little refrigerator and got a Corona.

A sinking feeling came over Gene. Things must be worse than he'd realized for Johnnie to be drinking this early.

That old demon alcohol had launched Johnnie into the business of saving dolphins from captivity in the first place. Johnnie had always been a loner, and eventually, the booze turned loneliness into hopelessness. Johnnie wasn't the sort who'd willingly submit to therapy or 12-step rehab programs. Instead, his answer to hopelessness had been to go out on a boat, drop anchor, drink a fifth of tequila and jump overboard in a fit of misery.

A dolphin happened along at that very moment and apparently decided to intervene, spoiling Johnnie's half-baked attempt at suicide. Every time Johnnie tried to slip to the bottom that nosy dolphin pushed him back to the surface.

When he'd sobered up, he and the dolphin had bonded, and Johnnie decided there was something worth doing with his life after all. He'd given up the binge drinking and redneck hangouts like the No Name Bar and Geiger Key Marina to dedicate his life to the cause of reintroducing captive dolphins to the wild. Every Monday he'd buy a six-pack and that was all the beer he allowed himself for the week. He could drink it all in one sitting or stretch it out and have one beer a day, but for ten years, Johnnie hadn't broken his promise to himself to never let drinking get in the way of his devotion to the dolphins.

With three dozen empty beer bottles littering his desk on this particular morning, it seemed that something had changed. Gene was not going to stick his nose into this one. So he decided to stick to his main reason for the visit, the dolphins. "Are they here? Alphie and Jake?"

"Sure. Nothing's changed since you were here two days ago." Johnnie moved his foot off the desk to kick a chair over for Gene to sit in.

"We missed you at the big meeting in town Sunday."

"Ha," Johnnie just laughed and took a big slug out of his beer. He slammed the bottle down a little too hard afterwards and foam bubbled out the neck.

"You're sure Alphie and Jake weren't out on the reef over the weekend?" Gene asked.

Johnnie shrugged, "What are you, the dolphin police?"

"Hell, sometimes I don't even know why I bother." Gene got up and headed to the door, about to give up and go back home.

A shoe flew through the air, past Gene's nose, and hit the door, and when Gene turned around to see where it came from, Johnnie was looking at him, his face looked more tired and worn than usual. "Pete left the pens open. Sit back down, Rock."

"Then they were out," Gene said. "You know you don't have to throw things to get my attention. You're playing right into the Navy's hands—you know that?"

Johnnie shook his head. "Aw hell, we're just letting them swim in the ocean. Pete wants to see if they'll catch their own food. They come back every time."

"J.R., any reason you can think of that a dolphin would kill a human being?"

"If a dolphin were human, he'd have a million reasons to kill somebody," Johnnie said. "They are being penned up, killed by the hundreds in the nets, washed up on beaches full of toxins. But since a dolphin's a dolphin ..."

Gene shrugged. "They're too cute to do that kind of shit, right?"

"You know better than I, cowboy." Johnnie went to the fridge for another cold beer. "You sure you don't want one?"

Gene shook his head.

"That freaking Navy with its freaking admirals," Johnnie said. "It's enough to drive a man to drink. That fuckin' Storm comes in here pretending like he was just showing around one of his damn relatives on vacation."

"Storm was here?"

"Didn't I just say that?" Johnnie said, raising and putting on his wide-brimmed straw hat. He stood up and picked up the beer, and began to move toward the door.

Gene had about enough of both of their tiptoeing around what was happening here like it didn't matter. Johnnie knew more about this whole dolphin situation than he was letting on, and Gene decided he wasn't going back to Key West without some information. He got up and stood between the door and his friend. "You know that Storm wants to mount some kind of operation against the killer dolphin."

"Dolphin hunting's turning out to an Olympic competition round here," Johnnie said. "Come on, man. I gotta go feed my critters."

Gene wouldn't budge from the door. "Who else?"

"I don't know. The Russians—the Cubans. Damned United Nations around here. When I started this little refuge, I thought I'd seen my last dipshit bureaucrat but I swear they are following me. Bunch of damned spooks."

"The Russians? You don't mean that creepy little guy in the bad suit?" Gene said.

"You know him?" Johnnie said, anger showing in his eyes at the mention of Ruykov. "He comes in here and tells me this bullshit story about a marine theme park under construction in Havana. Man tells me a big dolphin escaped. The old guy says the Cubans want him back bad and will pay a reward, since this is some big eco-tourism investment on the part of the Japanese and now the whole deal is going to be screwed."

Gene laughed. "A Cuban version of Sea World—that's a new one."

"Hell, everything everybody has said to me in the last week was a lie. Can I go now? I'm late."

Gene stepped aside.

Then Johnnie paused at the open door. "If Storm and his warrior friends were smart, they'd be looking about 90 miles to the south."

"Cuba?"

Johnnie shrugged and walked out, heading to the lagoon and his precious dolphins.

Gene followed him out and headed over to the Harley. All the way back to Key West, the thought of Cuba stayed with him. Mattie, Patcher and now Johnnie Reb. Everybody had a thing for Cuba these days.

Chapter 23

Mattie woke Tuesday in her room at the Plaza as the first gray streaks of Cuban morning slipped through the wooden slats of her shuttered windows. A fleeting dream had left her disoriented, unsure of time or place.

In her sleep, Mickey had visited, back from the dead to see her, to be with her. Had he entered her dream, or was it a nightmare, to warn her? Havana had been their city.

They'd made love for the first time, on one of the Plaza's narrow beds with faded sheets and a mattress hard as a board. But the shabbiness of the Plaza never bothered her for a moment. The thin towels had left them nearly as wet after drying off as when they'd stepped out of the cold shower. Even though the city was run down and lacking in nearly every practical matter, her heart had felt as warm and rich as the humid Havana air.

When she'd been awake a few minutes, she forced thoughts of Sam to push away the ones of Mickey. She had a fiance now; she didn't need to think about what might have been.

What an impossible choice Sam presented. If she added up all his good attributes – his money, his good looks, his easygoing attitude – she'd inevitably conclude that she was wise to accept his marriage proposal. But she couldn't work up the required level of enthusiasm that a woman ought to have before taking on such a commitment. It wasn't Sam's fault and it didn't make much sense.

How does a flesh and blood man compare to a ghost? Mickey had been drawn to danger to the point of being reckless, and for some reason, that recklessness held an attraction for Mattie, one that good guy Sam could never have. In death, Mickey had taken on the aura of a hero, when in reality, he'd been no such thing.

Today, Mattie had a few hours before they'd depart for Varadero. She decided to get out of the hotel room and explore the city a bit. She dressed and went to the Plaza's rooftop restaurant for breakfast. Way up high in the open air restaurant, waiters in black suits and white shirts poured fresh orange juice and dark, thick Cuban coffee into tiny cups for a handful of guests. The restaurant had a view of the Havana skyline and beyond it, the sea. She could just see the famous oceanfront promenade, the Malecon, in the breaks between the buildings.

From the buffet, one would never know there was a devastating embargo that had ruined Cuba's economy and made all but the most basic foodstuffs scarce. She filled a plate from a long, white linen-covered buffet table. Silver platters were piled high with tropical fruit, poached eggs, mounds of breakfast rolls, cartons of yogurt, platters of meat and tiny honey cakes.

Then she sat alone at a table in the sun, watching the brilliant sunshine paint ramshackle apartment buildings around the hotel in shades of blue, violet and yellow as she ate. The meal was good but she had a hard time enjoying it, remembering from the last trip how none of the beautiful food would be available in the small shops where the average citizen of Havana shopped. They'd make do with rationed coffee and cigarettes. The egg or two that each Plaza guest would consume this morning would be an average Cuban's allotment for the entire month.

When she finished eating, she took the wire cage elevator down to the lobby, went out the front door and into the street.

Ten paces beyond the door, a swarm of children surrounded her, smiling and holding out their hands, asking in Spanish for candy, money, and ballpoint pens. One thin little boy came up and tugged at the empty plastic water bottle that she carried like it was a piece of gold. She let him have it, shaking her head in amazement at how these Cuban children treasured items that Americans considered trash.

Mattie walked, the kids trailing behind her. The streets had almost no cars, just pedestrians overflowing the sidewalks into the gutters. She passed small neighborhood food stores that were open for business, but the stores had nothing to sell except for a few scraggly-looking yams and coconuts. She walked for blocks without passing a single cafe or coffee shop. Despite the rampant poverty, Havana's architecture was beautiful and grand like an old European city after a war, except that here the crumbling facades were due to politics not bombs.

Mattie consulted her map and headed in the direction of the old cathedral. She wanted to find the open-air artist's market in the cathedral's plaza.

Following the twisting brick streets, she reached the stone cathedral with its modest spires and gray walls. The doors would be locked of course; she knew that without even trying to go in. In the center of the warm, sunny plaza, the church looked cold and forbidding. All around it, artists and craftsmen had set up stalls full of handmade items.

Mattie browsed at the booths until she reached a table where a young man with dark, curly hair and lively black eyes was selling Noah's arks made of papier-mache. The arks were painted bright colors and filled with animals. He'd even created a small pair of dolphins to swim next to the ark. She picked up a dolphin.

"You like?" the artist said.

"Very much," said Mattie. "Did you make this?"

"Yes," he said. His brow went up in puzzlement and she could tell he was trying to tell her nationality from her accent. "Where are you from?"

"Florida," Mattie said.

The young man's eyes opened wider. "What are you doing in Havana?" He paused, then continued to question her with excitement. "From Florida? You are really from Florida? I have a cousin in Miami. You know Miami?"

"Sure," Mattie smiled at him. All Cubans had cousins in Miami. She waited for the inevitable request to carry a message back to the states or call someone for him and pass along word that he was okay.

"Here, you take this," the young man said, picking up the ark and thrusting it at her.

"How much?"

"A gift," he said. "You take."

He picked up the animals and loaded them into the little ark.

"I insist on paying you," Mattie said.

"No, you take," the artist said. "Really."

He shoved the ark and its little menagerie into her hands and she thanked him, feeling awkward and embarrassed at her suspicion that she was being taken in by accepting the ark. She walked back to the Plaza, ignoring the stares that she drew with the brilliant ark under her arm. The artist did not even have a used paper sack to put it in.

Inside the Plaza, Todd and Bud were waiting in the lobby with their bags.

She inspected her crew, looking for damage from the night on the town. "You survived your big adventure."

Bud nodded. His eyes were bloodshot and puffy but he looked happy. "You should have come with us, Mattie. The Malecon was incredible, an all night party. That old fort is a club after dark."

She moved closer to Todd. "You're looking a lovely shade of green today, Todd. Feeling okay?"

"I could use a con leche," he groaned.

She herded them into the palm tree-filled bar and ordered three Cuban coffees. "You guys are supposed to dive today on our way out of Dodge. I hope the alcohol's out of your bloodstream by then."

"I'm fine," Todd said, defiantly gulping down the steamy black fluid in one shot like it was tequila.

At the taxi stand out front, they hired a car to drive them back to Varadero. For the next two hours, the driver sped along the coastal highway at breakneck speed, windows down and balmy air blowing at them until they reached Varadero.

In town, Todd handed the driver a slip of paper with an address. A few minutes later, the car pulled up in front of a small cement building with a red and white diving flag snapping in the breeze out front.

Todd jumped out, the motor still running.

"I've got to find a friend of Dad's," Todd said. "I'll need a half hour or so."

"We'll all go," Mattie said. Then she saw Todd's expression and knew that he didn't want any help. Mattie knew that Todd wanted to show his father that he could handle business matters on his own, without Mattie looking over his shoulder. Coming back from Cuba with a deal would mean a lot to Bob Patcher.

"On second thought," she said, "maybe Bud and I will look around Varadero."

"Sure," said Bud. He pointed across the road at a tiny café with sidewalk tables. "We can get some lunch."

"Great," Todd said. "I'll join you when I'm through."

At the café, they took an empty table and waited a long time for a waiter to bring menus. The only other patron, a Cuban man about Mattie's age, was a few feet away finishing off a large plate of fish surrounded by mysterious orange vegetables.

The man wore a T-shirt and brown pants that were too short in the legs, the kind known as high waters in Mattie's elementary school days when anyone who wore them was classified a nerd. Although he wore ill-fitting clothes, he was handsome with smooth dark hair and black eyes.

Bud and Mattie ordered coffee and fish. The Cuban man was staring at her, but she ignored him. She looked out at the road in front of the café, which was deserted except for two dogs tangling over a bone. Their yellow fur stretched over ribs so clearly defined that the animals could have been used to teach an anatomy class.

"I never saw such skinny dogs," Bud said.

"Why should the dogs be better off than the people?"

"I don't know," Bud said. "What a mess this place is. I don't see how Patcher thinks he's going to run a business over here."

"I guess he thinks his customers will bring the money so it doesn't matter that the Cubans don't have any. It's his dream, Bud, and right now, all he wants is to get a connection so that he can make it happen some day."

"He'd be better off investing in the stock market."

"It's not about money, you know."

The waiter delivered their con leche in large white mugs topped with a thick layer of foamy milk. Mattie dumped sugar into hers.

"Over here, everything's about money, isn't it? The women in the bars last night were all over us, but not until they saw our money. It's pretty obvious that the Cubans aren't going to do anything unless something's in it for them."

"That makes them different from the rest of the world?"

The waiter brought the food. As they ate, the man at the other table stared at Mattie to the point that she grew uncomfortable. She kept checking him out from the corner of her eye until finally he arose and approached them, limping.

"Good afternoon. You are Americans?" he asked.

"I didn't realize we were talking so loudly," she said, noncommittally. Everybody here seemed to eavesdrop and the minute they heard you speak English, it was like an invitation to intrude.

"What are you doing in Cuba?"

"Visiting," said Mattie. He was a little too direct for her tastes.

"You are a diver?" he asked.

She looked at Bud, "Is it written on my forehead or what?"

"You come to Cuba for diving?" the man persisted.

"We'd love to," Bud interrupted, pointing to an empty chair. "Take a seat, tell us about the diving 'round here."

"I can help you," the man said. He looked around cautiously, then sat at their table and removed a clear plastic envelope from a pocket. From it, he took a carefully folded piece of paper, waving quickly under Mattie's eyes, then stuffing it back into the pocket. "Look. A very interesting place to dive."

"Near here?" Bud asked.

"Of course. Very close. You can find it, no problem," he said. His coal black eyes sparkled. "If you have this map."

"Can I see it?" Bud said.

"I must be careful. It is very precious, this map," the man answered, making no move to bring it back out.

"We're not interested," Mattie said.

"Oh, yes you are," the man said.

"It's for sale," Bud said.

The man smiled.

"How much?"

"In dollars?"

"Sure," said Bud. "You don't want pesos, do you?"

Mattie shook her head, laughing. At least Bud had learned something on the trip.

"One hundred U.S. dollars," the man said solemnly. "You want to find a treasure under the sea, this map can help you."

"Whoa," Bud held up his hands. "A hundred dollars is a lot of money."

"Forget it," Mattie said. Sure, there were many shipwrecks around Cuba. But that didn't mean this map marked one. And some Cubans had no qualms about ripping off Americans. Last time she visited, they'd bought a sealed box of cigars, only to find when they got home that the box was stuffed with shredded paper.

"You make the dive. If you find nothing, I give you the money back."

"If we can find you," Bud muttered.

He pulled out the map and unfolded it. This time he handed it to Mattie. "Here, take your time. The map is very old. It is real. You reach into your heart for the answer, to see if you believe."

She touched the paper, which was thick and yellowed. The contours of the map were drawn in black ink but features had been painted in rich colors. Off the black ink coastline was a spot marked with small golden symbols and tiny blue dolphins. On the far edge of the paper, more black lines appeared to be Florida. Just as art to hang on the wall, the old map was worth something.

"It's very beautiful. Is it handmade?" She saw that it was. "How old is it?"

He shrugged. "This map comes from the old days. I would like to dive myself, to explore this place, but you see, I cannot be a diver."

He rapped on his leg, making a sound like knocking on a door. Then he pulled his pants legs up a little until they could see the leg was wooden, not flesh. Suddenly, her doubts vanished. Perhaps it was pity for this man with his sad, honest eyes and missing limb, she didn't really know why, she just wanted the map badly.

"I will give you twenty dollars for the map," she said.

He shook his head. "Please, pretty lady. I cannot part with it for that price."

The man stood up. She thought of the gift of the ark in the corner, sitting on top of her backpack. She wanted the map. The money didn't matter.

"Wait," Mattie said. "I'll give you fifty. It's all I've got left."

Bud nudged her, whispering, "Mattie, you're being taken to the cleaners."

"I don't care," she said. "I want it."

"Yes, pretty lady. I think you will are the right person to entrust with this," he said, stroking the map affectionately. "You must promise not to share this map with anyone."

She nodded, then pulled out her money and shoved it into his hand, wanting the transaction to be over quickly.

He handed her the map, bowed politely and disappeared out the door.

"Mattie, I thought you were more practical than that," Bud said.

"Maybe it is a dive site—it'll help Patcher. If not, I'll just hang it on my wall. I like it," Mattie said. She pushed her food away half finished.

Then Todd came through the door.

"I waited all this time, but José still hasn't shown," he said. "Dad will be pissed."

"Wait till you see what Mattie bought," Bud said. "A treasure map. Go on, Mattie, show him what you paid fifty bucks for."

"Sshh," she said. She'd just promised not to show it around. "We need to go. We're late."

They hired a car to take them back to the marina.

When they got there, Mattie hurried down to their slip, expecting to find the hospital officials ready and waiting to take the supplies. Instead, the same somber customs officer who had issued their visas the day before was waiting. His excellent English was gone when he spoke to them this time. He barked out orders to her in Spanish, too fast for her to comprehend. He frowned and started screaming loud, his face turning red. Mattie couldn't understand what he was saying but she clearly got the message that things were not okay.

The doctor also was waiting and Mattie turned to her. "Dr. Rivero, what did we do to make him so mad?"

"You must leave as soon as possible," the doctor said. Her expression was still kind but Mattie also heard alarm in her voice.

"What about the the medicine? For the hospital?"

"You must take it back with you." The doctor shook her head sadly.

"Why?" Mattie felt frustration boil up inside. They'd come a long way and invested several days to get the medical supplies over; the Cubans clearly needed the donation; she wasn't about to just turn around and take the boxes home. "We can't take them back. We have gone to a lot of effort to get them here. The donors will be very upset."

"You do not have the proper approvals, captain. Our government rejects your charity. You must take them back," the doctor said, patting Mattie's hand gently as she spoke. Then she added quietly, "You must leave as soon as possible."

There was another rapid exchange in Spanish between Dr. Rivero and the customs agent. Then the agent turned away abruptly and headed back up to the office building, leaving Mattie and the doctor alone.

"There is a problem," Dr. Rivero said, lowering her voice. "A boat full of counterrevolutionaries from Miami came ashore this morning not so far from here." She whispered so that Mattie could hardly hear the words. "They shot some farmers. Leave Cuba."

Mattie shivered as if a cool breeze had just come up but the temperature hadn't changed a bit. She started to thank the doctor, but she was gone.

"Todd, Bud," she called out. The boys were hanging out on the dock, waiting to help unload the supplies. "Get over here. Load the boat, we're leaving."

"What about the needles and gloves?" asked Bud. "Por hospital, señora?"

"It's all off, so's the dive," she said. "Sorry."

"Dad's not going to like this," Todd said, miserably. "No dive, no contacts at the dive shop, no medical mission. Talk about three time losers."

"What a waste of gas," Bud added as he untied the lines. Mattie backed the boat out of the slip and a few minutes later, the Paradise Diver was headed out of Varadero harbor.

When they cleared the cement walls at the harbor's mouth, Bud joined Mattie on the flying bridge. He threw a brotherly arm around her shoulder.

"Now that we're out of Cuba safe and sound, let's talk about that dive." He grinned. "At least we'd fill one of the squares on Patcher's list."

"After what happened on the dock, Bud? We're not diving."

"Come on, Mattie. Just a quick jump in and out. It won't take more than 20 minutes. I promise."

"Bud, didn't you notice how eager the Cubans were to get us out of there? Something's wrong back there. Patcher's going to understand," Mattie said. She felt discouraged, and she didn't care if he knew it. "This trip has been a total disaster. I don't know why we came."

"How can you say that?" he said, his voice teasing. "You got your treasure map. Let's look at it."

Mattie pulled it from her bag. The coastline and landmarks around Varadero were accurately depicted. She could see the mouth of the harbor and two hills that jutted skyward a mile south of the town. The markings on the map matched the shape of the land on the horizon. Just looking at the ancient drawing gave her a surge of excitement.

"I'll bet we can find the spot," Bud said, pointing at the place where the blue dolphins swam on the page next to the gold symbols. "Hey, I've got an idea. Let's dive it. What better way to test whether you got ripped off or not?"

"I don't know," Mattie said. "The smart thing is to just go home and do some research; check the old records and see if we can figure out what might be down there."

"Hey, you've got a chance right now. Who knows when you'll be back," Bud said. He had a good point.

"The way the pros would do it is to check the old shipping logs, the storm records, insurance claims," Mattie said. "Not just impulsively jump into the water."

"Yeah, well we aren't pros. It might be a year before you get back. Five years, who knows? And in the meantime, that guy could sell the same map to somebody else who would beat you to it, steal that treasure right out from under you. You've got two great divers here, just waiting to go. All the equipment. It'll take, what, an hour?" Bud said. "What did that Cuban tell you? Let your gut make the decision here, not your brain."

What if there really was something of value down there, and she passed up the chance to find it? Hardly anyone had been diving in Cuba since the revolution more than 30 years before. It was entirely possible that the map could mark a shipwreck. Hundreds of ships had been lost in the area during the last 200 years. Havana had been the point of departure for ships loaded down with New World treasure. They had plenty of daylight left. Maybe she ought to take a risk in life once in a while. She'd been playing it safe ever since Mickey died and look where that had gotten her.

"Oh hell. Why not?" Mattie said. "Get me the Magellan. I want to match the drop coordinates with the map, on the slight chance that you do find something, I'm going to mark the lat and longitude very carefully so we know where to come back to. Then go get suited up. I want you guys in and out of the water as fast as possible."

Mattie navigated as close as she could to the spot marked with the golden symbols and tiny blue dolphins on the map. She checked the GPS location finder and plotted their location, writing the coordinates on a small piece of paper. The wreck, or whatever it was, appeared to be right on the boundary between Cuban and international waters.

When she had the boat lined up with the landmarks on the map, Todd and Bud were dressed in wet suits and dive gear, ready to jump in off the stern.

"Wait," Mattie yelled. She scrambled to the lower deck, pulled the waterproof video camera out of its aluminum case and handed it to Todd. "Take this. Document anything that looks interesting."

Todd gave her a thumbs up and the boys took giant strides off the boat into the water.

Paradise Diver's depth sounder said they were in 300 feet of water. This would be a pretty deep dive, but since they were going to bounce it, just a quick trip to the bottom and back, she felt reasonably comfortable. They'd do a deco stop, although not as long as she would like if they had all the time in the world. Mattie studied the depth finder, which drew an electronic profile of the bottom with shapes of whatever was down there on it. She waited for them to return. She blinked hard, thinking for a moment that she was seeing things. The instrument showed a sharp, well-defined object below the boat, something big rising up from the ocean floor right under her feet.

If it were a sunken oil tanker or big cargo ship, it would rise a hundred feet or more from the bottom. An old wooden sailing ship could be much smaller.

Were the lumps on the bottom a shipwreck, or was the bottom finder just acting quirky? Mattie felt anxious, and took to checking her watch every few minutes. The sun sat low on the western horizon. If the boys didn't come up soon, the entire trip home across the Florida Straits would be in the dark. But as long as clear weather held, the electronic equipment would allow the boat to operate nearly as well in the dark as during the day, and the cool night air would be welcome relief after two days in the broiling sun.

Mattie went below to get her binoculars. She wanted another good look around while there was still enough light to see. She wouldn't think about the complications that finding a sunken treasure would bring to her life. Even if she had no claim to the fortune, just discovering a wreck, a piece of history, would be enough to make the risk worth it.

Through the binoculars, she saw something moving in the water toward Cuba. Dark shapes on the surface. She focused the binoculars until she could make out dolphins, perhaps three or four together, coming right toward her.

As they got closer, she noticed the funny shapes of their heads. Their noses were fat and round instead of their natural pointy shape. A moment later, the dolphins arrived, swimming in jagged lines beneath her boat. They lifted their heads from the water and now she saw why they looked so strange. A small cage, like a baseball catcher's mask, was strapped over each animal's face.

Mattie was hanging over the side of the boat, trying to get a better look, when the big gray dolphin surfaced a few feet from her. He was huge and wore no muzzle. He gave her a long look, right in the eye, and she was certain that he was the same one she'd met out on the reef the day Jim Reynolds died. The dolphin that half of Key West was after, with a bounty on his pretty gray head, was right before her, not ten feet away.

She reached her hand out toward him and the dolphin raised up out of the water, then propelled his body backwards, like a performing dolphin at a show might do. He squealed at her and dove beneath the surface, disappearing into the dark blue water.

She was staring at the spot, waiting for him to come back, when the rumble of a boat motor startled her. Mattie turned around to see a Cuban gunboat approaching fast. But this time, it was not the meek little 1950s era pleasure cruiser that stopped them the day before. This was a sleek, new 45-ft fiberglass powerboat, cherry red and white. Its powerful Chevy engines, capable of doing 60-90 mph, roared, drowning out all other sound. The boat was a fuel hog, fast and sleek, the kind favored by drug smugglers and millionaire playboys. As it pulled alongside, she wondered where the Cubans got their hands on such a vessel.

She looked around for the dolphins, but they were gone.

On the gunboat, a half dozen men in camouflage stood frozen, their machine guns pointed at her. She felt a brief yearning for those harmless looking youths from the previous day and then one of tough guys stepped forward and called out, "Identify yourself."

He was a big man with a heavy mustache, good looking in a dark, ominous way, with a jagged scar across the right side of his face.

"I'm Captain Mattie Gold. I'm going below to get my papers," Mattie yelled at him over the rumble of his boat's engine, descending into the tiny cabin. She tossed life preservers and duffel bags aside until she located her backpack, where she found the waterproof pouch with their passports and State Department papers granting permission for the trip.

She was about to return topside when she remembered the map in her pocket. She turned back, looking for a safe place to stash it. In the forepeak, behind the head that no one ever used was a small teak compartment, its bottom shelf loose. Mattie had neglected to fix the loose board when she helped overhaul the boat the previous winter. She lifted the board and tucked the map into the space carefully, saying a small prayer that it would stay dry.

Then she climbed back up the ladder, the official looking papers clutched in her hand.

Up top, the Cubans had tied Paradise Diver to their cigarette boat. The guy with the mustache had come over to her boat. She handed him the papers.

"I'm Captain Gold out of Key West," she said. She hoped she sounded more confident than she felt.

He opened the pouch and, too late, she realized that in her rush to hide the map, she'd forgotten that it contained three passports rather than one. Before he could ask her why she carried three passports, Todd and Bud surfaced about 20 feet behind the boat. The Cuban officer's eyes got larger and his granite expression got stonier.

"What do we have here?" he asked.

"I was just about to tell you that I was waiting for my divers. Colonel, is it?"

Now he turned his full icy glare on Mattie. He studied the documents slowly, then looked up. His tone was calm and in control, which only made the gaze all the more chilly.

"Pardon me. I'm Colonel Díaz. I didn't mean to be rude. What were they doing?" Díaz asked, gesturing toward the boys.

"Diving," she replied.

"Obviously."

Bud and Todd climbed up the ladder and into the back of the boat. They removed their tanks and buoyancy vests, and Bud came back to join Mattie and Díaz.

"Is there a problem?" he asked, water dripping in a pool around him. "We thought there was a reef here."

"There is no reef here," the man said.

Mattie added, "I guess we must have got it wrong."

Díaz fingered the jagged scar on his cheek as he considered what to do next. "Who told you there was a reef?"

"He's right," Bud said to Mattie. "We went down 20, maybe 30 feet. Nothing down there. No reef. Couldn't even reach the bottom. It's just dark water."

Mattie looked at Díaz. "My mistake," she said. "We thought diving in Cuba was allowed."

"You are in a restricted area," Díaz said. The reptilian eyes ran up and down her body, leaving a trail of cold on her skin. There was splashing in the water on the other side of the cigarette boat. Mattie saw the dolphin. The dolphin was splashing and making a lot of noise. The men with the guns turned toward it, talking to each other in Spanish and then yelling commands at the dolphin, which it apparently was ignoring. Díaz suddenly crossed back over to his boat.

"I'm going to let you go, but you must get permission to dive in our waters," he said, reaching for the lines that his crew had attached to her boat. "Remember that."

"Colonel, I checked the GPS. This is international water," she said.

"It is not," he said, loosening the line. "This belongs to Cuba."

He stopped and held up a finger as if she were a small child who had gotten into big trouble. "This is not America; you cannot just come and go as you please here. You can go home now but see that I do not catch you here again. I don't think you are so sweet and innocent as you look."

"Sweet and innocent, humpff," she growled as she climbed back up to the flying bridge out of his hearing range. "You macho military types are all alike." The rumbling cigarette boat engines drowned out her words. She still felt invaded by those eyes.

As the sun sank below the horizon, Mattie headed Paradise Diver toward Florida. She noticed other small boats anchored toward Cuba and had the strange feeling that they were observing her. Bud climbed up the ladder, his face was flushed with excitement. "You aren't going to believe this, Mattie, that was the best fifty bucks you'll ever spend."

Then there was something down there. Treasure. Mattie could hardly believe what she was hearing even though she'd known to trust her instincts back in the cafe. "What did you find?"

"I might have been narced but I swear I've never seen anything like it. We only saw the top, but Mattie, I'm telling you there's something the size of a skyscraper down below. Made of glass, though, not like a building I've ever seen. And there were a few dolphins down there too.

We saw two of them coming back up."

Mattie caught her breath. "You mean, you found a building down there?"

"A glass pyramid, Mattie. Clear glass. With dolphins guarding it."

No wonder the Cubans showed up so fast. "That is very strange. Take the wheel a minute."

She went below to retrieve her map. Todd was waiting at the bottom of the ladder, looking gloomy.

"What's wrong?" she asked.

"I didn't want to mention it in front of the Cubans. I dropped it." He looked glum.

"What?" Mattie said, then she remembered. "The camera." The video and its housing were worth five grand. "What happened to it?"

He shrugged, as if it were no big deal. "I don't know. Something bumped me, one of those dolphins, and it just slipped out of my hands, when we were close to the pyramid."

"Great," she said. "This is just great. Oh hell."

She wondered if she ought to go back to the dive site now, get into the water with the extra tanks on and go look for the camera herself. It was the most expensive single piece of equipment on the boat. But it was already dark and too much had already gone wrong.

All the way back to Florida, Mattie thought about going back. Something strange was going on back there. A sick feeling came up in her throat and she wasn't sure if it was the lost camera or the creepy smile of Díaz playing over and over in her head.

Chapter 24

On the ride home from the dolphin refuge, the glorious orange and purple sunset made Gene remember why he moved down here in the first place. He had loved the look of the land here, really the water more than the land. And he'd just wanted to have enough time to really look at it for once, to just be on a small island surrounded by the sea. Then he reached town and the glories of sunset were replaced by heavy traffic that crept all the way around the island until Palm Avenue, where he turned off into Old Town.

As he passed the sport fishing pier, he noticed the cluster of Navy cars, obvious with their GSA lettering stenciled on the doors, in the parking lot. Men in uniform stood around doing nothing. He wondered what that was all about, but kept moving.

On William, he parked his motorcycle under the steps to the house and went up to his apartment. The long ride had made him thirsty so he rifled through the refrigerator's drawers until he located the emergency beer, the one stashed away under some rotting produce in the vegetable bin, and popped it open. As he drank it, he watched sugar ants parade around the counter.

"Meow." The cry came from down around his feet, accompanied by silky fur rubbing against his shin. Tugger, Gene's old tomcat, made a dignified appeal for a meal.

"Hey old pal, you in for the night already?" Gene bent to scratch the cat's head.

He found a box of dry cat food and emptied the dregs into the cat's dish, tossing the empty into the trash. If he or the cat were going to eat tomorrow, he had to go to the corner store, and for that, he needed money. Gene emptied his pockets and counted his cash. He had eight crumpled one-dollar bills and another two dollars in change. Broke. The inevitable job hunt could not be put off much longer.

In the living room, the light on the telephone answering machine blinked furiously at him. Gene hit the playback button and toppled onto the couch, expertly juggling the half-empty beer.

"Four calls," the answering machine said in a sexy female voice. Sometimes he felt like the voice was connected to a person, a very efficient, absentee roommate. He wanted to meet her, to talk with her. A little female companionship would be nice tonight.

Instead, he had the cat. Tugger climbed into his lap, purring and kneading his legs with his black paws, giving Gene an adoring, sleepy gaze. Gene scratched the cat's chin and together they listened to the messages.

Alexandra's voice came on first in a low purr, rambling about work, her mother, and her new boyfriend. "Jerry is so crazy, he's so funny. I call him Pirate. He says he's taking me to the Cayman Islands next month," she informed him.

Gene had no idea why Alexandra was telling him all this, confiding in him as if he were one of her girlfriends. Maybe she was trying to make him jealous. He stretched as far as he could until he reached the Skip button that fast-forwarded the machine to the next call. Tugger rolled off and thumped onto the floor, leaving a blanket of long black hairs on Gene's shirt.

The next call was from his landlord, informing him that rent was overdue and a late fee would be applied. If he didn't have the rent, where was he going to get a late fee? The machine beeped and Storm's voice, deep and serious, filled the little room. "Gene, there's been an accident. A bad one."

Gene sat up straight, almost spilling his beer.

"Two more victims. The dolphin got Loring."

That explained the cluster of Navy cars back at the fishing pier.

"And that damned reporter. I knew we shouldn't have taken him along. I need to talk to you. I hope you'll change your mind. It's going to get rough real fast, buddy. I need you."

A click and a dial tone, and Gene was alone again. He finished off the beer and decided to go into town. He walked to the Green Parrot, where he sat at the bar, nursing one beer that also qualified as dinner. Then he gave up on the night and headed back home. After midnight, his phone was ringing as he walked in the door. Suddenly, he was a very popular guy. He took his time picking up and the caller had hung up by the time his machine turned on. Five minutes later, the phone rang again and Gene picked it up this time on the second ring.

"There you are," Diamanda said accusingly, sounding as if they were in some kind of relationship and he wasn't supposed to go out without her. "Gene, Mattie just got back from Cuba. She found something over there. Well, actually, she found something and she lost something."

"Good for her," he said. "I got to get some sleep. Can we talk about this tomorrow?"

"No," Diamanda said, all businesslike now. "She wants to go back. We need your help."

He sighed. "I got plans. I'm busy the next few days."

"Gene, you're not going to get a job until this thing is over."

"How do you know?"

"I'm a psychic, remember?"

"If you're so psychic, tell me how I'm going to pay the rent without any money."

"If it's just the money, I'll pay you for your time. We're going to Cuba and you have to come with us."

"Dee, Cuba would be fun but this just isn't the time."

"Gene, there is no better time. You will get paid, and you can look for a job when you get back."

He had wanted to go to Cuba for years. Why did the offer have to come now, when everything seemed to be going wrong?

"I'd love to help you if things were different, but a joyride to Havana is not on my list of priorities. Can't it wait a while? Give me a few weeks, then I'd be happy to go."

"No, we're leaving the day after tomorrow. Gene, I'm not asking you for a lifelong commitment. I'm asking you for one day."

Gene heard himself say, "Okay." He hung up, wondering what he'd just agreed to.

Chapter 25

At dawn Thursday, Gene rode out to Spark's Marina. Diamanda and Mattie were on board Paradise Diver already, waiting for him. The boat was loaded with gear and boxes. In the stern, Gene lifted a blue tarp to discover boxes full of rubber gloves and syringes. Large blue plastic bins, the kind divers use to store equipment, were tucked under the gunwales. Two sets of dive gear were stacked next to the bins. A dozen cylinders of compressed air were strapped along the boat's sides.

Steel backplates that looked like a stubby set of wings and rubber air bladders were bungee-corded in next to the tanks. The rigs ran several thousand dollars each. Only deadly serious divers with unfathomably deep pockets, or pros, spent that much on their gear.

He was still checking things out when the engine roared to life and they got underway. Soon Key West was shrinking in the distance behind them. He went to the wheel to find the captain.

"Looks like you plan on some serious diving today, Captain Gold."

"It shouldn't be so hard. We dropped a camera on a dive the other day. We'll be in the water an hour or two; it's deep so we'll need a deco schedule. Then back on the boat and straight back home. With any luck, we'll be back by bedtime."

Gene leaned against the side of the boat. "As long as we're going to all the trouble of going to Cuba, why don't we stay overnight in Havana? Have some fun."

"Not this time," she said.

She was leaving the details far too vague for Gene's taste. He got the impression that Captain Gold was not going to tell him what they were up to until she was good and ready. He tried again.

"Who are all those hospital supplies for?"

"Just call it insurance. We have papers from the government granting us permission to go over and deliver humanitarian aid."

"I thought we were going over to dive."

Mattie hesitated. "Just in case the Cubans give us any trouble. This could be just a little risky."

Mattie wasn't the kind of woman who scared easily and he was surprised to hear her admit this. Gene asked, "What kind of trouble?"

Mattie gave a shrug and turned her attention to piloting the boat. "Don't worry. I'm sure everything's going to be okay."

The sea was dead calm and the boat made good time across the water. Quite a while later, she pointed at the distant water. Dolphins were jumping. "Same as Tuesday. A good omen."

Dozens of dorsal fins seemed to keep pace with the boat.

Gene whistled. "I've never seen so many at one time. How the hell do those idiots think they're going to find the one that killed those guys?"

She shaded her eyes and watched the dolphins. "Diamanda believes he's a messenger."

"So I've heard." Gene shook his head. "And I'm the next queen of Fantasy Fest."

"Okay, okay," she said. "You don't believe anything until you have proof. I'm like that too, sometimes."

"But not now?"

"Ask me on the way home." She paused as if considering whether to go on. Then she returned her attention again to the boat and the water.

He went to the stern, intending to keep Diamanda company for a while but instead fell asleep in the sun. When he woke, he stood and stretched until he felt alert again and then went up front, where Mattie was squinting into the distance through a pair of high-powered binoculars, with Diamanda alongside her.

"You want a break? I'll drive for a while," he offered.

"I'm okay," she said.

She handed him the binoculars. "They're still with us." She pointed. A half dozen dolphins leaped into the air a few hundred feet in front of the boat. Diamanda came up, clapping her hands and smiling.

If Mattie was all somber mystery, Diamanda was as light and carefree as a child on holiday. "He's nearby, I can feel it. It's time to call in a blessing."

She opened a velvet bag and pulled out a bundle of dried green herbs, sticks of incense and two rattles made of small gourds.

"What is that?" Gene asked, picking the herb bundle and sniffing. The aroma was rich and earthy.

"Sage," Mattie said. "You know, smudge."

No, Gene didn't know, but he wasn't going to admit it.

Diamanda lit the incense and then the sage. She held them in her hands and made three circles around the boat, waving the smoking sticks in the air, while Mattie shook the rattles. Sweet smoke drifted over them and out across the water.

Then Diamanda pulled off the big hat and red hair tumbled to her shoulders. She raised her arms to the sky.

"Grandmother moon, father sky, mother Earth," she chanted. As Diamanda started her ceremony, she became even more beautiful than usual, with her hair shining like polished copper in the light, her hands lifted to the sky. "Bless this boat. Give us safe passage across the water and guidance from the dolphin spirits."

She moved around the boat with the smoking stick, praying to each direction in turn.

"Spirit of the North," she began, "eagles, herons, pelicans, all our feathered friends, we call to your great intelligence, guide us to act with sureness today."

To the East she turned, calling out: "Spirit of the East, rising sun, your fire burns bright today. We call to the reptiles, the 'gators, the geckos, the fish in the sea, the rays, the crawling creatures, and our special cetacean friends, the whales and dolphins. Protect us today from any harm."

She turned again. "Spirit of the South, we call to you, great mother, Moon mother, protector of small children and all the four legged ones that roam the Earth. Our hearts, our emotions, our fears are in your hands. Let us walk with compassion and understanding and strength today."

She turned again. The wind caught the sage stick, which glowed and burned more furiously until the air around them smelled of sweet sage.

"Spirit of the West, we call to you, to the darkness, to the place where our ancestors walk and where the Earth is honored for her greatness and beauty. We ask our spirit guides to show us the path, we ask you to give us the strength to follow our convictions into the fire, into the water, into the sky, to travel the Earth as your emissary in honor of the greater good."

Then she began to sing a beautiful song in a strange language, shaking her rattles. Gene watched, feeling like an outsider.

Mattie seemed to know the song, and he saw her lips move along quietly with the words.

And so they cruised into Cuban waters, the women singing a

prayer and Gene observing silently as he leaned against the gunwale, his arms crossed over his chest. When Diamanda finished, she promptly began to pack up her shamanic tool kit and Mattie went back to the business of driving the boat.

The thin dark silhouette of Cuba appeared on the horizon. Mattie studied her little handheld Magellan GPS receiver and steered the boat in a circle. Finally, she slowed the engine.

"Hold these." She handed Gene a map and a lead weight attached to several hundred feet of line and a float. "When I say the word, drop the marker over the side."

The boat circled for a few more minutes until Mattie called out to drop the marker. The float splashed into the water and the line unreeled, marking the spot where Diamanda was to pick them up two-and-a-half-hours later.

Mattie spent five minutes briefing Gene on the dive. He was to follow her down, and they'd be going pretty deep.

"We're looking for a camera, and a structure. A pyramid shape," she said.

"Pyramid? What would that be?"

She kind of shrugged and then started talking about depths and deco schedules. "Just hope we find that camera," she said, finishing her brief.

Mattie went back to assemble her gear, leaving Gene with one or two unanswered questions. Gene had put his rig together on the way over. They'd each use a double set of tanks attached to two regulators. They'd carry primary and back up dive computers and spare tanks of gas and pure oxygen.

Diamanda watched them suit up in silence. As he got ready to jump into the water, she reached out to touch his arm. "Gene, you must find the pyramid for me. It's 50,000 years old, you know. Part of a grid of 12, spread around the Earth. One of the lost remnants of Atlantis and Lemuria."

"Atlantis? Everyone I meet wants to talk about Atlantis." He wasn't going to tell Diamanda that he was beginning to think she was nuts.

Mattie patted his other arm. "How're you doing, partner?"

"Let's go diving," he said.

Mattie gave him a thumbs up as she shuffled over to platform on the stern. She looked at Diamanda. "Head out a half mile. Come back to the float in two hours, fifteen."

Gene looked at the two women. "Why doesn't she just wait here?"

Mattie took the regulator out of her mouth to answer him. "The

Cubans may be watching this spot. No need to draw attention to ourselves."

"What Cubans?"

"The gunboats. You know."

Gene shook his head. "What gunboats? No, I don't know. Never mind. Just get in the water. That's great. Just great."

Mattie had her regulator back in now and jumped into the water.

Gene had come this far; he wasn't sure how or why, but he decided he had reached the point where he could not turn back. He stuck the regulator into his mouth, breathed the compressed air and plunged overboard.

Chapter 26

Gene followed Mattie down the float line stretching toward the sea floor. The loud rumble of a boat engine sounded overhead as Paradise Diver moved away.

As he descended into the green water that seemed to go on forever, he ran through the dive in his mind. Visualization was an old habit from his days as a SEAL and he envisioned the dive unfolding exactly as planned—a perfect ending, Diamanda coming back unhassled and alone, with no Cuban patrol boats around.

Ahead in the water, Mattie turned and looked at Gene through her black-framed mask, checking to see if he was ready. She seemed confident. He found that reassuring until he remembered the conversation about Atlantis and his suspicion that she was just as crazy as Diamanda.

He followed her anyway. They dropped the first thirty feet at a leisurely pace, equalizing the pressure inside their sinuses every few feet by holding their noses and blowing.

Once they hit a depth of 30, adjusting the pressure in the body cavities was easier and they practically flew down the next 100 feet of descent line. Time was precious. Gene hoped Mattie had dropped them directly over the target. They wouldn't know until they had gone deeper.

He looked down and saw nothing but dark green water. Neither the bottom nor a mysterious crystal pyramid was in sight.

Mattie leveled off ahead and Gene looked at his computer. Depth, 130. If they were in the right place, the tip of the pyramid should be just below them.

She moved her arm in a circle to tell him to follow her in the search pattern. The water flowed around their bodies gently, and she headed straight into the current. Gene kicked to catch up, wishing they had wireless comm gear to talk as they scouted around. The silence was disconcerting. While sound traveled well in water, the absence of voices or other auditory distractions during a dive somehow always lured Gene into listening to his own body, sinking deep into his inner thoughts, deeper than he ever did on land.

His breathing was steady; his heart beat slow and constant; he could feel the blood rushing through his veins. He followed Mattie's slender shape, the curve of her breasts, waist and hips nearly hidden by the heavy gear, into the stillness. He liked the closeness, the intimacy of being the only two humans in the sea together.

She turned a sharp left, checked her instruments and looked back to measure his progress. She was setting up a classic search pattern. Four right angle turns plus a specific number of kicks would put you back where you started. Except that normally divers could rely on the sandy bottom as a reference point and here there was nothing. Just water in every direction. Like being in outer space.

The endless water made Gene feel like an astronaut on a space-walk. He felt euphoric. Gene noticed that his thoughts were wandering, that the focus he usually had while diving seemed to be drifting away.

The concern that he'd had when he had jumped off the boat was fading. He felt good about the dive, about the women. They might not be crazy after all. Mattie and Diamanda were both smart, competent. Diamanda was his friend, and Mattie—well, she was something else. Gene hadn't yet figured her out.

Ahead, her sleek form reminded Gene of the essence of woman, like the figures he'd seen in the sculpture hall in the Louvre Museum in Paris. Indeed, she seemed as graceful as a bird of paradise in a tropical garden. Gene wasn't usually poetic but at this moment, everything was beautiful. Lyrically beautiful. He was the helplessly entranced fool, following an enchantress down to a watery lair. He glanced at his computer. 180 feet. He needed to concentrate on the dive. Gene hadn't been this deep in years.

A large game fish swam by. When the fish danced and played before his eyes looking a little too much like a scene from Disney's Fantasia, Gene recognized the blissful dream state of nitrogen narcosis. Divers called it "being narced." He felt invincible, drunken, stupid and happy.

Through the pleasant fog, Gene had his wits about him enough to realize that being narced could get him into big trouble. He needed to pay attention. She'd set the limit at 300 feet, 15 minutes bottom time. Right now the rules called for him to ascend and wait for the narcosis to vanish. However, he had no intention of allowing her to finish the dive without him. Whatever ride she was in for, he was coming along.

At 200 feet, she angled right. They were deep and still no pyramid.

She didn't pause, just kept kicking in the search pattern, changing direction every few minutes. They floated like snowflakes suspended in one of those little plastic bubbles with a wintry scene inside. Perhaps this was how death felt.

The light was dim at this depth, but not so dim that Gene couldn't see the shadow pass over his body just then. It sent a chilly sensation up his skin under the wetsuit. He looked up to see what had caused it and saw a large creature near Mattie.

In the green water, Gene could just make out a long silver shape approaching her, twenty feet away. Moving closer, the fuzzy shape resolved itself into an enormous dolphin, twice her size, with thick white scars on its sides and near its head. Jagged flesh covered places where the animal's skin had been torn. Gene recognized the scars. Devices that were once strapped on the dolphin's head to keep it from eating or to do more sinister work had left their mark.

Gene's heart pounded as he realized this most likely was the same killer that had struck in Key West, 90 miles away. Dolphins could travel 150 miles in a day, so the crossing would have been possible, but Gene wondered what would make the creature travel so far. It had shown up at least three times in Florida, and now here it was in Cuba.

Gene wondered if this one had been trained back in San Diego, perhaps even by him? The creature did not look familiar but Gene wasn't close enough to be sure.

The dolphin was within an arm's length of Mattie but she still didn't seem to pay it any attention. Gene kicked hard, trying to get closer, but the heavy gear slowed him down. He watched as the dolphin came up beneath her and rubbed against her wetsuit where it was not covered by the bulky tanks. Now Mattie saw the creature.

She reached down and touched the silvery skin, as naturally as if she were petting her dog. She wrapped her gloved hand around his fin and let the dolphin pull her along. The pair quickly disappeared into the dark water. Gene's throat tightened as he realized Mattie was going deeper and he was alone.

Chapter 27

The gray felt the cool pressure of the water against his skin. The water was always there to remind him. Water was denser, more powerful than air, so abundant that it connected all forms of life on the blue planet. He was privileged to be able to move so easily through the very substance of life. The sea gave him life, connected him to all living things. At the temple he would pay homage.

The temple reminded him always of duty, honor and obligation. He swam toward it now, reaching it first with his sonar, detecting the symmetry of its lines, then the crystal center emanating the warmth. As the sonar bounced back, the pyramid came alive in bright red, green and blue; the colors recorded in his imaging center brighter than his eye could see. Energy burst from it like a rainbow.

He swam toward the pyramid and painted the temple's sloping wall with sonar waves. Above, two shapes descended. Humans. The companions of the red-haired one.

The woman led. The gray's sonar touched her and returned quickly to him as an outline of her shape, two round breasts like perfect small mountains rising out of her flesh, most of which was hidden behind a bulky steel and rubber device. The larger human, a male, descended more slowly behind her. The gray found the female human more interesting; indeed, he was attracted to her.

He would not kill today, had no taste for blood. In fact, he knew the killing was over now, now that the red-haired one had come.

He wished he could give the female human the power to breathe beneath the sea, to swim with him forever. She had answered his call, not like the other humans on the boats, the ones whose frequencies had been so damaged that they could function only slightly better than tiny children. He liked her, and again he felt desire. He imagined the red-haired one swimming through the water too, with no tanks or equipment, alone in the water, free. She had been his kind a long time ago, and if she came back as a dolphin, she would be his mate. The image of the red-haired woman came not from sonar but from another store-house of information.

He kicked his flukes until he reached the diver. She drifted down, unaware of the temple though it was near. The gray approached her, swimming close until she reached out with a gloved hand to touch him. Her fingers pressed against his skin and he shuddered. He turned, trying to get closer, wanting to feel the electric touch of her small human hand on his body again.

She reached out and put her hand around his fin, then pulled her body into alignment with his. The gray pressed against her, wanting her to stroke him, for her to touch his velvety skin. As if she heard him, she removed her glove and rubbed his side with one hand, still clutching his fin with the other. He pulled closer until his body ran alongside hers. She seemed small and fragile.

He swung his flukes hard to reverse direction until they headed to the temple. The male human had been left behind. The gray had sensed the man reacting to his presence like a guardian. They swam a short distance and then the temple loomed up before them, reflecting silvery light through the darkness of the water.

Chapter 28

Gene waited for Mattie and the dolphin to swim back to him. He was hot and sweaty even though the water temperature was probably 60 degrees this far down, which meant he should be shivering and cold instead. When they didn't return, he checked the computer and considered his options, given a depth of 250 feet with twelve minutes elapsed time since the dive began. Three minutes before he needed to ascend for the long series of decompression stops.

Mattie and her biological propulsion unit were nowhere to be seen. The seconds ticked away. The narcosis no longer seemed amusing or pleasant, and he cursed the false inebriation, blaming it for his slow reaction to the dolphin's kidnapping of his dive partner.

He moved in a slow circle, kicking and thinking about what to do. He was looking down, wishing desperately that she would emerge from the shadows when his head rammed into a hard smooth surface. He reached out to touch a glass surface that extended in all directions as far as he could reach.

Gene unclipped his underwater flashlight to get a better look and its light bounced back in his eyes like it had hit a mirror. He adjusted the angle until the glare no longer blinded him, and then he could see that he was on the side of a steeply angled wall. The flat surfaces were tilted, like a pyramid, and he'd smashed straight into it. He'd been so distracted by the disappearance of Mattie and the dolphin that he'd nearly forgotten what they'd been searching for.

His computer read 17 minutes, 280 ft. Gene didn't have a choice now, he had to start up. He looked around again but Mattie was nowhere to been seen. Two minutes ticked by. Gene had exceeded his limit at the depth. He'd compensate by adding to his decompression stop, and then just take his chances. Getting bent this far from home could be deadly. He had to leave.

He swam up the pyramid's side, examining as much as he could on the way up. Her instructions had been to complete the dive and decompression independently if they were separated.

Gene kicked in the direction of his rising bubbles, making sure he ascended more slowly than the bubbles did. He kept his fingertips on the structure, wondering all the while what this big Plexiglas paperweight was and how the hell it got there.

The object was as big as a building. He pulled a slate out of his vest pocket and noted the depth, the number of feet he'd ascended while traversing the surface of the pyramid. At 140 feet, he reached its uppermost point. He paused and felt an eerie stillness. He centered himself directly over the pointed top of the pyramid and looked straight down into its glassy depths. A gentle blue glow lit its center like a candle would light up a sanctuary.

Diamanda's affinity for extraterrestrials and lost underworlds might be crazy. But Gene could touch the monolith. It was real. It didn't have to be sent from outer space.

It could be a military installation. The Soviets wasted their rubles on some pretty far out military weapons back during the Cold War. Granted, none of them worked, but the object could be part of a missile defense system or Star Wars beam weapon.

He stared at the blue glow for another minute, then ascended to 60 feet, where he made his first decompression stop. The current was weak at this level. He'd hoped to end up somewhere near the dive boat and find Mattie and Diamanda waiting and now he began to think about what he'd do if he were swept far offshore as he drifted during the decompression.

He had a long time to think, two hours of hanging in the water waiting for nitrogen to wash out of his system so that he could surface. The current had subsided and he hung stationary, no longer drifting. At 30 feet, he unclipped a reel and inflatable lift bag from his side. When the bag was full of air, it floated toward the surface, cheery as a circus balloon. Now Gene could only hope that Diamanda would spot the bag and pick him up.

He ascended another 10 feet and switched to the tank of oxygen at his side to accelerate the process of washing nitrogen out of his blood. Mattie had seen to all the right equipment. She knew what she was doing. Undoubtedly she thought she knew what she'd been doing when she grabbed that dolphin's dorsal fin. Dumb ass thing to do, Gene thought. He only hoped, in fact, he prayed that she wasn't still down there with the crazy fish. If she were, she'd be dead by now.

Chapter 29

With his two hour decompression stop over, Gene ascended through turquoise blue water, becoming more buoyant and moving a bit too fast as he rose, then slowing himself by releasing air from his vest, holding the ascent line and creating drag with his body. Finally daylight shimmered overhead on the surface of the sea. He breathed steadily in and out as he dangled ten feet below the surface. He was calm and relaxed despite every logical reason not to be.

His bright yellow lift bag floated overhead tethered to him by the line and reel hooked to his rig near his waist. He heard the rumble of a boat motor and the familiar clean white bottom of Paradise Diver moved into view overhead. Gene kicked his way to the surface, reeled in his line, dragging the yellow bag behind him.

He surfaced and saw Mattie behind the wheel, maneuvering into position to pick him up. Diamanda stood in the stern, waiting to help him get his gear out of the water.

"Good dive?" She smiled as she caught the fins he tossed them into the stern.

Gene pulled himself up, sea water flying as he climbed the aluminum ladder. He strained against the weight of the diving gear, which felt much heavier in air than it had underwater.

Mattie came up behind Diamanda, smiling and apparently unscathed from her encounter with the dolphin. The missing video camera lay on the deck beneath her dive gear.

"I'm a little surprised to see you, captain," Gene said, sounding more casual than he felt. "I thought the dolphin might have got himself another one back there."

He unbuckled his tanks and vest, then used a bungee cord to strap them into a rack on the side of the boat.

"You weren't worried, I hope." She smiled. "He took me right to it."

"To it?"

"The camera," she said. "And then to the pyramid."

"The pyramid? You saw it too, then. I guess we can rule out a mass hallucination. Enough of us have seen that damned thing, whatever the hell it is." Gene felt exhilarated if more than slightly mystified at what they'd just encountered.

At least they could talk about it. At least it wasn't classified and something that had to be carefully compartmentalized away. All of a sudden he was feeling like part of a team again, just like in the old days when being a SEAL was new and the job seemed pure and worthy. But Mattie didn't notice his change of heart.

"That pyramid is older than the oceans. This is the archeological find of a lifetime," Mattie said. "We are going to rewrite the history books."

"Hold on. That didn't look like anything built by an ancient civilization to me," Gene said. "It wasn't made of stone; it wasn't prehistoric. It looked like modern technology."

"In Cuba?" Mattie said incredulously. "No way. That was an old and powerful place. Besides, the dolphin took me down the side of it. There's a doorway. This is a sacred place, like one of those temples in the jungle in Mexico. I could feel it in my bones. The only question is, what's it doing underwater?"

"She's right. There's a vortex out here, too," Diamanda said. "I could pick up the vibrations."

Mattie continued to pack away gear. "It reminds me of when I went hiking in the mountains in northern Arizona. It's like an electrical buzz in the air that charges your whole body."

"Hold on," Gene said, shaking his head as he sat to unload the dive tanks. "Before you two get any more carried away with your vortexes and magic, maybe we ought to look for a realistic explanation. What I saw was not mystical; it seemed more threatening than anything."

"Threatening?" The excitement in Mattie's voice was replaced by anger. "Are you nuts? We know that the Fisher boys have been telling people they are close to finding Atlantis. Maybe it's not Atlantis, but it's got to be part of an ancient civilization. What could be dangerous about that?"

"That's not the only possibility," Gene said.

"Okay, then, what's your explanation?" she asked, her eyes challenging his.

Gene snapped a bungee around the double tanks. The boat bobbed up and down gently with the waves.

"Weaponry. Something put there by the Russian military during the Cold War. Either for communications, or to focus a laser at space. A big crystal object could be useful for either."

Diamanda wasn't buying it. "Why are you so convinced the crystal is the work of human hands?"

"Because it's too high tech to be anything else. I'm damned sure the U.S. wouldn't install anything this close to Cuba. So who else could have done it?" Gene asked. "I didn't even think the Soviets would be capable of something as advanced as that. But a few years ago, before the collapse of the Soviet state, most of their money was pumped into military black holes. I wouldn't give you a dime for most of the equipment the Russians have, but you see something like this, who knows?"

Mattie and Diamanda exchanged a look. Gene saw they were ready to argue their metaphysical points some more but the sight of a large, fast boat approaching cut it short. Mattie muttered softly, "Damn."

Gene nodded at the speedboat. "If this is a temple, I guess those cowboys are here for a prayer meeting."

The long red boat drew near, riding low in the water. A crew of khaki clad men armed with automatic weapons were on board.

"Hey, they'd be out here to protect a historical site just as fast as some secret space weapon, if they knew it was down there. And I'm beginning to believe they do," Mattie said softly, adding, "We should have skeedaddled."

"Too late now," Gene said, peeling off his wetsuit. "Stay calm. We'll find out what they want."

Mattie frowned, her hands on her hips, studying the men on the boat as they got closer. Then she said, "Oh hell, it's Díaz."

"A friend of yours?"

"Not exactly," she said. "He is going to be royally pissed if he finds out we've been diving here."

She had turned pale.

"Don't worry, kiddo," Gene said, sorry now that he'd given her such a hard time. "They probably just want to check us out." He hoped he was right, but he knew these men were too well armed and in the wrong kind of boat to be any ordinary patrol. Whatever was beneath the surface here must be pretty valuable.

"All they gave me last time was a warning," she said.

"A warning?" Gene asked.

"Basically—Díaz told me not to come back."

Mattie went to the wheel when the Cuban boat was only 20 feet away. "Gene, Dee, stow whatever is loose and get out some fenders."

In an aft compartment, Gene found pillow-shaped foam fenders to place between the two boats. Then the Cubans lashed the boats together and a tall Cuban officer with jet-black hair and decorations pinned to his uniform came aboard.

"Captain Gold," he said, his expression was dark as a thunderhead. "I'm surprised to see you. I thought I made myself clear the other day."

"Hello, colonel," Mattie said. "I had to come back, I lost a camera the other day. I just wanted to get it back. We didn't touch anything."

Díaz went to the ignition and removed the key. Mattie trailed behind the Cuban officer.

"You must come to port," Díaz said.

"I can explain everything."

"I'm sure you can." Díaz walked over to the camera. "Very nice. Very expensive," he said as he opened the camera, removed the videotape, and then tossed the camera overboard.

"You see? Your camera is worthless and you were a fool to come back for it. Now we go to shore. You have been warned not to dive here. But it would appear you do whatever you please. We have laws; we have rules. You have broken them."

Díaz returned to his own boat, leaving a crewman behind on Paradise Diver. The man went to the wheel, his holstered gun bumping clumsily against his leg as he passed Gene. A few moments later, they were underway, the cigarette boat rumbling noisily ahead, Paradise Diver trying to keep pace.

At the mouth of the harbor, Mattie whispered to Diamanda, "Go below and get the papers out of my bag. The ones with the State Department seal at the top."

A few minutes later, Diamanda emerged from the cabin with the plastic pouch of papers. Gene was hoping the Cubans would give them another slap on the wrist, detaining the Americans for an hour or so, and then letting them go home.

"Let's see if they want the supplies," Mattie said, nodding at the stacked up boxes of syringes and rubber gloves under the blue tarp in back. "Maybe these guys will take them and sell them on the black market. Whatever."

"Thank God for bribery," Gene muttered, knowing that a few soggy boxes of rubber gloves and hypodermic needles would not get them out of this mess.

The tall buildings of a resort came into view as they neared the Cuban coastline. The high rise luxury hotels of Varadero lined up along the white sand beach like soldiers on parade. Mixed among the big hotels were small opulent villas that had been planted in the sand like magical castles.

The Cuban soldier who was driving their boat passed the regular entrance to the harbor; then they reached a smaller inlet surrounded by woods where they turned in. Tall trees lined both sides of the pretty little harbor. As the boat churned ahead, Gene noticed signs of a military zone. On shore, a tall concertina-wire tipped fence surrounded a small group of low, modern cement-block buildings. The razor sharp wire extended into the shallower water a few hundred feet offshore. The boat passed through an unmarked opening in the wire, which was set up to make sure anyone trying to sneak in would almost certainly become ensnared.

Finally Paradise Diver was tied up to a long dock with several smaller boats. The big speedboat came in ahead of them and a half dozen Cubans on the dock scrambled to tie it up, then hurried back to assist with docking Paradise Diver. Díaz made his way down the dock toward them.

He climbed on board. "Give me your passports."

Mattie handed the documents over along with the plastic pouch of State Department papers. "Please," she said, "take a look at this."

Díaz glared at her and nodded toward one of his men. "Follow him. He will take you to a place where you will wait."

The young soldier had a large sidearm strapped to a belt around his thin waist. When he looked up, Gene saw that the soldier had only one good eye. His left eyelid drooped lazily down.

Mattie tried to protest, saying, "I don't want to leave my boat."

"Captain Gold," Díaz said, "what you want is of no importance. I will deal with you later."

Díaz turned and hurried up the steps toward the cinder block buildings at the top, leaving them in the care of the lazy-eyed guard.

The guard led the trio up the steps, then to a two-story gray building surrounded by sparse patches of grass. Cuba's red, white and blue flag flew from a pole in front. Three bony dogs slept in the shade of the building.

The guard took them to the second floor of a nondescript building, then down a long corridor with a dozen or more doors, all of which were closed. Up high, the view improved enough to get a good sense of the facility.

Gene could see the perimeter of the facility that they were in. It was secured like a military base but the layout of the buildings seemed more suited to research than for use as a fortress. A few hundred yards down the shore from the boat docks, in the direction that Díaz had headed when he left them, were rectangular underwater pens. Gene was reminded of the Navy's dolphin cages at San Diego and Key West. The pens appeared deserted at first but then he saw a dorsal fin break the surface inside one.

The Cubans were keeping dolphins here. What in the hell were the Cubans up to?

The setting sun reflected off the water. Gene squinted, thinking about his sunglasses, back on the boat with the rest of their belongings, probably being plundered at this very moment by those nice, polite soldiers.

Mattie was in front and he deliberately speeded up his pace until he bumped into her.

"Sorry, captain," he said as she turned. He nodded toward the pens. She followed his gaze, looking directly at the pens in the water, just as he had hoped she would.

"Dolphins," he said softly.

The soldier stopped and turned around. "Silence."

He unlocked a door and waved Mattie through.

"Wait," she said, "I think we should stick together."

The soldier put his hand on her arm and pushed her into the room. The shove was enough for Gene to see that he wasn't kidding. The soldier nudged Gene and Diamanda down the corridor. They passed a few more doorways, then he unlocked another room and motioned Gene inside.

The door slammed closed behind him and Gene heard the fading sounds of the guard taking Diamanda further down the corridor. He thought he heard the guard call her, "La Roja."

So much for his theory that the Cubans would merely detain them an hour and then they'd be on their way. Gene used to have pretty sharp instincts back when he was a SEAL. How had he allowed himself to sleepwalk his way into this?

He studied his surroundings. He was alone in what appeared to be an office that had all the furniture removed except for a metal chair with a torn gray cushion. A tiny window with no glass, just bars over the opening, was high on the wall, providing a small amount of fresh air. Gene tried sitting in the hard little chair but it was designed for discomfort. He moved to the floor. The cinderblock gray walls and brown tile floor were caked with mud that left soft powdery grit on his arms and legs. He sat down to wait.

Chapter 30

When Gene awoke, an orange moon was rising in the dark sky. Moonlight came through the bars of the window high on the wall in the tiny room. He guessed it was midnight or later. At home in Key West, the night would bring cool respite from the subtropical heat but here on the gritty concrete floor of the small Cuban holding cell, the air felt as hot as the devil's playground. Gene's clothes clung damply to him. His hair and face were crusted with a thin layer of salt leftover from the late afternoon dive, which now seemed an eternity ago.

He lay there, thinking about his fickle, female travel companions and what he should do next. After what seemed like an eternity, he heard footsteps and loud voices outside, then a key turned in the lock and Díaz came in.

Díaz nodded at Gene. His thick black hair and dark eyes resembled the other Cuban soldiers, but his military decorations and fancy uniform told the world that this was no ordinary soldier. He carried a small black baton.

Gene got up off the floor when he entered. Díaz pulled the metal chair to the center of the room and motioned for Gene to sit.

He would have prefered to remain standing, to stay eye level with Díaz, but then he thought better of it and took the chair.

Díaz began to pace, tapping the baton in his palm in a steady rhythm. "Mr. Rockland, I have a few questions for you. Your cooperation would be most appreciated."

The Cubans would have run a background check on the passports by now. Díaz would know that he'd been in the Navy, probably even in the SEALs. Unless their intelligence was so poor that he could continue to pass as an out of work bartender.

"What were you doing in the waters off our little island today?"

Díaz prowled and tapped the baton into his palm as he waited for an answer.

"I didn't realize recreational diving was illegal over here," Gene responded.

"Diving? You dive at a resort. On the other side of the island. Your papers say you are on a humanitarian mission. If you come to dive, you must enter as a tourist. But you Americans cannot come here to dive; your government won't allow it. So tell me why you came to Cuba." The baton beat harder against his palm.

Mattie wanted him to act like a hapless capitalist adventurer who had stumbled into Cuban waters out of ignorance and misguided entrepreneurial fervor. Gene couldn't play dumb but he could keep his mouth shut. "You'll have to talk to the captain. I was just following orders," he said.

"Ah yes, the captain. The second such mission in two days for your lovely captain. That's a lot of humanitarian kindness if you ask me." Díaz stopped the baton and wrapped his fist around it."And your boat is about to sink with the load of fancy diving equipment. You have more diving equipment than you do hospital supplies. Or perhaps all those hoses and tanks have a medical use. You mean to donate them to Cuba as well?"

Díaz smiled. The officer was enjoying himself.

"Ask the captain."

Díaz lowered his face to Gene's, his eyes narrowed menacingly. "What makes you think Cuba needs your hospital supplies? Your medicine? Your rubber gloves? Cuba is strong. We provide well for our people. If it weren't for your embargo, we would have all the medical supplies we could hope for. Who asked you to come over here loaded up with charity? No one. You arrogant Americanos."

Díaz backed off until just his white knuckles against the black stick were at the level of Gene's face again. Like a bundle of kindling soaked in gasoline, all Díaz needed was one little spark and boom.

"Colonel, maybe you'd answer a few questions for me, as long as we're having this friendly little conversation."

"Friendly? Yes." The baton tapped in the hand. "You amuse me."

"You're keeping dolphins here. What for?"

"My friend, you aren't in Miami now. What makes you think you have the right to ask questions?" The baton began the sharp slapping again.

"Well, I should be entitled to a phone call at least."

"All in good time. If your trip was authorized by the U.S. government," now the baton pointed at Gene's chest, "they'll notice that you're absent soon enough."

"Colonel, there's a killer dolphin on the loose in Florida. The U.S. authorities are going to get over here sooner or later to see if it was one of yours. They're bound to notice that we're here, and then you're the one who'll have to do the explaining."

Díaz stuck the baton in Gene's face. "They will find nothing. You aren't going to be around that long." He moved the baton away from Gene's chest. "This area is restricted. What were you doing out there? Spying?"

Gene didn't answer.

"Mr. Rockland, you obviously enjoy trouble. I will see to it that you get your fill."

Díaz turned and opened the door.

"Enjoyed our little talk," Gene said to the door after he'd gone. He heard voices speaking in Spanish outside.

A few minutes later, another soldier came in and motioned Gene up and out of the room again, leading him down the corridor. He unlocked another door and shoved Gene through it.

Inside, Mattie was alone, slumped against the wall. She was sleeping. Her long legs jutted out awkwardly, and she reminded Gene of a gazelle trying to sit on the ground when its body was built for running.

She rubbed her eyes, then when she saw it was him, jumped to her feet and gave him a warm embrace. The affectionate gesture took him by surprise. She must be more upset than she's letting on, he thought.

"Glad to see you too," he said. The lock clicked shut and the light bulb flickered to dirty brown. "You okay?"

She nodded. She had changed clothes, which meant she must have talked one of her guards into bringing her bag from the boat. Her hair was out of its long braid, tumbling loose around her face. The girlish look of the long hair, all soft and dark, transformed her. She was no longer the tough grownup tomboy who ran the boat so well.

"Your old friend Díaz been by?"

She nodded, pushing her hair back nervously, twisting it and then letting it fall again like a veil. He had never seen her so jumpy.

"He was in here for nearly three hours," she said. "He's pretty pissed off. I asked him to contact the U.S. consulate and inform them that we needed assistance. He didn't seem to be in a hurry to do me any favors."

"This is probably the most entertainment he's had in months."

She shrugged. "Do you think this is a military base?"

"It sure looks like it, but I hadn't heard of one being here," he said. "If it's not run by the military, then it's protected by them. The question is why? What's the research?"

The bulb flickered again and then the room went dark.

"Where's Diamanda?"

"Díaz wouldn't tell me," she said. "I'm worried. When I ask about her, the Cubans get all wierd."

He could see the outline of her face in the moonlight coming in the little window. She looked unhappy. "They aren't going to hurt her," he said.

"How can you be so sure?"

"They're still trying to figure out what we're up to, and what we know. It's the only reason they put us together, hoping we'll talk about it. The best thing we can do for Dee is to just stay quiet."

She nodded and then took his hand and led him over to where some clothes and her duffel bag were piled, then spread a couple of shirts beneath them on the floor. They lay down close to each other. She was close to the wall, and he faced away from her.

He felt Mattie snuggle up close to him. Her arm slipped around his waist and up to his chest. Her breasts and thighs fit tightly against his back and legs. The room was hot and the close contact only raised the temperature but he liked the way she felt. Maybe a little closeness wouldn't hurt him either.

"Gene," she whispered. "I'm sorry for dragging you over here."

"It's okay. I knew what the risks were." He may not have been thinking about them, but he sure should have known. When did he become such a good guy?

She snuggled closer and moved her hand tighter around his chest.

He touched her hand and thought about rolling over to face her, to reassure her, but he decided to just let things be. The last thing they needed was to complicate things more than they already were tonight. And Mattie finally seemed to trust him.

"Hang in there, captain. We'll figure out what to do."

"We," she said very quietly. "We. That's nice."

Gene shut his eyes and drifted off.

Chapter 31

aint light from the little window announced the dawn. Mattie was still wrapped around Gene's torso as tight as moss on an old tree. She breathed steadily, exhaling warmth that tickled his neck. When he rolled onto his back, groaning as his spine scraped the cement, all she did was pull in closer and tuck her head under his chin.

He watched her sleep until a key turned in the lock and the door swung open. Mattie opened her eyes as a Cuban soldier came into the room carrying two trays.

The trays held two mugs of tepid black coffee and hard bread. The guard had been out there all night, listening to them no doubt, and he watched as they disentangled themselves and brushed the dust off, then raised his eyebrows knowingly and left them alone in an awkward silence.

She brushed her hair away from her face and looked at him out of the corner of her eye. "I hope I didn't keep you awake," she said.

He could hear the formality creep in as she backpedaled away from any promise that might have come from having her arms wrapped around him just a few minutes earlier. "I was out the minute my head hit the nice soft floor," he said, hearing himself sound just as cold and formal as she had. "You didn't bother me a bit."

They ate the bread and drank the coffee. When they were done, the guard came back and led them down the corridor to a primitive bathroom where they used the toilet and washed up with cold water. After, Gene felt better, the itchy salt finally gone from his skin.

Then they returned to the small barren room until midmorning, when the door opened again and Diamanda sauntered through.

Her long red hair was combed and shining. She looked terrific, even though she wore the same clothes as the previous day. Unlike Mattie and Gene, her outfit was fresh as if she'd been traveling with a personal maid and her freckled skin was scrubbed clean. Either she really was a magician, or the Cubans had treated her to a hot shower and warm bed, Gene decided.

Mattie was disheveled, her hair in tangles, dirt streaked on her skin and clothing, looking like a wild woman out of the jungle next to the regal Diamanda. Mattie didn't seem to notice the difference as she rushed over to throw her arms around her friend.

"Are you okay?" Mattie asked, relief in her voice. "We were worried to death."

Diamanda smiled, tossing the red hair back. "I'm fine. But what about you? This isn't where you spent the night, I hope." The psychic wrinkled her nose in distaste as she looked around the barren room. "This place is awful."

"We managed to survive," Mattie said. "I kept asking after you, but they wouldn't tell me anything. You must have been scared to death all alone."

"It wasn't so bad. I had a nice room in an old house about a mile up the beach, with a bed, clean sheets, my own bath."

Gene shook his head. "We've got to talk to our travel agent, Mattie. I thought we'd booked first class."

Mattie finally stepped back and took a good look at Diamanda. "So what happened to you last night?"

"The guard took me straight down to see Ruykov."

"That little Russian? You were with him?" Mattie said, sounding shocked. "He catches dolphins for a living."

"We had quite an interesting conversation. That man knows a lot about dolphins. Then they gave me dinner and sent me off to bed," Diamanda said, sounding a bit guilty. "I asked about you and they told me you were talking with Díaz and would be taken care of. I had no idea they'd put you in this little jail. We'll get you out of here today. I'm sure Ruykov can take care of everything."

"What's he so interested in you for?" Gene asked.

"He wanted to talk about psychic phenomena. He's building it into his research here," Diamanda said. "With the dolphins."

"Oh, come on, Dee. It's a military compound. This isn't for science," Gene said.

"Ruykov is a scientist. And there are dolphins here. Quite a few of them." Diamanda frowned. "Gene, what are you so angry about? Just because I didn't stay here last night?"

"Hell, no. You had your luxury hotel. More power to you. I just can't figure out what your motives are for cooperating with these goons."

"Cooperating? How do you think we are going to get out of here, let alone get the dolphins out, if it isn't by dealing with them on their own terms? Ruykov is listening to me. Russians take psychic powers very seriously. And we might get a chance to work with his dolphins in exchange."

Gene frowned. "Wait a minute. I didn't come over here to work with the dolphins. This was a quick trip to the coast and back. Remember? You said we weren't even coming ashore."

Diamanda held up a hand. "The situation has changed."

"What about the big gray?" Mattie asked. "Is he here?"

"I don't know. I need more time," she said.

"More time?" Gene said. "When I hired on for this little cruise, you told me it was a one-day job. Let's figure out how we're going to get Mattie's boat back and head on home."

Diamanda's eyes flashed defiantly. "After what you saw yesterday, you want to rush back home? If we stay here a few more days, we might actually make a difference."

"After what I saw yesterday?" Gene asked. "I thought we agreed that we didn't see a damned thing."

"Gene, there is something going on over here, and I for one, want to know what it is." Her emerald eyes challenged him. "You have gotten a glimpse of the past, and of the future. You were the diver. You are in a position of privilege. You saw something down there, and I believe it was one of the ancient temples of Lemuria. We've known the temples are there, either buried on land or at sea. We've had that information for these past 100 years. The structures are 50,000 to 60,000 years old."

Mattie leaned forward. Gene could see she was caught in Diamanda's excitement. "Diamanda's right. When I was down there, I felt the power of the place. Gene, we can make archeological history if we could get permission to run an expedition over here. Maybe it could even become a project that would pull Cuba and the U.S. together, if we can just forget about the politics for a minute. Just think, the Cubans and Americans working together, rewriting the history books."

"You're both being terribly realistic," he said. "What a couple of dreamers. You ought to be in Hollywood."

Diamanda shook her head. "Gene, that is a completely small-minded attitude."

"Small minded? No way. It's rational, reasoned and logical. What I saw can be explained by science, no matter how mysterious it was, and there's nothing as mysterious as an advanced weapon," Gene said.

"The only thing we're arguing about is perspective. Once upon a time, the Earth was flat and the sun rotated around it too. Remember?"

she shot back. "Since the '70s, more specific information has come through about 100 channelers who've been tuning into information from the Pleidians. The Atlanteans and Lemurians built 12 crystal pyramids in a grid pattern around the Earth. They're used to receive information and energy from other star systems. The grid was covered with water when the planet was changed."

"And that's what you think we've stumbled on?" he asked. He was about to try to reason with her when the door opened again and the guard came in, pointing at the lunatic redhead.

"La Roja. We go." He motioned at the door.

Diamanda didn't budge.

"Now. Por favor."

"I'm not going anywhere without my friends."

"Everyone." He waved at Gene and Mattie. "You come. Now." He repeated, "La Roja," then bowed slightly as if she were royalty.

"La Roja?" Mattie whispered, nudging Diamanda with her elbow. "So now you are La Roja?"

"I'll explain later," Diamanda said.

As Gene passed through the doorway, he remembered Hecate's premonition on the pier about coming to a door and going through it. What would he find on the other side? More trouble, that was for sure.

The soldier led them single file across an open field that ran along the ocean until they came to a compound where old buildings that predated the revolution were mixed with cheap, modern cinderblock structures. They came to a grand old house with a wrap around porch that faced the sea. The building had been a beautiful mansion in its younger days but its conversion to government use had made it as anonymous and lifeless as the cinder block pillboxes they'd just passed.

They went up a short flight of wooden steps, through the front door and beyond to a dark hallway that divided the house. Turning left, the soldier ushered them into a large room, filled with wide wicker sofas with plump cushions in a gay tropical print and heavy antique furniture that looked old enough to have been brought over from Spain by Columbus. Against the wall, a table was piled high with platters of avocado, oranges, roasted meat and a huge cooked lobster, its white flesh bursting from a bright red shell. A bin of ice held Cuban Hatuey beer, cola and juice.

Gene's mouth watered at the sight of the food. The lobster was one of the largest he'd ever seen in his life.

A small man with bushy gray hair, neatly dressed in an ill-fitting polyester suit, was sitting in a big chair in the far corner of the room.

Gene recognized Dr. Ruykov. Díaz stood near the windows in his green uniform and black boots, looking solemnly out at the sea. As the three Americans entered, Ruykov shuffled over and held out a grizzled hand.

"Buenos días, honored guests." He pumped Gene's arm and then Mattie's. For Diamanda, he had a special welcome, kissing her on both cheeks with a warm greeting, "La Roja, I am delighted to see you this morning."

She smiled back at him. The coziness sent a chill up Gene's spine.

"We will talk, then have some lunch, yes?" Ruykov shuffled over to the bar and opened a beer, then went to one of the sofas and settled in. He took a few sips from his glass and then finally noticed that his guests were empty-handed and called to Díaz, "Colonel, colonel, get our guests a drink."

Díaz looked at the old man with disdain, obviously resenting the direction to wait on the Americans. But he did as told.

When the tray came around, Gene took a beer and a Coke. The Coke went down in a few quick swallows, and he refilled his glass with the Hatuey. Ruykov was fawning over Diamanda, and referring to her again and again as La Roja.

Diamanda took Ruykov's hand and pulled him a bit closer to where Gene and Mattie were sitting on the overstuffed couch. "Dr. Ruykov, tell Gene and Mattie about your work here."

The Russian cleared his throat as if he were about to deliver a lecture to a hall of students. "As La Roja knows, I have spent my life studying the dolphins and whales. I have published hundreds of papers and spent 40 years doing research on cetaceans. But of course, since my work was done for the Soviet Union, you would never have heard of me or any of my findings, unless of course you are an oceanographer in Moscow," he said sadly. "And there aren't very many of those, are there, La Roja?"

Gene shook his head. "Wait a minute. What's with this La Roja business? Her name is Diamanda Full Moon."

"La Roja is the red-haired mermaid who brings knowledge and good tidings. It's a legend. Her appearance marks a time of abundance." The old man smiled. "In the paintings, she looks a lot like Ms. Full Moon. The dolphins and sea turtles are around her."

That explained the special treatment she was getting. Ruykov and the Cubans thought Diamanda was some kind of magician. If she was, Gene thought, why didn't she just magically get them out of there?

"What I don't understand is why you would choose Cuba for a

research center," Mattie was asking the Russian.

"If that's what it is," Gene interjected.

Ruykov shrugged. "Why not here? I like it here."

"Come on. You can't get food or basic necessities here, you can't even make an international phone call," Gene said.

"What do you call that?" Ruykov pointed to the table that groaned beneath piles of mangoes, shrimp, beans and rice. "Don't believe all that U.S. propaganda. Cuba is beautiful, it's cheap. The Cubans are lovely people. The waters are warm and clean, and the dolphins are at home here. You've seen it for yourself."

"The only thing I've seen is the inside of the jail cell. And the only Cubans I've met are the colonel and his goon squad," Gene said, nodding at Díaz. "What I see is a cover story. It looks like science—but it's not." Gene glanced at Díaz, sitting by the window. He hadn't moved or spoken, just sat glowering at the Americans. "Why else is he here?"

"The colonel is not a scientist, you are correct. He is here to ensure security. You picked the wrong place to jump into the water yesterday." Ruykov laughed like this was all a big practical joke among friends. "It's not his fault you decided to go diving in a military zone. He had no choice but to bring you here."

Gene rose to his feet. "Look. We weren't trying to cause trouble. Why not let us just check into one of the Varadero resorts while you figure out what to do with us? Why all the guns if this is just for science?"

Ruykov held his arms out wide. "There is much to protect, the reef, dozens of shipwrecks. History and science both need protection, my friend. Some scientific secrets are worth guarding."

The old Russian smiled again, exposing his broken teeth.

Mattie leaned forward. "Dr. Ruykov, if there are underwater ruins offshore here, wouldn't it be better to make them public? Encourage some exploration?"

"Not if they really aren't ruins, Mattie," Gene said. The two women looked at him as if he'd just suggested that the moon was made of fruitcake. Everyone else was buying this Atlantis theory, except maybe for Gene and Colonel Doom, sitting like a pit bull in his corner.

Ruykov shuffled slowly back toward the buffet table. "I'm sorry you've chosen not to trust me, Mr. Rockland. I was hoping that we could work together."

Gene was losing patience. "Work together? Doing what? Terrorist training for dolphins?"

Mattie interrupted. "Hold on, Gene." She looked at Ruykov. "He didn't mean that."

Díaz stirred from his parking spot by the window. He stood, and then came to where Gene was planted in the middle of the room.

"Now it is your turn to answer some questions, Mr. Rockland." Díaz said. The pit bull eyes were black as oil. "How long have you been a bartender?"

"For a while."

"Why is a bartender working on a diving boat?"

"Call it an odd job," Gene said.

Díaz moved closer. Gene could smell the garlic the man had eaten with his beans and rice the night before.

"Why don't you tell us what you did in the U.S. Navy?"

Gene shrugged. So he knew.

"I'm talking about San Diego, Combat Swimmer School, the years you spent as a SEAL."

"What's to tell?" Gene replied.

Ruykov got up and shuffled over to wedge himself between the two men, who towered over him like giant trees over a scrubby bush.

"Colonel, these are our guests," Ruykov said. The little Russian had flecks of spit at the edges of his mouth.

Díaz glared at the Russian, then turned to Gene. His index finger poked Gene's sternum hard. "Just wait."

Ruykov put his hand on Díaz' chest and gave him a look that ended it there, the Cuban backing off like a dog that had been kicked too much. "Colonel, just leave us for a while," Ruykov said, and then Díaz turned and left the room.

"My friends, there is no need to play games," Ruykov said, smiling once again. "We know who you are. A former SEAL; a dive boat captain. Ms. Full Moon, we know that you have special talents. Perhaps America doesn't appreciate them, but in Russia, you would be treated well."

Ruykov made a move toward the buffet. "The Cold War is over. There is no need for us to be enemies. In fact, we have common interests. You want a business partner here in Cuba? I'm ready to make you a deal. You could make certain arrangements back in Florida, and we could help you set up a dive business here. You could make a lot of money."

"Dr. Ruykov," Mattie said, "We need a little time to talk things over among ourselves."

"Yes, my dear, that's an excellent idea."

"Wait a minute. We're not making any deals," Gene said. "Not till we are free and clear, on our way out of here."

Mattie turned to Gene. "Didn't I just say we'd talk about it?"

"You're making a mistake, Mattie," he said. "The only deal is we go back to the U.S. now."

"Are you going to let us leave?" Mattie asked the Russian.

Ruykov shook his head. "Leaving immediately is not going to be possible. You have violated Cuban security rules. Don't worry, a few days is all. I thought you understood."

"Just let us go to a hotel," Diamanda said. "We promise won't leave until this is resolved."

Ruykov shook his head. "How are you going to pay for a room? You are not allowed to spend money here. Your government makes those rules, not Cuba. You should be grateful we give you a place to sleep instead of throwing you in a real prison."

Gene moved over closer to the window. Outside the sugar white sand and topaz blue water beckoned as if it were a dream. Gene turned his attention back to the Russian.

"I insist that you let us call the U.S. interests section in Havana." he said. "Now."

Ruykov's eyes narrowed and the pleasant, welcoming tone disappeared from his voice. "Mr. Rockland, you were engaged in dangerous activities in restricted waters belonging to the sovereign nation of Cuba. You do not have enough fuel to make it home, even if we let you go. Who's to say what happened if the bodies of several divers turn up floating in the Straits of Florida 90 miles from home? Who's to even say that bodies would be found? The sharks are very hungry round here."

"We do have enough fuel. We brought it with us," Mattie protested.

"When you broke the law, your boat and everything on it were confiscated," Ruykov said. "The fact is you cannot leave without my help."

He edged a bit closer to the buffet. "But come relax. We can have some lunch and talk about my proposal. We can work together on an international dolphin research project."

"Not until you level with us, " Gene said. "No one is going to work with you while this business is going on about a killer dolphin. The Americans are going to be over here before you know it to find that dolphin. It's not a game anymore."

Ruykov closed his eyes and shook his head slowly before responding. "We have plans for that one. He will not be around much longer."

Diamanda sat up in alarm. "What are you saying? What are you going to do with him?"

"You don't want to hear the details," Ruykov said. "We all make mistakes. But this one is correctable."

Ruykov turned to Gene. "If they come, they will find nothing."

Gene looked at the women. "You see, he's admitting it. This is not something you want to get mixed up in. There is nothing but trouble ahead."

Ruykov sighed, then shuffled over to the door, opened it and spoke to the guard who was posted outside. "Tell Colonel Díaz that Mr. Rockland is ready to return to his quarters. Ms. Full Moon, you and I will have some lunch. Captain Gold, are you hungry?"

Díaz returned with two other solders and escorted Gene out of the room. One of the Cubans stuck a rifle in his back, and its muzzle prodded him down the dark hallway. On the grand old porch of the old house, Díaz produced a pair of handcuffs and snapped them around Gene's wrists.

The group walked back on the deserted beachside road. No traffic passed them, either in a car or on foot. "You wanted to see Havana, commander?" Díaz asked as they walked in the hot sun.

Gene shrugged. "Someday."

"Tomorrow, you get your chance." He paused. "You are going to see a judge in Havana, and then commander, we'll finish your tour of Cuba with a visit to a real Cuban prison. You will get a taste of Cuban hospitality."

Díaz began to whistle a shrill piercing sound, a song that Gene did not recognize, and he kept it going as he walked with Gene and the two soldiers all the way back to the building where he'd spent the previous night. Inside his little cell again, Gene slid to the floor. Díaz was wrong. Gene was not going to a Cuban jail, no matter what he had to do to avoid it.

Chapter 32

The sea and Mattie's boat were only a hundred yards away from the hot little room where Gene once again waited. The trick was finding a way to get to them. The Cubans had been casual about guarding the Americans; sooner or later, they'd make some small mistake. All he really had to do was wait.

He was finished following orders—Mattie's or the Cubans'. Gene would keep his eyes open, watch for a lapse in security. Mattie's belongings, a knapsack and a change of clothes, were piled in a corner. He remembered how she'd curled up close to him the previous night, holding on as though her life depended on it. And then when morning came, another sudden shift in attitude. Suddenly, she was the boss again, cozying up to the little Russian scientist just as she'd cozied up to him.

Daylight was fading. He was hungry and began to regret his righteous decision to pass on the big buffet. It had been hours since he'd last seen the women, just as they were sitting down to their Cuban feast.

When darkness fell outside and the room was illuminated by only the dim lightbulb, Mattie and Diamanda returned, both with slick-backed hair and rosy cheeks, looking for all the world like a couple of sun-drenched tourists who'd stayed on the beach too long.

"Welcome home," he said, sitting up, a little surprised to see them. "I thought you two diplomats had changed sides."

"Gene," Mattie said excitedly. "We swam with the dolphin."

"How did you talk Ruykov into that?"

"When Diamanda got near the pen, the dolphin went crazy, practically leapt out of the water. He loved her. Ruykov didn't want to let us in the water—it was really dirty and oily—but Dee persuaded him."

"Great. I hope you got his death sentence commuted."

"We're working on that."

Diamanda sat down beside him on the concrete. "Gene, can't you see that the real reason we're over here, although maybe we didn't know it until this afternoon, is for that dolphin? The dolphin has a message to deliver and I have heard it now."

The mystic routine had worn thin and Gene wasn't in the mood for games anymore. "Ruykov is a con artist," was all he could find to say.

"Aren't you even willing to listen?" asked Mattie. "Things are done differently over here, Gene. He offered to help us set up a diving operation."

"And you fell for it?"

"It wasn't a matter of falling for anything. He was serious. I wanted to see what you thought about..."

"Now all of a sudden you want my advice—"

"Would you just listen? Diamanda can explain everything." Mattie looked at her friend. "Tell him. When she was with him in the water, something happened."

Diamanda closed her eyes and took a deep breath. She exhaled and began her story. "The big dolphin is the guardian of the temple. The temple where you dove yesterday."

She opened her eyes and looked at Gene solemnly. "The dolphin was patrolling it. The Cubans don't know what that big underwater crystal is, all they know is that it's strange, a mystery, and they want to keep it quiet. They've done some free diving on it, and a little scuba diving but they don't have the technical equipment or training to go down there and really check the place out like you and Mattie did. The dolphins live there. They are here to protect the temple, but the Cubans have caught several of them and are trying to train them, you're right about that."

"Ruykov lets the big gray out of his cage out each day. He stays out of spiritual duty, not because the Cubans want him to. He is carrying a message from his species. That's why he came across to Florida. The dolphins have got to be set free. This practice of taknig them into zoos and theme parks, putting them on display because they are so cute, it's all got to stop, as does the abominable stuff the military is doing. It's no better than kidnapping."

The woman waited for his reaction. Darkness had fallen and Gene decided that his companions liked ghost stories and fairy tales a little too much. "You already knew all that before you came over here, Dee." he said. "You think that's the reason behind all the deaths? If he's trying to get a message across, he picked a helluva way to do it."

Diamanda's brow wrinkled in a frown. "Do you have any idea how many dolphins have died?"

Gene ignored the question, and continued his argument. "For

another thing, that pyramid looks more like a modern weapon than an ancient temple. The shape, the material, it all seems to be consistent with a focusing or firing mechanism for some kind of laser space weapon. If you could only raise it up over the sea, it would be a perfect defense mechanism; if I were a weapons designer, I'd love to keep it underwater until I was ready to use it. If I'd had a little more time to examine the thing I might be able to prove it."

"That was no weapon," Diamanda said. "You can find information about the temples in the Mayan prophecies. When the civilizations fell and the cities were destroyed, some of the Atlanteans chose to be human and live on the land. They wanted to create, to build more cities. Others chose to take on the dolphin form. They rejected the idea of acquiring possessions and building material things. They went to live in the water, evolving into a whole new species that didn't need to work to survive. The human species became the builders, but they lost their connection to much of their power. Look at our condition. People have become highly creative, but at the same time, we're oppressed and miserable. Look at the dolphins. They spend their lives, the same life span as man, playing and eating and making love. That is, if they're not held captive in tanks."

"That's a nice bedtime story," he responded. "But somehow I just can't buy that a creature that can be trained to kill is constantly emanting love."

"Think about your own experience, Gene. You learned to kill, didn't you?"

"You're stretching things to make a point. Military operations are done for necessary reasons."

"Exactly," Diamanda said. "The dolphins' agreement has held for 50 million years, but now they want out. They want to be released from the contract. They want to go home."

Diamanda shook her head, growing visibly tired of the argument. "Truth is a very personal thing, Gene. You touched the crystal temple. You felt its smooth cold surface with your own hands. You have more concrete proof than most people ever get in life. It's up to you to decide what to believe. If you want to think it's a weapon, you can help justify military intervention. If you accept the possibility it's a temple, maybe things will be different."

"And what about the big dolphin? What becomes of him?" he asked.

Her calmness disappeared. "Gene, we've got to get him away from Ruykov."

"I don't think that's going to happen," he said. "The dolphin is dangerous."

"No more so than you or I. In the olden days, in Atlantis, he and I were..."

"Would you stop with that?" Gene said in exasperation. "Atlantis is a fairy tale, for Christ's sake." He crossed his arms over his chest and leaned against the wall. The women exchanged a look and remained silent. The stalement hung over the room until Mattie yawned and gave him a suspicious look. "I don't know about you, but I'm going to get some sleep," she said.

The women inched away from him and curled up with Mattie's extra T-shirts and backpack as pillows. He sat against the wall, watching them sleep for a while. He felt disconnected and wondered why he'd argued his point so hard when it didn't really make much difference. It didn't matter if the sea contained a Russian weapon, an Atlantean temple, or a figment of someone's imagination as long as they were stuck here.

As the night stretched on, Gene drifted off too. Hours later, a faint sound disturbed his dreaming. The humming was quiet enough to be a mosquito but then, its steady, mechanical drone broke through his subconscious. The hum was the sound of a small outboard motor. He sat up with a start.

As he did, Diamanda pushed herself upright and rubbed her eyes. He pointed at his ear, indicating that she should listen. She nodded, then pointed at the window and whispered, "Go and look."

Gene got up and went to the small barred window. He could hear the guard singing softly in Spanish just outside the door. The guard was smoking, his cigarette smoke drifting into the room. He grabbed the bars and pulled himself up high enough to see out. The corridor was dimly lit; several hundred feet beyond the edge of the sea there was nothing but darkness.

Far beyond the shore, Gene thought he saw a faint green glow, so small that it was almost undetectable. To a person who hadn't spent much time on the water, the glow might be taken to be a small boat or starlight, but Gene knew it was a chem stick. Divers use the small green chemical sticks to signal and mark objects at night. He considered the possibility that Cuban operatives were training out there. But you couldn't even get a newspaper or a stick of gum over here. There was no way the Cuban security forces had chem sticks.

Something was happening. He rummaged through Mattie's canvas bag until he found a small mirror. At the window, Gene used the tiny mirror to signal toward the green light. He had no idea who was out there or what they were doing, but he wasn't going to sit in the little cell like a helpless victim. He boosted himself to the window and looked out again, searching the darkness for the green light but it had disappeared.

He returned to the women. Mattie was awake now, and he motioned to them to stay still and wait. It seemed like an eternity until footsteps sounded in the cement corridor, followed by a scuffling outside the door. A thud, a heavy sliding sound against the wall, more thuds. The Special Forces' calling card. Then, the door exploded open, the wooden frame in fragments, with its flimsy lock still attached.

The stubby barrel of a black automatic weapon appeared in the door frame, followed by a man dressed head to toe in black. Gene stood against the wall, and waited to decide if he should put up a fight. But the man's black garb was new and professional looking. It was either an American military operative or the security force of some drug lord. Nobody else was as well equipped. The dark figure looked at Gene and took off his hood. It was Storm.

"Yo, Skunk. Came to buy you a Mojito, what do you say?" Storm grinned, his black hair spiking straight above his head like it was electrified, his blue eyes sparkling.

"Ladies, the cavalry has arrived," Gene said. "Come on, we'll make introductions later. Glad to see you buddy."

Storm looked around the little room. "Get your bags, kids. It's check out time."

"How'd you find us?" Gene asked, as Mattie gathered up her belongings and her pack.

Storm grinned. "We keep an eye on things over here. The guys have been watching this little operation for a while. The satellite spotted your boat this morning."

Storm stuck his head out the door, looked around and then turned to Gene and the women. "Everybody ready to move? You ladies stay close behind me. Skunk'll bring up the rear."

They trailed Storm's dark silhouette down the corridor, with Mattie and Diamanda close behind and Gene bringing up the rear. They moved fast and running felt good to Gene.

Down the stairs and across the open yard, they moved single file past three Cuban guards, all of whom were flat on the ground as if they were sleeping, small pools of blood spreading on the ground around them like blankets. Diamanda and Mattie stepped over the bodies as casually as if they were trees across the trail, and Gene was relieved that neither of them flinched at the sign of Storm's trail of violence.

At the water's edge, a rubber inflatable boat with an outboard motor was beached with another Special Forces guy at the helm. He was dressed in camouflage and black paint.

"Everybody into the Zodiac. Come on, come on, step it up," Storm said. He reached his hand out to help the women into the boat.

Diamanda was going along with the plan, but Mattie stopped and planted her feet in the sand. The look on her face was enough to tell Gene she wasn't about to get in the little rubber boat. She pointed to her boat, bobbing in the water 100 feet away.

In the dim moonlight, they could see that it had been emptied of everything that wasn't nailed down. "I can't leave the Diver here," she said.

Then she darted off before Storm could stop her. Gene glanced at Storm, who was frozen momentarily in disbelief, then hurried after Mattie. He looked up toward the buildings, expecting to see Cubans running out in hot pursuit any moment now. But no sound came from the compound. Storm had done an efficient job of clearing the way for their departure. By the time he got to the Diver, Mattie had untied half the lines and was at the wheel.

"They took the keys," she said. "But it doesn't matter. I don't need them."

"No fuel either," Gene said. The stern, which had been loaded with big fuel drums and all her diving gear, was empty. Gone, along with the electronic navigation boxes near the driver's seat.

"Leave the boat, Mattie," Gene said. "It's not important."

She shook her head. "I can't."

"You don't have a choice."

"Do you have any idea how much a boat like this is worth? How's a guy like Patcher supposed to run a business without..."

"Patcher isn't going to give a damn. Your life is worth more than this." Gene took her hand and tried to tug her toward the Zodiac but she wouldn't budge.

"I stay with the boat," she said firmly.

"You can't stay here now. Not after..." His voice trailed off, with neither of them wanting him to finish the sentence about how three Cuban guards, just kids who hadn't asked for any of this trouble, were now dead. "I'm not leaving you behind."

"Who appointed you to take care of me? If I want to stay, I will."

"Mattie, there is going to be hell to pay if Díaz finds you here and me gone."

"If I lose the Diver, Patcher will be ruined." Gene detected a slight tremble in her voice. "He's lost too much already this year. I can't let him down again."

Then Diamanda came clattering down the dock with Storm right behind. She rushed over to Mattie. "Let's go home, sister. It's getting too rough."

Storm was right behind her. "I want you three to get your sorry asses over to the Zodiac pronto. This is no joke, and we're not going to stand around having a democratic discussion about it. This is an order."

"I'm not in your Army, pal. You can't order me." Mattie had already stuck her head into the engine compartment, and was fiddling with some wires.

Storm shook his head and cursed. "No wonder women aren't allowed in combat."

Then the boat's engine rumbled to life. She stood up. "Can we get out of here?" she asked Storm.

"For expediency's sake, I'm going to say yes. You've got a radio and an emergency beacon?"

She nodded.

"You know the compass headings for home?"

She nodded again.

"How far can you get on the fuel left in her tanks?"

"Ten miles, maybe twenty, if we're real lucky."

"You should be able to make international waters. Go for it," he said. "Get out of this cove and head for Key West. Run like hell till you empty the fuel tanks. Then turn on the distress beacon and sit tight. Someone will come and get you."

"Gene, you stay with the mule-headed captain here." Storm tapped Diamanda's shoulder. "Red, you're with me. I came all this way for you three and I'm not going home without at least one of you."

Storm took Diamanda's elbow and propelled her toward the Zodiac.

With Gene's help, Mattie got the Diver underway and through the narrow opening in the concertina wire at the mouth of the harbor. In the open water, she headed due north toward Key West. She ran the engine at full throttle until the gas gave out a half-hour later.

Paradise Diver bobbed gently in the small waves as Mattie switched on the emergency transmitter. Gene was fairly sure they were still in Cuban territory.

"What's the wind direction?" he asked.

"From the North," Mattie replied, not bothering to add that it would swiftly push them back to Cuba. They both knew it. Now it was a race to see if Storm's people would reach them before the Cubans did. Gene thought about Díaz's cigarette boat and how easily it could catch them.

Overhead, the sky was imprinted with the brightness of a thousand stars. Mattie scanned the northern horizon with her binoculars. "I wish we didn't have to leave him back there. Any of them for that matter," she said.

Gene touched her shoulder. "You did everything you could. Sometimes you've just got to walk away."

She put the binoculars down and looked at him. "Isn't there some tiny part of you, maybe buried away deep inside, that's just crying out to help those dolphins? I don't see how you can be like that. You saw what was going on back there. It's like you don't feel a thing."

"I learned a long time ago that sometimes you have to let your dreams go, Mattie."

"I'm not talking about a dream. I thought you used to be a SEAL, a man of action. Break heads first, think about it later."

When he didn't answer, she picked up the binoculars and looked out at the water again, then quietly added, "Surely you weren't always so cold, Gene. What in the hell happened to you?"

She put the binoculars down and looked at him. "I mean it. What happened?"

"I just got tired."

"And then what?"

The familiar wall of silence dropped down. Gene wanted to tell her but he could not go there.

Then Mattie stood and turned her attention to the horizon once more. "Here comes a boat."

A large SportFisher approached, its top deck towering forty feet above the water, bristling with poles and wires from three stacked decks. As it drew closer, they saw Storm's rubber inflatable Zodiac dragging along behind it. For the second time in a single night, they were rescued.

Chapter 33

A half-hour later, Gene found himself staring in a round mirror at a ferocious-looking man with a two-day growth of beard and dirt stained skin.

He was in a small cabin below deck on the SportFisher. He looked older and more worn than when they'd started across the water two days ago. His black hair was tangled and matted down to his scalp, making the streak of gray that started at the center of his forehead and ran to the back of his head more prominent.

He poured a tumbler of whiskey from a bottle on the small round table next to the bunk. He took a big drink, feeling the alcohol settle in his midsection with a pleasant burning sensation. The edginess ebbed.

Some sleep and a shower would help erase the weariness, but until then, he'd rely on the whiskey to keep him going. The little cabin even had a small television, although nothing happened when Gene hit the power button. The shower was clean and hot water flowed when he turned on the spigot. The sport-fishing crowd sure knew how to live.

He stepped into the head and climbed under the steaming spray. Mattie would be showering in the other stateroom down the hall. He tried to push her image out of mind, but there she stayed.

When the salt and sweat and Cuban dirt were washed away, he shut the water off, shaved, dried off and looked in the mirror again. Better. He slicked his hair back tight into a rubber band.

A dinner tray had appeared in the room. Canned chile, a bag of fritos and an ice-cold bucket of beer beckoned from the tray. It may have come out of cans and cellophane bags but since it was the first real meal in two days that hardly mattered.

He was ready to dig in when a knock sounded. He opened the door to find Mattie standing in the gangway in a heavy terrycloth robe, a towel around her head. She held a dinner tray.

"Can I join you?" she asked.

"Sure," he said. He let her in and rearranged the small table to make room for her tray. "Do you want a drink?"

She nodded.

Gene filled a second tumbler with whiskey and ice, and handed it to her. She took a few sips in silence.

"I came down here to apologize. I haven't been completely fair with you," she said.

He wasn't sure what she meant, but said, "Okay."

"What are you going to do when we get back home?" she asked.

"Back to bartending, I guess. Soon as I find a job."

"If you ever want to get back on the water, I'm sure Patcher could use you." She pushed the tray away untouched and put down the drink. They sat in awkward silence for a few moments until she stood up, saying, "I guess I'd better get back to Dee."

It was now or never. Gene went straight to her and put his arms around her. He bent to kiss her. His lips touched hers, and he felt her melt into him, lips open, a fire inside that had been burning for a long time. Neither backed away, and the kiss became an exploration, until it reached the place where each small brush of flesh against flesh only heightened the hunger. In the deepness of the kiss, one of seemingly interminable length, the line between bliss and yearning vanished, and there seemed to be no stopping.

The boat lurched as it hit a wave, knocking them off balance. Gene grabbed her tight around the waist and her arms flew up around his neck as naturally as if they'd been together a thousand times before. Gene felt her melt into him, her lips finding his again as her fingers traced down his neck, leaving a trail of heat in their wake, like the whiskey that had warmed his belly, only much better. The kiss was interrupted by a loud banging at the door.

Storm's voice came through the door. "Key West is 30 minutes off, kids. We need you topside."

They disentangled themselves and Mattie excused herself. Gene composed himself and made his way to the main deck. As they pulled into the dock at the Key West Charter Boat Marina, the high noon sun beat down fiercely from straight overhead. The white rays reflecting off the water were bright enough to blind a person.

A small cluster of people were waiting at the marina as the boat pulled into the slip. Most were in uniform. Storm's people, Gene assumed, but one man, neatly dressed in civilian clothes, stood out, his hair a shade too long to be military. His nicely pressed tan slacks, a polo shirt and a $100 pair of Docksiders looked like they'd just been taken out of the box. He looked to Gene like one of those congressional staffers back in Washington who used to show up in his Pentagon office on occasion trying to appear inconspicuous and harmless, like he was just one of the guys, when everyone knew he was there for all the wrong reasons.

Diamanda emerged from below decks as Storm and his crew finished tying up the SportFisher.

Mattie came out then, blinking in the bright sunshine. She put on her sunglasses, took one look at the pleasant-looking man on the dock and visibly shrank back from the rail.

"What's wrong?" Gene asked.

"It's Sam," said Diamanda, answering for her. Sam had spotted them and was now waving as though his life depended on it. "It looks like he decided to surprise her. The guy's got a great sense of timing."

Mattie raised her hand to wave back, a smile frozen on her face. But her expression was not one that Gene would have been pleased to find on a woman he'd decided to surprise.

As soon as the boat was tied up, Mattie made her way down to the dock. Sam Harbor threw his arms around her and they embraced, oblivious to the commotion around them. Diamanda took her time going down the gangplank, saying slow good-byes to the captain and the crew, inviting them to come by sometime for a reading on the house. Gene followed her in silence.

On the dock, she took Gene by the arm and steered him away from Sam and Mattie and their ongoing reunion.

He tried unsuccessfully not to stare at Sam Harbor ushering her towards a white convertible, the two of them deeply immersed in conversation.

Mattie waved in their direction.

"Sam will take her back to the Casa Marina, where he undoubtedly has booked a suite," Diamanda said. "Mattie can recover from the trip with room service, massage on the beach, anything she wants. He's got money, you know. But it's not particularly good for her."

Sam Harbor's car sped out of the parking lot and Mattie was gone.

"Come by the house. I want to pay to you," Diamanda said, still holding onto his arm.

"Forget it, forget it. You don't owe me a thing. I'm going home."

"Don't worry too much about Sam. This isn't over yet, Gene."

"Who said anything about Sam? I need to get some sleep," he replied.

"We'll talk about this tomorrow," Diamanda said, kissing him on the cheek, then headed off. Gene decided to walk the short distance home and started across the parking lot towards Palm Avenue. Then he heard a voice call out, "Gene, not so fast."

Gene turned to see Storm jogging in his direction. He threw an arm around Gene's shoulders. "Nice going, Skunk. You found the killer for us. But this little mission isn't over yet. We've got to talk."

"I'm tired, I'm going home," Gene said.

"You owe me a Mojito. Didn't I just save your ass?"

"I got to get some shut eye. Maybe tomorrow."

"A quick pop, that's all. It'll help you get to sleep in the middle of the day."

"Oh hell, why not?" Gene said. If nothing else, he could use a drink to wash the taste of Mattie Gold out of his mouth.

Storm took him over to Finnegan's Wake, the Irish place on Grinnell, just a few blocks from the marina. Inside they found a quiet table in the corner and ordered two pints of Guiness.

The beer came and Storm finished off half his in a single swallow. He licked his lips and leaned forward, a familiar glint in his eye. "Now about that Mojito you owe me. I want to drink it in Havana."

"You had your chance. I hear they make a great Mojito over at Pepe's."

"I mean it. Cuba Libre. Let's go back."

"I didn't have such a great time last time I went. So I think I'll pass. What in the hell would you want to go back there for, Storm?"

"You think we went to all that trouble just to bring you home? I was happy to help you out buddy, but the mission was to check out the dolphin training camp there. Now we intend to do something about it. We've found our killer."

"Why don't you just let that dolphin be? Don't you think he's in enough trouble with the Cubans taking care of him? Besides, nobody's been killed in two or three days. Let it blow over. Hell, if you got to lose an admiral, at least it was Loring."

"That's just the point. What are those Cubans teaching that dolphin to do? Recce time, Skunk," Storm said. "Waitress, bring us two more beers."

"Every time you buy me a beer, I get into trouble. I'm not going drinking with you anymore. It's too dangerous. And I'm sure as hell not going back to Cuba with you."

Storm was rolling a cardboard beer coaster back and forth under his forefinger. He looked at Gene, his voice low and calm. "Loring's buddies want revenge. The brass are hot for another go at him. And a little recon of what Fidel's boys are up to over there wouldn't be so bad either, with the defense appropriations bill coming up before a whole slew of committees in Congress in the next few weeks. I want you to help me net that critter. We'll treat you as a consultant, give you a per diem. From an operations standpoint, you'll be a full member of the team."

Gene shook his head. Going back to Cuba was definitely not a good idea. "Any chance I can talk you out of this?"

The waitress delivered two more pints and Storm winked at her.

Gene cupped his hands around the mug and stared at the white foam on top as if the froth were tea leaves that might tell him where to go from here. Storm, meanwhile, continued to pitch him.

"Extraction is the operative word." Storm's eyes were bright as a schoolboy on the first day of summer break. "The research weenies are going to want to study him. What a prize! How in the hell did the Cubans actually get him to come over here and terrorize the coast? Is it possible that they succeeded where our finest people failed? Thirty years and a couple of hundred million dollars and we haven't been able to teach a dolphin to execute a hit. And here Fidel's got himself a swimming strike force. You bet the intel boys are interested. We've gotta find out how they did it. Plus, we'll make sure he doesn't strike again."

Gene remembered what Mattie said last night under the stars. She'd wanted to bring the dolphin home too. Storm and Mattie couldn't have been more different but they both wanted the same thing.

Finally Gene interrupted. "You want to bring him back then, that's it?"

Storm nodded.

"Then you'll let it go? Retire him into a lagoon on Fleming Key?"

Another nod. For once, maybe Gene should do something for no other reason than his own. Gene finished his beer.

"If I say yes, I'm not going to be your damned apprentice. I want something out of it besides a paycheck."

The waitress came over and Storm ordered a third round of beers. "Honey, bring us a couple of corned beef sandwiches, would you?" He winked at Gene. "Whatever you say, Skunk. Just name it, it's yours."

"I want to be the handler for the dolphin."

"Fine."

"Not just when we grab him. Afterwards too," Gene said. Maybe it was time to make amends for all those years in San Diego.

"After?"

"Yeah, consider it my consulting fee," he said.

"Done," Storm said. "We leave in 48 hours. Better get some shut-eye."

Chapter 34

Gene took a deep breath and tasted cold, dry air coming through the rubber mouthpiece that was attached by a thick black hose to its LAR V rebreather. He was in open ocean, about twenty feet beneath the surface two miles out and swimming toward Cuba in the dark. Visibility was limited to a soft orange glow from the control panels of his gear. Storm was an arm's length to his left, marked only by a little green chem stick.

The LAR Vs, high-tech diving toys borrowed from Trumbo Annex, had been provided by Storm, who, true to his word, mobilized his best men and newest equipment for the operation. Even more impressive than the rebreather was the big underwater bus, officially known as a Swimmer Delivery Vehicle or SDV, that Storm had somehow conned the Navy into providing for the ride from the support ship to their drop off point. Six other divers were still on the SDV, being ferried over to the underwater pyramid, where they would dive down to investigate. Storm acted like he didn't believe Gene about the big structure but he'd sent a team out to take a look anyway.

But Gene knew that what the military really wanted was the dolphin. The pyramid was only a footnote.

The SDV had been so dark inside that Gene could barely make out Storm's fingers motioning at him to get ready to head out. He followed Storm silently through a hatch that was barely large enough for two men loaded with every imaginable piece of gear to squeeze through. Inside the bus Gene had felt protected, but now with nothing but water below and stars overhead, he felt small and insignificant.

He ascended, surfacing into midnight darkness broken by the light of a waning moon. A few seconds later, Storm's black hood popped up and they floated together for the minute it took to get a reading from the GPS satellites overhead on the navigation receivers on their wrists. Gene held the navigation instruments level on the surface. When the receiver locked on to three satellites, it automatically gave him their position and he calculated the angle that would point them directly at the dolphin base in Cuba.

"Two-six-four. Range two miles," Storm read out after performing the same calculation with his own equipment. His black wetsuit and the black paint smeared on his face obscured all but the whites of his eyes. When he smiled, pearly white teeth glimmered in the faint light but other than the grin, Storm was invisible.

"Roger that," Gene replied.

Even this far out, they would keep conversation to a bare minimum. Sinking back underwater, they mounted two underwater scooters and prepared for another ride all the way to shore. Gene flipped a switch to get the small electric motor on his scooter humming. Storm blinked a small red light on his scooter three times, the signal that all was fine and they should go. Gene flipped the switch into the drive position and the scooter carried him forward. Now it was just a matter of keeping the underwater bike on the correct heading.

Twenty minutes later, they stopped and abandoned the scooters on the bottom. They'd leave the scooters behind when they were through but not the electronics, which they snapped off and took with them. The most the Cubans would get, if they found them at all, was some scrap metal.

Gene surfaced again. They had come to shore right on target, hopefully out of range of the Cuban's rusty Russian-made machine guns. On shore he could see the silhouette of the squat two-story buildings where he'd been held with Mattie and Diamanda and the spot where Paradise Diver had been tied a few days before. The dock was deserted. No sentries were in sight and only a few ragged looking small boats were tied to the dock, plus the long sleek cigarette boat that was Díaz' pride and joy. Gene used a compass to take a heading the old-fashioned way directly toward the pens.

Then they sank back into the dark water. The moonlight was reflected by large shapes on the bottom but he couldn't tell whether they were boulders or large pieces of debris.

He kicked to reach the shallow water, the muscles in his legs burning and twitching as he slowed down, his legs tiring from the long swim. He hadn't worked so hard in years.

When his navigation board told him the water was only 15 feet deep, Gene crashed headfirst into an underwater chain link fence, bouncing back, his head stinging. Storm had also stopped. He fumbled in his bag to find a small flashlight. Gene signaled him to wait on the bottom, then surfaced for another look around. He left Storm opening the black bag and unpacking wire cutters and other tools for cutting through the chain link fence.

On the surface, Gene got his first good look at the dolphin training camp since their midnight departure two days earlier. The place was quiet as a cemetery at midnight. Too quiet. Inside the pens, a few dorsal fins circled. He counted six dolphins. The mission only called for grabbing one but now it occurred to him that it might not be a bad idea to set the others loose as well.

Gene pulled a waterproof infrared camera out of a zippered pocket and shot a few frames of the facility. Then he sank back to the bottom, where Storm was hard at work. The plan was to cut through the fencing until they got to the big gray dolphin. Then they'd hold a big net over the hole until the dolphin swam through it. They'd corral the animal in their net like a couple of underwater cowboys herding a cow. On the blackboard back at Trumbo Annex, at least, it had worked like a charm.

Storm cut a hole through the first fence, and the two men swam though to the next layer of fencing. Storm kept busy with the wire cutters while Gene surfaced to try to look for their target again. He raised his head quietly and watched the dorsal fins circling. The dock was still silent.

Then Gene spotted the big red cigarette boat that Díaz was so fond of and swam to it. He had a special treat for the good colonel. From a zippered pocket, he removed a small plastic bottle that he had filled with honey, unscrewed the silver-plated cap of the fuel tank, and turned the bottle upside down to drain into the tank.

"Have a sweet ride, colonel," Gene said, patting the boat.

As he swam back past the pens, the piercing shriek of an excited dolphin about 15 feet away stopped him. It was the big gray dolphin, chattering in an uncanny imitation of a human voice. The dolphin swam closer and turned his head to the side as if he wanted to get a better look at Gene. It was the same dolphin from the pyramid, Gene was certain.

"Sshh, sshh, quiet," Gene said, trying to calm him but it was too late. Voices rang out in Spanish, and a minute later, men on the dock turned a bright light toward the big dolphin's pen.

"All right, big guy. It's checkout time," Gene said, ducking back down, hoping that they hadn't noticed the black lump of a human head sticking out of the water. If the men understood the dolphin's alarm, there'd be trouble and fast.

Storm had almost finished cutting into the pen. Gene picked up another pair of wire cutters and hurried to the next fence, the last barrier to the big dolphin. He snipped away until it too had a large hole. Several dolphins waited in the murky water a few feet away, waiting and watching. He only hoped they'd be smart enough to leave once the big gray was gone. Their pen was open now. He swam back to Storm.

The men positioned themselves and the net around the hole in the fence and waited. On the other side, the dolphin hovered, watching them intently.

Then he began to move. The dolphin came toward them, through the opening, and they tightened the net, trapping him. Gene heard a boat motor running in the distance. The red speedboat. He wondered how long it would take for the honey to seep into the engine. And then they began to move, hanging onto the net, which was being pulled by the dolphin.

Gene clung to the net and tried to relax. He was hot and sweaty under the wetsuit. He checked his breathing, concentrating on keeping it steady, checking his gauges to make sure the air was flowing correctly. The dolphin was like a huge locomotive pulling the divers out to sea. They had planned on pulling him, stunning him, floating him, and getting him out into the open sea by brute force. In hindsight, Gene would realize that their plan had been fatally and ridiculously flawed -- to think that they could manhandle a 600-pound dolphin to sea while being pursued by angry, armed Cubans. But now the dolphin had taken over.

Gene tried to read his navigation panel and depth gauge but the rush of water kept him from holding his arm up in front of his face. They were headed out to the open ocean, and for the next few minutes, he was going to have to trust the dolphin.

When the sound of the pursuing boat faded, Gene thanked the heavens for honey and switched on a button on the side of the rebreather to activate a tracking beacon. Storm's men would find them with the help of the small electronic pulse generated by the beacon.

After a while, the dolphin slowed down and Gene wondered if the big creature was tiring. In the moonlight, Gene saw the glint of light on silver and knew that Storm had the small stun rod out. His gloved finger flicked the cap off and the tip pressed against the dolphin's flesh. The dolphin stopped moving and became very docile.

As Storm held the dolphin, Gene set up the lift bags. They had only a few minutes to float the dolphin before the animal would go limp and drag them all to the bottom. Two bright yellow lift bags and a harness strapped beneath the dolphin would float him on the surface until help arrived.

Gene shot air into the first lift bag with his regulator until the bag floated nicely above him. He repeated the procedure with the second bag, shifting back and forth, pumping more air into four bags until the net supported the animal's weight like a baby in a cradle. Finally four bags hovered above them like balloons. Another few blasts of air and the doped up dolphin rose to the surface, graceful as a saint ascending into heaven.

Gene clung to the floating dolphin and they surfaced together. He felt invigorated. Mission accomplished. It wasn't supposed to be this good, Gene thought, remembering why he'd quit in the first place. On the surface, he could hear Storm moving around on the other side of the dolphin.

Gene shifted the dolphin's weight around to keep his blowhole above the water line, making sure the creature got air. He patted the dolphin's side. "After all the trouble we went to, old buddy, don't drown on us now," Gene said quietly. He didn't notice Storm next to him in the dark until he grinned.

"You calling him buddy now?" Storm said. "You know one of the worst things a guy can do is get emotionally attached to a hostage."

They bobbed up and down, small waves slapping them in the face every few seconds.

"Hostage? Where'd that come from?" Gene asked.

They could hear a motor running then. A few minutes later, the dark hull of the SDV popped up nearby. Six frogmen swam over and took the floats, and then the sleeping dolphin out of Gene's hands.

Gene reached out to give the dolphin a final pat before the frogmen took him, then kicked his way to the hatch.

Chapter 35

Gene stood on the dock at Trumbo Annex watching the big gray circle in the old dolphin pen. Diamonda and Mattie were in the water splashing around in their swimsuits and snorkeling equipment. Gene kept an eye on the dorsal fin each time it got close to the women but there was nothing to worry about. The dolphin was behaving like a puppy that had been rescued from the pound.

The women took turns letting him tow them in circles around the pen. Mattie was holding his fin, tucking her body close to the dolphin. They sped through the water like a single being. She let go, and then lifted her head and waved at Gene.

"Want a break?" Gene yelled.

"Five more minutes," she answered, then dove down, mermaid woman, beneath the surface.

An armed guard stood a hundred feet away, courtesy of Storm. The guard had a machine gun in his hands and a sidearm strapped to his belt. He'd been acting jumpy all morning. Gene hoped the guard wouldn't be crazy enough to think the gun was for anything other than show. The thought crossed his mind more than once that Storm might have offered some kind of bounty on a dolphin that had allegedly killed an admiral.

The dolphin towed Diamanda over to the dock. She let go and climbed up the ladder and out of the water. "The dolphins must be set free," she declared as she came over to Gene, dripping water in all directions. "It's very clear."

"That's what's coming through, huh?" He laughed. "I'm glad the com lines are open."

Gene tugged the wetsuit over his swimsuit. Today he planned to try out a few commands that U.S. dolphin trainers used to see if they would provoke a response from the big gray. Gene still wasn't sure how this particular dolphin had become so aggressive. Had the Cubans trained the creature, or had he somehow slipped out of the U.S. milino better than leaving him in the hands of the Cubans. Gene watched him and knew, just as clearly as Diamanda had seemed to know, that the dolphin would not live much longer in captivity.

Gene checked his air gauge. 500 psi. He was about to ascend when he sensed a fast motion behind him. He turned to see the dolphin coming again, hard and fast as a torpedo. This time the creature did not veer. He struck Gene in the midsection, knocking his regulator out of his mouth. Gene was out of breath now, flailing around trying to get his hands on his air hose, trying not to inhale, but the hunger for air was too much, and without intending to, he sucked in a mouthful of salty warm seawater. As he choked, a vision of dolphins, hundreds of them, in small cages or floating dead on the surface, came to him.

Gene reached the surface and inflated his vest. He bobbed, sputtering and trying to catch his breath.

Storm's voice came from the dock. "Having fun down there?"

Up here, no one had seen the attack.

"Oh yeah, he's in a playful mood today," Gene answered.

Mattie's voice came back, asking Storm, "Do you think we can open the pen for a while tomorrow, let him do some swimming out in the harbor?"

"You'll have to ask the bossman," Storm said, gesturing at Gene. Then he turned to Gene. "Skunk, can I see you a minute in my office?"

The office turned out to be a the closest pine tree. Gene got out of the lagoon, took off his gear and followed Storm.

"We've got to make a few changes around here," Storm looked down, avoiding Gene's eyes. "I know you wanted more time with that dolphin but we've got to turn the project over to the scientists sooner than I thought. You'll have to tell those two that they can't come back. This is it. Today's the last day."

"Wait a minute," Gene said. "When I agreed to help you, the deal was that you were going to let us work with the dolphin. You gave me your word."

"And I kept it. It's just coming to an end a little sooner than planned." Storm's voice took on an official "I'm in command here" tone. "And I never promised you could keep bringing civilians onto the base. My ass will be in a sling if word gets out that I let your girlfriends swim with the killer dolphin. This is supposed to be classified."

"They aren't my girlfriends," Gene replied. "Give me a little more credit than that. They aren't the enemy, neither is the dolphin. You can't prove he killed those people anyway. Nobody knows for sure."

"I don't need proof," Storm said. "The Navy wants an end to this, pronto. The scientists are going to study his brain instead of his behavior. That's the new plan."

"What's that supposed to mean, study his brain?"

"He's the one, Gene. You know it as well as I do. All your instincts ought to be screaming that this is the one. We got him. Thank God he was one of theirs. We're going to classify your report as top secret, but if it does leak out and something tells me it will, at least we can blame this one on Castro and the Russians."

"What do you mean, study his brain? You're flying him out to San Diego?"

"Nothing quite so complicated, Rock. More like a harvesting date in two days."

"Harvest?" A sick feeling rose up in Gene. They were going to slice the dolphin up like a laboratory rat. "You can't."

"Oh yes we can. Government's got the right to harvest up to 50 dolphins a year for research. They've got no constitutional protection. You know that." Storm's expression softened. "Look Gene, I got nothing against the dolphin. There's just got to be an end to this."

Gene's blood turned to ice. "You are making a big mistake."

"I get your point, Gene. He's a warrior like the rest of us. But, hell, he never should have killed the admiral. He wrote his own death warrant with that little stunt."

Gene looked at the dolphin swimming in the pen. Open water beyond stretched out toward Boca Grande and the Dry Tortugas. Only a few pleasure boats were visible in the distance. He was only one small fence away from freedom.

Storm was blithering on about patriotism and national security, rather mindlessly, Gene thought.

"We've got to certify that the threat to human safety has been eliminated. Otherwise the community and the Navy are in danger. All that's going to lead to is more dolphins killed." Storm took a deep breath. "How many times did they tell you not to let your emotions get in the way, Skunk?"

"At least I'm not a damn hypocrite. First you manipulate me into getting involved, then all of a sudden, I start caring about something other than myself, I'm some kind of bleeding heart."

"Skunk, if you really want to save the dolphins, why don't you go get a job up at the refuge with Johnnie Reb?"

At this moment, Gene only cared about one particular dolphin.

Storm shifted his weight around impatiently and looked out in the distance, as if Gene would come to his senses given sufficient time. "It's only one lousy dolphin," he said. "There's a thousand more out there, just like him."

Gene thought about the wild dolphins. How many were left? Thousands, maybe hundreds of thousands.

Gene heard Diamanda's words echo in his mind—'he's a messenger'.

"Yeah, but this one is special. Let me talk to whoever made this half-assed decision. If they hear what is really going on over in Cuba, maybe they'll give me a little more time to work with him," Gene said.

"Sorry, buddy. The decision's been made, the orders signed. There's nothing you can do."

"What about the pyramid, Storm?"

Storm looked mystified.

"You had six guys videotaping it while we were off grabbing the dolphin."

"Gene, I honestly have no idea what you're talking about." He crossed his arms over his chest. "Those women are filling your head with all kinds of nonsense. These new age gals must be getting to you, huh, pal? They're a little old for my tastes, but what the hell."

"Knock it off, Storm," Gene said. "I did the dive myself. There's a big, clear, perfectly shaped pyramid off the shore of Cuba at a depth of 250 feet. It's too big for you guys not to know about it."

"That's sounds downright crazy," Storm said. "Nothing's down there. Video came out blank. The guys didn't see a thing except black water."

"I saw it with my own eyes." Gene said. "Touched it."

"Makes a nice yarn, Skunk, but you tell anybody, they're going to think you're nuts. 'Course look at where you're living. Key West! The whole island might as well be an insane asylum."

Gene gave up. Storm wasn't going to listen.

Storm's expression was dead serious. "My advice to you, friend, is to forget about that pyramid. Stirring up trouble for the Navy is never good for a man's health."

"Are you threatening me?"

"Come on, Gene. Just forget about it."

Gene crossed his arms defiantly over his chest. He could be just as pigheaded as Storm. "Let's say I do. Let's say I just forget about you and the mission, and everything I saw this week."

Storm smiled. "That's my man. There's nothing you can do anyway. Decisions been made. I'll call you later. We'll grab a beer, and I'll keep you posted on the dolphin."

tary dolphin program?

He was all suited up now, scuba gear on his back. He put his regulator into his mouth and stepped off the dock into the water. He sank beneath the surface momentarily, then popped back up and swam over to Mattie.

"Your boyfriend still in town?" he asked.

"He left this morning," she said.

"I never got a chance to meet him," he said.

"Well, it was time for him to go," she said. She got quiet for a minute, then added, "We broke up."

Then she turned and swam toward the ladder, before Gene could ask what happened.

He deflated his buoyancy vest and descended to the bottom where he swam the perimeter of the pen. The gray kept his distance. From beneath the surface, Gene and the dolphin followed Mattie's progress toward the ladder. She held the rails and they watched her pull off her fins and toss them onto the dock, then disappear up the ladder.

Gene moved to the center of the pen, while the dolphin stayed along the outer fence. His sonar was more effective than the dark little dolphin eyes. Gene hadn't planned any drills or brought any dead fish or other rewards. He was just going to see what happened when the dolphin encountered a military diver in full gear. Just how aggressive would he get?

They kept a good distance apart at first, and then the dolphin began to swim faster, much faster than when he played with the women, his circles tightening with each revolution. Gene was reminded of a shark circling a wounded fish.

Then, before Gene had time to react, the game turned and the dolphin came at him, mean and aggressive. Three times it happened. On each approach, the dolphin veered off at the final moment. Gene turned to face him each time, tensed his muscles, and waited for the blow that didn't come. The pattern reminded Gene of the Native American warriors who were supposed to have counted coup on their opponents by simply touching them in battle, without killing or drawing blood. On the fourth pass, the dolphin careened around Gene and slammed into the metal fencing.

And then the dolphin went into a frenzy, hitting the fence again and again until his skin was streaked green and brown from algae and rust. As Gene watched the dolphin ram the fence, he realized that the women were right. This dolphin had to be set free. Turning him over to the U.S. government to be poked and prodded like a laboratory rat was

Gene walked away. This time nobody was asking his help or his permission. This time, he was just being asked to step aside and take a seat on the sidelines. The very thing he'd wanted all along, and now he had it. The problem was that it wasn't going to work.

Chapter 36

Mattie headed Paradise Diver through Cow Key channel to the open water. The sun had begun to drop toward the horizon to the west. Darkness remained a few hours off but already the sky was peach and blue, like looking through one of those tiny glass kaleidoscopes the artists sold at Mallory Pier.

Gene stood close to her as she held the wheel, a breeze gently ruffling his hair. The air was so warm that clothes, as usual down here, were a formality rather than a necessity. They wore shorts, T-shirts and Teva sandals, looking like any casual boaters out for a sunset cruise.

The boat turned and ran along the shore. To their right was the beach and the long sidewalk than ran for a mile along the island's tiny airport. A small turboprop buzzed overhead as it landed, its noisy engine drowning out all other sound. Then they passed the big, boxy hotels lining Smathers Beach, the famous and expensive Casa Marina, a sprinkling of big homes, then the gay resort Atlantic Shores with its clothing optional sundeck.

The boat rounded the southeast end of the island where Ft. Zachary Taylor stretched, its rocky beach shaded by tall Australian pines swaying in the gentle wind. Finally, they motored past the docks of the old seaport to the end of the island where the Navy base began.

Mattie didn't talk. The quiet was a gift. He liked the way she didn't fill the air with chatter like other people did. He wouldn't let himself think about the danger he was putting her into. They could be shot or arrested, he supposed, but he needed her, and she hadn't hesitated a moment when he told her what he aimed to do tonight.

Since the kiss on the Sport Fisher a few days before, they'd seen each other a half dozen times at the dolphin pen but the kiss was not mentioned. It was as if it had never occured. It was all business between them now.

"Things could get dangerous tonight," he said to her. "Can you think of any angle we haven't covered?"

Gene and Mattie had gone over their plan again and again, trying to think of as many unforeseen circumstances as possible. What if military personnel were in the pen with the dolphin, or what if he had been moved? What if the dolphin refused to follow them out once they set him free? Gene didn't have the net or the tranquilizers this time, just a couple of pairs of wire cutters. Diamanda had told them to go ahead and just cut the fence, that the dolphin would know what to do, and Gene believed her.

"It's going to be fine." Mattie's voice was calm and confident. "Go get the gear ready, SEAL, before it's too dark for your old eyes to see."

He headed toward the stern. This time they'd use high tech Prism rebreathers borrowed from the shop instead of the old LAR Vs from the Army diving school. The Prisms were small and light and souped up with electronic controls. Gene wasn't sure he liked them any better than the rugged old LARs workhorses. Too many things could go wrong when the electronics went underwater.

He turned the controls on and each Prism's panel lit up with an orange glow. He ran through a check and the computers seemed to be working fine. Weights, masks and fins were lined up, ready. The last few days of diving had given him his old confidence back. The equipment once again seemed like an extension of his body instead of a fifth limb.

Gene filled the mesh gear bags with two pairs of heavy duty wire cutters, four flashlights, extra compasses, spare dive computers, waterproof flares and an emergency transmitter in a Plexiglas canister. He checked the power and electronics on the underwater scooter, which rested in its saddle in the middle of the boat. The scooter was silver and shaped like a torpedo. It had a small propeller inside a cage on one end and little chrome handles for the rider on the other.

Then Gene came back to Mattie at the helm. He climbed up onto the bow to smooth the anchor line, checking for any stray knots, and waited for her signal. When she waved, he let the anchor fall and the line grew taut. He tugged at it to check that it was securely lodged in the sand.

By the time he got to the stern Mattie was suiting up. She wasted no time at this task, or any others, which maybe explained how she'd gotten engaged to Sam Harbor in the first place. That subject was just as taboo as the kiss. Maybe when this was all over, he would ask her what happened.

They had more important things to concentrate on for the time being. He got out the night vision goggles and scanned the shore. The

Navy base was quiet. Unless you counted the occasional raft full of Cuban balseros, nothing much happened out here. Fishing boats and sailboats often spent the night on the moorings just offshore from the base. The presence of an odd dive boat anchored offshore for a few hours wasn't likely to set off any alarms.

In silence, Gene smeared waterproof black paint on his face. Then he went to work on her, applying black paint to her forehead, cheeks, nose and chin until he had carefully covered all the visible white patches of skin.

"How do I look?" she asked, grimacing in an imitation of a fierce warrior.

"Like the angel of death," he replied, pulling on his wetsuit and lifting the Prism onto his back. It fit like a large backpack, encasing his torso like high tech armor. Mattie stepped off the side of the boat into the water. Gene handed the scooter down to her and jumped in.

Now the waves were small and moving around was easy, but the weather forecast called for a front to blow in later and seas to pick up to four to six feet. Gene wanted to get going, to get this thing done and be back on the boat before the rough seas arrived. He pulled the regulator out of his mouth to take a final breath of Mother Nature's finest air before descending. They treaded water face-to-face.

"Good luck, captain," he said, "I'll either buy you a beer at The Frog tonight, or see you in Ft. Leavenworth."

She came closer, holding out a small leather pouch. "Here," she said, handing it to Gene. "I almost forgot. Diamanda sent it."

Gene gripped the little sack. "What's in here? Feels like stones."

"It's a medicine bag. Just stick it in your pocket. For protection."

He shrugged and tucked it away. "Why not? We can use all the help we can get."

Gene took a compass heading, aiming directly for the mouth of the little lagoon where the big gray waited in the pen. They descended through the dark water to the bottom where they stopped to adjust their buoyancy until they floated a few feet above the sand. Now she was just a faint green glow in the dark.

She got on the scooter, mounting it like a kid on a sled, lying down with her face and hands close to the controls. They had only one so Mattie drove, and Gene hung on. As she took off, he balanced his body against hers, legs touching, only the clumsy rebreathers separating them. He was thankful for the barrier, not wanting the distraction that would have come from being pressed up so close to her.

When they got close to shore, Gene surfaced for a look around while Mattie attached a small white strobe light to the scooter. The flash would help them find it for the ride back to the boat.

They had navigated well and when they surfaced, they were within a few yards of the dolphin pen. A guard slouched on the dock, his weapon slack at his side, lulled into inattentiveness by the heat or the monotony of guarding a single dolphin. In the water, a single dorsal fin slowly circled. The dolphin was waiting for them.

He sank back to the bottom. He touched Mattie's hand and pointed to the fence that caged the dolphin. The light reflecting from shore was enough to let them see in the dark water. Gene took the metal shears out of the bag. If he never cut another dolphin out of a pen as long as he lived, that would be all right with him, as long as it worked this time. As his eyes adjusted to the dark, he made out the dolphin on the other side of the chain link watching him.

Mattie picked up the second pair of wire cutters. Working together, they cut a sizable hole in the fence in a few minutes. As the fence fell away, the gray slipped through, coming straight to Mattie, nuzzling her affectionately, letting her stroke his head. Gene could almost feel her happiness around them like a bubble. She reached out to touch his arm. Time to go.

They kicked away from the pen until they spotted the white flash of the scooter's strobe. Mattie flipped the switch to turn on the motor, but nothing happened. Gene floated next to her, listening to the clicks as she switched the motor off and on with no response. She turned, a thumb extended upward.

At the surface, they conferred in whispers. "Something's wrong," she said. "The motor gets sand in it sometimes."

"Can you fix it out here?"

"I don't think so."

The dolphin popped up next to her and began to chatter.

"Hush," she said.

He stuck his snout back in the water and brushed against Mattie, inviting her to take his fin and go for a ride.

"Let's leave it. We need to get out of here before they realize the dolphin's gone," said Gene. "I'll swim, you take the fin."

"Oh no, I'm not leaving you behind," she protested.

"I'll be right behind you," he said, brushing his fingers against her lips to silence any more argument. He wanted her gone. "Wait for me on the boat. If I'm not there in an hour, go back to the dive shop and wait for my call. The tide is coming in. I may have to swim for shore."

"I can't leave you," she said. "If they catch you here," she stopped, not finishing the sentence.

"I'll think of something clever to tell them," he said, "after all, Storm owes me one. Go. There's no reason for both of us to be stuck."

"You wouldn't leave me in Cuba. I'm not going to leave you here." The water was getting choppier by the moment.

"Mattie," he said, "you can't leave your boat out there now. They'll be looking for whoever did this in no time. Don't argue."

The dolphin nudged her with his snout. Mattie treaded water and pleaded with him, "Gene, you have to come back, you have to."

Once more the dolphin offered his fin and this time Mattie took it, disappearing into the blackness without another word.

Gene began the long underwater swim in the direction of the boat. He'd only gone a few hundred yards when the orange lights on his rebreather blinked off and on. A malfunction or a false reading. Something was wrong. He played with the controls, but the orange warning light continued to flash. The air might be fine, but it could just as easily go toxic on him, and he wouldn't know until it was too late. He was going to have to swim on the surface to breathe. He kicked and rose until his head was above water.

The waves had picked up during the last half hour so that every couple of feet Gene rose up and then fell on towering walls of water so high they nearly blocked the sky. Each time he hit a crest, he'd rise ten feet on a ridge of water, which allowed him to get a very disheartening glimpse of shore. Although he was swimming as hard as he could, he was making no progress away from the land. He thought about dumping the Prism to make it easier to swim but the rebreather was worth a few grand, plus he didn't want to leave more evidence of their visit behind. Waves slapped him in the face in fast succession, and he began to swallow water.

His legs ached and his calf muscles formed tight little knots. He reached down to pull at his fins, holding his breath. A nauseous, seasick feeling hit him as he tried to remove the knifelike cramps from his tendons. He gave up trying to swim or stretch and just floated in the water face down, waiting for his locked muscles to let go. Gene considered swimming to shore, letting the waves push him into the mangroves that were on the edge of the base. He'd probably end up on the front lawn of the base commander.

How would he explain landing there, a commercial rebreather on his back, the Navy's prize dolphin missing? No matter what he'd told Mattie, he knew Storm wouldn't believe him or forgive him for freeing the dolphin if he were caught. There was only one way to go.

He doubled his efforts to fight the sea until a giant wave washed over him, burying him. Then water filled Gene's lungs, dragging him beneath the surface. He kicked hard but the water was like a weight holding him down. He kicked harder but moved no closer to the surface. He needed to breathe, with every fiber of his being wanting to inhale, but knew that if he did, his lungs would only fill with water. He kicked and kicked but rose no closer to the surface, and then he looked up and down and it all looked the same. When he realized he no longer knew which direction the surface was in, he knew he was going to drown.

Was this it, he wondered? Life ends as easily as it begins with no control over either end of the process? His legs were not responding now, the kicking slower, the surrender started, and then something brushed against him in the water. Gene thrashed a bit, beyond panic, wondering if it was a shark that had smelled his fear, or a piece of debris. The thing brushed his leg again, and then he saw a familiar scarred fin. Gene reached out and the fin slipped into his hand, pulling him up smoothly as an elevator to the surface.

He broke through the wall of water, gasping, greedy for air, clinging to the dolphin. The dolphin's tiny eye was black and shiny as a bottle of ink as it looked back at him. In it, Gene saw his own reflection: a dark hooded figure with eyes magnified by goggles, ominous and unnatural.

Then Gene's fingers closed around the ridge of the dorsal fin again and the dolphin moved through the water, pulling Gene along behind, keeping him at the surface where he could breathe.

In the distance was a light, and as it drew nearer, Gene saw it was the boat. Overhead the night sky was filled with stars and the waves lay down as if some kind of dolphin magic had tamed them. A sense of peacefulness filled Gene. There may be trouble tomorrow when Storm discovered what they'd done but things were right in this moment.

He closed his eyes. The water washed over him.

Gene would look back later and realize that this was the moment in his life when he stopped thinking, stopped planning every step in meticulous detail and decided to live or die or take whatever life flung at him next without questioning it.

He wouldn't think about getting back to the boat or to Key West or even about Mattie. Or about what would happen when Storm found the fence cut and dolphin gone. He wouldn't dwell on next week or next month, or having a job, or those unspoken questions about loneliness and what was true about his life. He would be fine. The big gray would survive as well. The dolphin would find an isolated, remote place where he would no longer be hunted.

Gene opened his eyes a few minutes later. The dolphin had brought him a few yards from the boat. He released the fin, and treaded water. The dolphin came up to examine him again at close range with dark little eyes that glistened like mysterious pools of knowledge. Gene reached out to pat his scarred flesh. "Thanks, partner. Safe journey," he said.

The dolphin nudged Gene with his snout. The creature apparently wasn't quite ready to leave.

"Go! Go! You're free," Gene said, waving his arm. "I'll help. It's a promise."

The dolphin nodded, and then arced gracefully into the air and disappeared into the water.

Gene treaded water, thinking about what he'd just promised. All that had happened during the last week had happened as if it was a dream. But half the things he'd done in his life seemed that way. Maybe this dolphin business was no different. An adventure, a dream, a story that he wasn't supposed to tell. Nobody would believe him anyway if he ever did.

He swam to the boat, reached out for the aluminum ladder and pulled himself back onto it, back into reality.

Mattie was waiting, standing there, looking worried as she reached to take his fins and mask out of his hands.

"You okay?" She said, lifting the rebreather off his back.

He nodded. She took his fins, mask and weights and stowed them under the bench.

"Had me worried for a minute there, SEAL." She sat across from him, watching, as if she couldn't quite trust that he was there. When his gear was stowed along the sides of the boat, she sat to remove her wetsuit, wriggling her shoulders and her wrists to get clear of its rubbery grip. Gene leaned back, worn out, and watched her.

When the suit had been peeled down to her waist, she stopped. Gene still hadn't moved, just sat, watching, and thinking how beautiful she was. Her body was long and angular, made even more so by the tight black suit. Her breasts were visible like small round fruit beneath the silkiness of her swimsuit.

He wondered what would happen if he tried to kiss her again, to once more taste the sweetness they'd shared on the way back from Cuba. Had that been just her relief that the ordeal was over? Had it been a mistake?

He moved across the boat to sit next to her. He placed his hands on her shoulders and turned her to face him, and then took her chin in his hand to tilt her face up so he could see her eyes.

Her eyes searched his, and Gene thought of the sphinx who had posed an impossible riddle as a test to be passed before her portals would open. Gene saw his own impenetrable curtain reflected in her, one that he had employed for so long. No one could reach him. Distant, remote, independent—those qualities had served him, and he saw them in her too. The hardness may have been a necessity for survival. But all that didn't amount to much in the end. You could need me, he thought, not daring to say the words aloud.

Gene waited for Mattie to speak, to react, but she was still as a statue. He thought of the dolphin, who had taught him a lesson that all his years in the Navy hadn't. The dolphin's ability to communicate without words—to use instinct, not logic, to know the right thing to do. Following one's own instinct to the end, even when failure or rejection seemed certain.

He did just that, leaning toward Mattie until the silky fabric of swimsuit brushed against his arm. He felt her breath against his cheek. The lightness in his stomach, the numbness of his skin, it was like being in a dream again. He wondered if this was how love felt.

He pressed his lips to hers, tasting the wet, the salt, the texture of velvet. She would have to decide whether the kiss meant nothing or everything. If she pushed away, he would let her escape, to reclaim her chilly professionalism before it was too late.

When he kissed her, she didn't move. Then she closed her eyes, reached her arms up to him. She kissed him back, gently at first, then harder, until his mouth was full of the taste of her. Her hands wrapped around him, her fingers traced his hair back to the small ponytail at the back of his head. Her body arched to him, her hair, still in a braid, tickled his arm. He pulled her in closer and dropped his hands down to her waist, feeling the rubbery wet suit clinging to her hips.

"Can we take this off, captain," he whispered, touching the wetsuit.

She kept her mouth against his, her tongue still exploring as she moved her hands down to pull at the wetsuit. She fumbled and he felt her tremble.

Gene dropped to his knees on the hard fiberglass deck and she leaned back onto the bench, elbows on the gunwales, extending her legs toward him. He gripped the wetsuit firmly with both hands and leaned back until her knees popped out, the rubber rolling down around her ankles. One yank freed the left foot, another the right.

He took her hand and led her to the front of the boat, where life jackets were piled into a soft heap. They lay down and Gene felt as if those orange flotation devices were the sultan's most luxurious pillows. He ran his finger along the edge of her swimsuit, the feel of fabric and flesh raising the hairs on his arm straight into the air. She pulled his face closer and her tongue began to do its magic with him again.

Gene slipped her strap down over her shoulder and then ran his hand inside the suit to her waist, down toward her knees and ankles. Their bodies came together, skin still warm and scratchy with salt from the sea, the texture like some exotic emollient at an extravagant spa.

"Mattie," he said. He wanted to reassure her that this was nothing easy or casual.

"Sshh," she whispered her voice soft now. "Don't talk."

So he stopped trying to use words and simply licked her body slowly, inch by inch, tasting the salt, cleaning it off like a cat might clean its baby. When he paused, she protested, "Don't stop. There will be time to figure it out later."

He smiled and put his tongue back to work, kissing and tasting his way down, down, to her belly button. She stroked his shoulders, then ran her fingers through his hair. Gene placed his hand on her stomach, then moved his fingers down slowly to touch her. Where he touched, she was wet and warm, like a small furnace with a wood fire was locked up inside. She gasped as his hand played against her. Then he lifted his body over hers and they were together, the image of the dolphin swimming, undulating through the water away from them, in Gene's mind. Her warmth surrounded him like the sea must be wrapped around the gray dolphin, so far from them now.

Gene rode the wave of pleasure for a long time, rode the water, rode her body, wondering if he was inside the dolphin's mind purely by imagination or if animal and man had somehow really connected. Could he really tune into the dolphin's thoughts? The dolphin might be his better half, his brother, his fellow warrior. The dolphin had earned respect and allegiance. Then he let his musings go, no more questions, just feeling Mattie, like the dolphin would feel the water as he moved gently against the sea. Finally, a warm flood began at the base of his neck and spread slowly down his chest, to his legs.

Gene trembled, the muscles on his legs tightened all the way to his toes. He heard himself emit a noise, a primal sound like an animal might make during a full moon. He'd always remained silent when he loved a woman before. Then he pushed all the dizzying thoughts from his mind, no longer able to think of sounds or what made sense, to make room for the ecstasy, letting the terror and joy rush through him until he felt electric, wired to the universe, and nothing mattered in the world but the current running between his body and the woman beneath him. Rough, sweet spasms racked his body until he sank into Mattie's beautiful flesh, letting his eyes close, finally able to rest, caught in a place between prayer and surrender.

Chapter 37

The dolphin swam slowly away from the two humans, leaving them safely behind on their boat. He turned south, toward the island of his birth. Although nearly 30 years had passed, he still instinctively knew the direction home.

In a few hours, he passed the crystal pyramid for the last time, but he did not stop. As he picked up speed, he bypassed a pod of dolphins heading the opposite way, back toward the pyramid and the long island close by. He imaged the group with his sonar and recognized their leader as the new guardian of the temple. His part was done; others would now take his place.

The men remained on the island, unable to unlock the temple's secrets despite their weapons and the cunning of the old scientist who helped them. Neither the old man Ruykov, nor his younger adversary, the one called Storm, had learned the truth from the dolphin about the sacred place. The military man and the scientist—so different, yet so alike: always in conflict, always in a struggle for power. That was the human mystery, one that he would never understand.

The dolphin swam on, day turning to night, without stopping. It gave him pleasure to leave the small troubled patch of sea between the two islands in the distance. He was alone for a long time and turned his thoughts to his dolphin family, wondering if he'd meet up with them on his return and live out the days he had left with his own kind. Nothing could be certain; so many dolphins had died. In the years since he'd left, surviving in the water became more difficult each day, the fish fewer in number, the human's nets wider and deeper, and the toxins and oil and garbage in the water everywhere.

As he swam, in the center of his brain, an image of a blue planet appeared, glistening and clean from a distance, but so troubled from up close. He did not know if the world would change. In the old days, the humans and dolphins shared the planet as equals, in harmony, for thousands of years. It seemed that he'd known the red-haired one that long.

The red-haired one stayed behind as well, carrying the flame of hope for the dolphin, for all the dolphins. She would continue the work. She would speak quietly, yet powerfully to her people, and she would be heard by a few humans. It only took a few to make a difference, that he also knew. She was his true ally, his companion, though physically, he knew they would never again be together. There were other ways.

The red-haired one and her friends had proven that a human can possess a large heart, a fiery spirit. As long as some of them could hear and understand, and have the courage to act, there would be hope.

They'd shared the battle for an eternity. She would be there again, the dolphin knew, without knowing the form that she'd take or her purpose the next time. He was wise enough not to seek an answer, to simply swim through the silken blue sea toward his home island, the place where he was born and where his days would end.

The End

Resources

If you want to help the dolphins or learn more about them and the marine environment, the following organizations can help:

Reef Relief
P.O. Box 430
Key West, FL 33040
USA

Reef Relief Environmental Center & Gift Shop
201 William St.
Key West, Fl. 33041
Email at reef@bellsouth.net
www.reefrelief.org
Phone: (305) 294-3100 Fax (305) 293-9515

Purpose: To preserve and protect living coral reef ecosystems through local, regional and international programs.

Marine Mammal Stranding Network
1-800-9Mammal
5001 Avenue U
Suite 105C
Galveston, TX 77551

Maintains a hotline for marine mammal strandings.

Center for Marine Conservation
1725 DeSales St NW
Suite 600
Wash DC 20036
www.cmc-ocean.org
Phone (202) 429-5609 Fax (202) 872-0619

Purpose: Works on a national and international level on ocean issues, endangered species protection, dolphins, turtles.

Wildlife Rescue of the Florida. Keys
PO Box 5449
Key West, Fl. 33040
(305) 294-1441.

Purpose: Wildlife rescue and rehabilitation, including active stranding and nurturing programs for marine mammals in the Lower Florida Keys area.

Acknowledgements

Many thanks to my friends, family and colleagues who lent their support during the years of work on Cetacea. Special gratitude goes to John Foley and Marilynn Foley, my parents, and brother Matt Foley, whose love, encouragement and advice helped bring the book into print.

My friends, teachers and mentors in the water and on land, especially Captain Velora Peacock, DeeVon Quirolo and Captain Victoria Impallomeni. Thanks to Michael Menduno, for introducing me to the complex world of technical diving, and to Captain Billy Deans for more than a few adventures at sea. On land, Mari Red Moon and Cindy Rank, my sisters, and wise women both, are recognized for their mentoring, teachings and support.

Last but not least, thanks to the writers who have so generously given their counsel, their time and their eyes and ears: Rosalind Brackenbury, Margit Bisztray, Colleen Rae, Deanna O'Shaughnessy, Sheri Lohr, Robin Orlandi, Allen Meese, Jennifer Eggers and Peter Shann Ford.

Biography

Theresa Foley lives and writes in Key West, Florida, the famous island at the southernmost point of the continental United States. Ms. Foley is an internationally recognized journalist, having written thousands of stories and articles for magazines and newspapers since the early 1980s. She specializes in business and technology journalism, focusing on subjects such as satellites, telecommunications, the Internet, broadband and mobile infrastructure and financing for high tech projects. With *Cetacea*, she adds Key West, dolphins and diving adventure to the list of subjects that she has written on.

Cetacea is her first published novel. Short stories by Ms. Foley are included in the two Key West Author's Coop collections, *Once Upon An Island* and *Beyond Paradise*. Her writing also can be found on her website at: www.theresafoley.com.

To order copies of *Cetacea, Once Upon An Island* and *Beyond Paradise*, contact Amazon.com or send an email to: Theresa@theresafoley.com.